Spirits of the Pirate House
A T. J. Jackson Mystery

by

Paul Ferrante

$\mathcal{F}$& $\mathcal{I}$

by Melange Books

Published by
Fire and Ice
A Young Adult Imprint of Melange Books, LLC
White Bear Lake, MN 55110
www.fireandiceya.com

Spirits of the Pirate House ~ Copyright © 2013 by Paul Ferrante

ISBN: 978-1-61235-713-3 Print

Cover Art by Stephanie Flint

To my teammates and coaches of the Iona College Gaels Football Team.

"We few, we happy few, we band of brothers."

Acknowledgements

Thanks to Caroline Ferrante for her excellent typing skills and proofreading, Sarah Martin for her information on Bermudian burial customs, Deb Perry for the Bermuda map, and my editor Denise Meinstad for her continued patience and guidance.

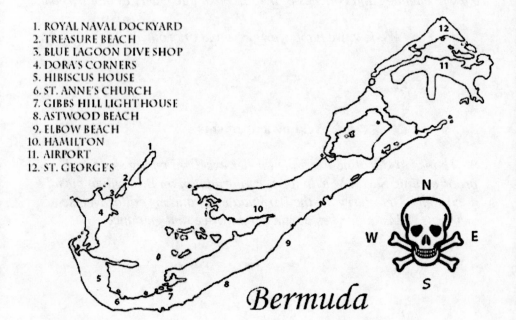

1. ROYAL NAVAL DOCKYARD
2. TREASURE BEACH
3. BLUE LAGOON DIVE SHOP
4. DORA'S CORNERS
5. HIBISCUS HOUSE
6. ST. ANNE'S CHURCH
7. GIBBS HILL LIGHTHOUSE
8. ASTWOOD BEACH
9. ELBOW BEACH
10. HAMILTON
11. AIRPORT
12. ST. GEORGE'S

N

W   E

S

Bermuda

Prologue

"Thanks so much for your patience and attention. This concludes our tour of Hibiscus House. Enjoy the rest of your stay in Bermuda." Winnie Pemburton flashed her most dazzling smile as she shook hands with the small group of tourists who had come to visit the estate of Sir William Tarver. All were retirees from the States, taking advantage of the lower air fares and hotel rates in the off season. Indeed, there was a chill in the late afternoon November air, and a light jacket or sweater was most welcome.

Winnie accompanied the group through the front door and down the steps to where a minivan taxi awaited. After helping them into the vehicle and gratefully accepting a few tips, she waved them off as the taxi coasted down the crushed shell and coral path to the imposing wrought iron fence 100 yards away. She stood there a moment in the oncoming twilight, drinking in the magnificence of her surroundings.

Though the vast majority of Bermuda's historic houses were privately owned, Hibiscus House was a National Trust site. The grounds, which featured hundreds of varieties of flowers, most prominently its namesake, the hibiscus, were meticulously maintained. A host of guava, palmetto and royal Poinciana trees provided areas of shade for strategically situated benches and a nesting place for tropical birds.

Since its acquisition by the government in the early 1900s, some of the acreage had been sold off and subdivided; other sections of the former plantation were now overgrown jungle. But the immediate lawns of freshly mown Bermuda grass, framed by flower beds and punctuated

1

with fountains, gave the effect of a tropical palace.

The house itself, built in the early 1700s by Sir William, was modeled after the West Indian plantation homes of the era, with wraparound two-story verandahs that provided sweeping views of the countryside, and the numerous windows at each level allowed ocean breezes to pleasantly pass through, precluding the need for air conditioning even in the hotter summer months.

Once inside, Winnie shut the heavy front door, with its anchor-styled knocker, and turned toward the imposing cedar staircase that led to the second floor. All the rooms of Hibiscus House were trimmed in cedar, and the walls were adorned with paintings of clipper ships and the English countryside. The furniture, dusted twice weekly by a cleaning crew, was almost exclusively of the finest period mahogany, and the dining room table was perpetually set with elegant Chinese porcelain and English silver. Most of the fixtures had been reacquired by the government after having been sold off in the mid-1700s by Sir William's wife after his death. The house had then stood vacant for nearly a century and had fallen into a state of disrepair, compounded by the ravages of the occasional hurricane that hit the island between July and November. But now it was the jewel of Southhampton Parish, and it was all hers.

Well, kind of. Winnie was a working class girl from the "back of town" in Hamilton. Her parents, descendants of free West India blacks who had migrated to Bermuda in the 1700s, had done fairly well for themselves. Harry Pemburton was a barman at the Southampton Princess Hotel and Resort nearby, and Allison Pemburton taught grade school in Hamilton, Bermuda's capital. It was from her mother that Winnie had developed a love of history; it was understandable, then, that after knocking about in a few dreary office jobs in town, she was overjoyed to hear that a position as tour guide was opening at Hibiscus House, which she would gaze at wistfully from her pink public transportation bus on the way into Hamilton each morning.

She had sweated through the interview with the National Trust representatives who were quick to point out that a person in her position would have to epitomize Bermudian manners and charm. Although Winnie doubted that her color would affect their decision—blacks formed the majority of Bermuda's population and maintained a fairly harmonious relationship with whites primarily of British descent—she wondered whether they felt she measured up to their standards. She was also surprised to learn that the position had a high turnover rate, especially within the past year. Had the previous tour guides fallen short of expectations, or had they simply become bored with the same humdrum routine, day after day?

It was no matter. Winnie assured her interviewers that this would be a dream job for her, and after a surprisingly quick consultation amongst themselves, she was hired.

And now, a month or so into her tenure, she'd fallen into a pleasant routine, opening the house for the first tour at 10:15 a.m. and locking up at 5:00 p.m. Winnie loved to imagine herself as mistress of the mansion, gliding through the many rooms with her tour groups in tow, relating local Bermudian folklore and discussing the somewhat mysterious background of her benefactor, Sir William Tarver, who was rumored to have made his fortune through piracy. She heard some disconcerting odd noises now and then, but attributed them to the ocean breezes wafting through the upstairs rooms or the odd animal making its way into a crawlspace or the attic. Nothing could disrupt her fantasy world.

As always, she closed off the top floor first, then ventured to her favorite place, the elegant drawing room, which was dominated by a Waterford crystal chandelier and ornately carved mantel that represented the height of Bermudian artisanship. Above it hung a large William and Mary molded mirror, into which Winnie would cast a last look before exiting the building and strolling around back to the gardener's shed where her Vespa scooter was discreetly parked.

While she was arranging a vase of cut flowers on the mantel, something in the mirror's reflection caught Winnie's eye. She blinked—hard—then looked again. Over her right shoulder, sitting in a corner wing chair, was a man. His shoulder-length, dark brown hair was pulled back and fastened into the short ponytail style of the 1700s, though nothing like the foppish, effeminate powdered wig look Winnie associated with those times. A full dark beard and mustache framed his tanned face and accentuated cold blue eyes that seemed to bore into her back. The man appeared to be wearing some kind of blue velour waistcoat with a ruffled white shirt underneath. Cream-colored breeches were tucked into high, black riding boots. Overall, he looked like the cover of one of the Harlequin romance novels Winnie so enjoyed on her trips to the beach at Astwood Park.

She closed her eyes again and fought to slow her breathing. "All right, then," she said to herself quietly. "I'll open my eyes and turn 'round, and he'll be gone." She counted to three, then cautiously wheeled and cracked open one eye.

He was still there, one leg casually crossed over the other, a flintlock pistol stuck into his wide leather belt. Winnie froze in fear. How did this man get in here? And why was he dressed in period clothes? As she stood trembling, an odor came to her, a strange mix of burning tobacco and something else. The man's eyes grew more intense, even hypnotic. When he finally said, "Come forward, girl dear," something in her broke loose. She bolted out of the room, through the front door, and into the gathering twilight, her screams mixing with the pleasant sounds of the evening tree frogs.

Chapter One

"It was the winter of their discontent," said the shaggy-haired boy with a sigh to his friend as they peered out the frosted bay window to the tumbling snowflakes.

"You've got it wrong. The quote is 'Now is the winter of our discontent.' *Richard the Third.*"

"Well excuse *me*, Professor Shakespeare."

T.J. frowned, mad at himself for taking out his frustration on his best friend. Bortnicker could be annoying, but it wasn't his fault that it was snowing again. Because it was *always* snowing. The first storm had arrived the day after Christmas, with blizzard conditions creating ten-foot drifts against the houses of their hometown of Fairfield, Connecticut. After that, it seemed they came every four days or so. You'd just be digging out from the last one and BAM, another foot, causing traffic snarls and falling trees and something he'd never heard of before—ice damming, a situation where snow and ice built up on rooftops, broke off sagging gutters, and leaked water down the inner walls of living rooms such as his own.

T.J. regarded his distorted reflection in the window. "A young Paul McCartney" is what he usually got from adults. "Cute" was the consensus of his female schoolmates, who considered him non-threatening in a Justin Bieber kind of way.

As far as his buddy, Bortnicker was, well, different. He took showers and washed his hair and everything but always seemed unkempt, from the brownish locks that fell across his Coke-bottle glasses to the always mismatched attire that drew snickers from the student

5

population of Bridgefield High School, where the boys were halfway through their freshman year. T.J., who was fairly social and athletic— he'd just finished his first season of junior varsity cross country and was considering JV baseball—more or less looked out for Bortnicker who, try as he might, was only slightly less inept socially now than he'd been in middle school.

But though Bortnicker tested his patience almost daily, T.J. couldn't turn his back on his longtime friend. The previous summer the two of them, accompanied by T.J.'s feisty cousin, LouAnne had shared a life-changing experience which created an unbreakable bond. T.J. still had trouble fathoming their encounter with the ghost of a Confederate cavalier on the battlefield in Gettysburg, PA, where LouAnne lived year round. In fact, the trio had faced down the homicidal specter in the middle of the 2010 reenactment as the "battle" swirled around them. Though it had fallen to LouAnne's dad, Mike Darcy, to fire the shot that had blown Major Crosby Hilliard, CSA back into the past, all three teens, especially Bortnicker, had exhibited extreme bravery under pressure, and the experience had forever altered T.J.'s perspective on life and the existence of a hereafter.

Not that there weren't some rocky patches down in Pennsylvania. It didn't help that both boys had more or less fallen in love with LouAnne, who was T.J.'s cousin by adoption. It led to a rather uncomfortable competition for her attention, which had seemed to tip in T.J.'s favor by the end of the boys' visit. He could still remember the woozy sensation he got as she innocently kissed him one night on the roof of her Victorian house. But Bortnicker, to his credit, hadn't thrown in the towel, not by any stretch. In fact, he'd ditched his eccentric allegiance to the 70s progressive rock band, Steely Dan, to immerse himself in the music and lore of The Beatles, LouAnne's listening choice. To that end, he'd purchased every Beatles CD he could find, as well as DVDs of the movies *A Hard Day's Night, Help!, Magical Mystery Tour, Yellow Submarine, Let it Be,* and *The Beatles Anthology* boxed set. He'd even taken to, when the inspiration hit him, affecting a Beatlesque Liverpudlian accent in his responses to questions, both socially and—to the mortification of T.J.—in school. Just a couple days ago in Biology class, the teacher was talking about the likelihood of global warming flooding the continents and Bortnicker had intoned, "Well isn't *that* wonderful" in his nasally best John Lennon voice. Of course, most of Bortnicker's peers, who thought he was just being stupid, didn't get it.

The Beatle thing was only a byproduct of T.J.'s angst at the moment. Here it was, February Break, also known as President's Week, and Fairfield was under siege again. But what made it worse was that for the second straight vacation, LouAnne had been forced to cancel a trip north to visit her cousin and his friend. T.J., who had deflected the advances of a few girls during the school year, as he carried a torch for his adopted cousin, felt especially cheated.

Winter sucked.

"Okay," said Bortnicker, "here's a good one. On *The White Album*, who is the song 'Martha, My Dear' written about?"

"Martha Washington," said T.J. tonelessly.

"Nope."

"Martha Stewart."

"Uh-uh."

"I give up."

"It was Paul McCartney's sheepdog! Can you imagine?"

"No, I can't," said T.J. tiredly.

Blessedly, the phone started ringing.

"Aren't you going to pick up?" said Bortnicker, while drawing designs on the foggy window.

"It's ten in the morning on a Wednesday. Probably a sales call or a business message for my dad."

"What if it's LouAnne? I bet she's at home, cooped up just like us."

That was another thing. Bortnicker had been texting or emailing his cousin all winter with Beatles trivia questions, which she deftly answered. At last count, he'd stumped her but twice out of 47 attempts. T.J. had kept in touch with her also, usually by phone, because her voice always lifted his spirits. It could get lonely in the huge house he and his dad inhabited, one that had lacked female warmth after the death of his mom a few years back. It was even worse when his architect father was away on one of his periodic business trips, overseeing building projects all over the world. Thomas Jackson, Sr. provided a cushy life for both of them, but there was a tradeoff; rarely was T.J.'s dad around for a cross country meet, and he'd only barely made Open House Night last fall at Bridgefield High. As a result, T.J. had become largely self-sufficient, though he cherished time spent with his dad. Of course, Bortnicker, whose own father had walked out on him and his mom years ago, was usually on hand to round out the bachelor trio.

"It might be your dad calling to tell you his flight's delayed," offered Bortnicker. Of course. Dad was on his way home from Phoenix that night. T.J. sighed and reached for the phone on its sixth ring.

"Dude, what's up?" said a gregarious voice on the other end.

"Wh-who's this?" questioned T.J. suspiciously.

"Dude, it's me! Mike Weinstein! You know, from *Gonzo Ghost Chasers*?"

T.J. couldn't help but smile. Mike Weinstein was the star of The Adventure Channel's hottest paranormal-themed show, which was entering its third season. The concept was simple: Weinstein's team, which included three 20-something guys and a girl, would visit paranormal hot spots around the country and try to make contact with the spirits who reportedly resided there. Their methods were confrontational and prevocational, which made for great TV. It didn't hurt that all of them were buff and wore skintight *GGC* shirts, either. They were also armed with every possible gizmo invented to capture spirits on audio or video; but what set them apart from other shows was the fact that they served as their own production crew, creating a *Blair Witch* atmosphere that kept audiences tuning in every Wednesday night.

T.J. and LouAnne had met Mike quite by accident the previous summer when Weinstein, having barely escaped being murdered by the ghostly Major Hilliard on a midnight expedition in the battlefield park, overheard the teens discussing T.J.'s own paranormal encounter with the phantom horseman. Though Weinstein had played no role in the solving of the Hilliard case, they made sure to call him and proudly tell their tale, reaffirming Mike's already strong belief in the supernatural and keeping them on his radar. Weinstein could be a bit over the top at times, but T.J. and Bortnicker loved watching *Gonzo Ghost Chasers*, secure in the knowledge that it wasn't all a bunch of baloney after all.

"Oh, yeah. Hi, Mike. What's new?"

"Well, as you know, the show's doing great. The episode last week at the mental asylum in Alabama was off the charts in the ratings—"

"Yeah," said T.J., "that was pretty intense when Josh thought he was getting possessed by the ghost of the axe murderer."

"No doubt. That was a real creepy place. Anyway, like I said, the ratings are great, and The Adventure Channel's making big bucks on us. Have you seen their online store lately?" Indeed, *Gonzo Ghost Chasers* hats, tee shirts and other accessories were popping up everywhere—even at school. The boys found it especially amusing, what with their real-life adventure in Gettysburg and all.

Bortnicker had now come to the phone, and T.J. put them on speaker. "So, what can we do for you, Mike?"

There was a pause, surely for dramatic effect, then Weinstein said, "How much snow is on the ground there?"

"Eighteen inches, give or take," said Bortnicker.

"Kinda makes you wish you could go somewhere warm and tropical, doesn't it?"

"Yes," said T.J. slowly, raising an eyebrow at his friend. "But, what's the point?"

"The point is, dude, that The Adventure Channel, in its infinite wisdom, is thinking of having some kids accompany me on a case, which might lead to a spinoff of my show!"

"You mean, like, *Junior Gonzo Ghost Chasers?*"

"Something like that."

"Sounds cool," said T.J., "but what does that have to do with me?" Bortnicker quickly cuffed him on the shoulder. "I mean, us?"

"Well, when the suits pitched the idea to me for, like, a pilot episode, the first thing I thought of, honest to God, was the three of you guys. Why go through the trouble of conducting a nationwide search for serious ghost hunters when I know three dudes who've already done it?"

"Makes sense. But we have this thing called school—"

"No problem. How does Spring Break in Bermuda sound?"

Bortnicker was jumping up and down, feverishly whispering, "Yes! Yes! Yes!" when T.J. shook his head. "Can't do it, Mike. First of all, the district superintendent has already cancelled spring vacation because of all the snow days we've had to take. Second, I'm playing baseball in the spring, and that's when the season starts." At which point Bortnicker collapsed to the floor, rolling around in agony.

"Hmm," said Weinstein. "Well, what about the beginning of June?"

T.J. winked at his friend, who immediately ceased with the histrionics. "That could happen. I'd have to ask my dad, of course, and Bortnicker's mom probably wouldn't mind. But what about LouAnne? Is she invited?"

"*Invited?* Dude, without her you have *no shot*. Don't you understand how TV works? You need at least one girl, and it just so happens your cousin is a teenage fox. Or haven't you noticed?"

Bortnicker was now grinning from ear-to-ear, nodding his head knowingly.

"Yeah, well, I'd have to talk to her and her folks. That's near the high season in Gettysburg, and she works in that inn doing the reenacting thing, remember?"

"Dude, she'll make a summer's worth of loot in a couple weeks, which is how long I figure it'll take for us to shoot."

"Well, I guess it's worth exploring," said T.J., who was cautious by nature. "But why Bermuda?"

Weinstein's reply got their blood running: "Pirates."

"Get out."

"No joke, dude. And oh, another thing … are any of you guys certified SCUBA divers?"

Chapter Two

"Pirates? You mean like, 'Arrgh, matey'? You can't be serious," said LouAnne as she painted her toenails before a crackling fire in Gettysburg.

"This is the real deal, Cuz," answered T.J. as Bortnicker stood by. "According to Mike Weinstein, The Adventure Channel will put us up in some beachfront apartments for the whole time we're there filming. The hotel and airfare are free. We'll just need one adult to come along as a chaperone."

"Well, you can count out my parents. Mom's afraid of flying, and Dad's not going to take time off as a park ranger during the Battlefield's high season."

"We're going to work on Mr. Jackson," offered Bortnicker, "and save my mom as a last resort."

"I don't know, guys," said LouAnne, "you know how it gets in Gettysburg near Reenactment Week."

"You'd be back with a couple weeks to spare," assured T.J. "Besides, Weinstein said we're gonna get *paid* for this. Just think—getting paid to go to Bermuda and hunt ghosts!"

LouAnne chuckled. "Listen, Cuz, I know it sounds too good to be true, but don't you think it'll just be a cheesy TV thing? Do you really think *anything* like last summer could happen again?"

"Probably not," said Bortnicker, "but even if it's a wild goose chase, who cares? Look out the window, my dear. How cold is it in Gettysburg, like 20 below? Can't you just see those palm trees swaying in the breeze? And that famous Bermuda pink sand? The turquoise water—"

"Okay, Bortnicker, I get it. It's a vacay opportunity I'd never otherwise have, at least until after college. And you're sure you two can't do this without me?"

"That's what Weinstein said," answered T.J. "And besides," he added, shooting Bortnicker a wink, "we're a team. No way can we function without you."

"All right, I'll work on my parents. But, guys, one thing I'm going to have to hold firm on—there's NO way I'm scuba diving. It's hard enough for me to stay on the surface with a snorkel."

"Fair enough," said T.J. "Talk to your folks and get back to me ASAP so I can call Weinstein and tell him it's a go. Then Bortnicker and I can book some SCUBA classes. You're *sure* you're not into diving? The Adventure Channel's picking up the tab."

"I'm dead sure, Cuz. When I was little I almost drowned in a lake, and ever since, I've been terrified of being underwater. I'll swim in a pool and occasionally salt water if it's crystal clear, but that's where I draw the line."

Bortnicker, trying to lighten the mood, broke in. "What was the original name of *Help!*"

"The song or the movie?"

"The movie."

"*Eight Arms to Hold You.*"

"Right again." He frowned, then produced a devilish grin. Affecting his best Beatle voice, he said, "You know, luv, we've never been told which one of us Liverpool lads you fancied as your fave. And who might that be?"

T.J., a dead-ringer for the young Paul McCartney, smirked at his friend's obviously leading question.

"That's a no-brainer," she said airily. "It's gotta be Ringo."

"*Ringo!*" the boys cried in unison.

"Oh, definitely. Without his backbeat they were *nothing*. Besides, I always go for the underdog." She chuckled. "Gotta go, boys. Dad's cranking up the snow blower and he's gonna need help with the driveway."

"Keep thinking of the swaying palm trees."

"I will. Talk to you soon, guys."

As T.J. hung up the phone, Bortnicker started rummaging around in the pantry for the ingredients to create his masterpiece snack, spiced beef nachos. He'd really gotten into the cooking thing after whipping up a series of gourmet-quality breakfasts with LouAnne's mom the previous summer in Gettysburg, and though he never seemed to gain a pound on his spindly frame, both of the Jackson men looked forward to his impromptu feasts. Removing a can of refried beans from the top shelf he asked, "So you think this ghost thing's gonna happen?"

"I'd say right now it's 50-50. But I've got an ace up my sleeve. I went online and checked the Bermuda tourist calendar of events, and the second week of June there's a 5k road race for teens. I'll bet she'll want to enter, especially if I say I'm entering too."

"Yeah," said Bortnicker with a smile. "I remember you two got pretty intense last summer on those morning runs through the battlefield. So you're figuring she'll want a little friendly family competition?"

"You got it. If chasing pirate ghosts doesn't get her psyched, kicking my butt in a race will!"

Chapter Three

"I think I'm going to be sick," moaned T.J. as the dive boat rose and fell in the blue-gray swells of Long Island Sound.

"Yeah," said Bortnicker, wiping his mouth after he'd heaved up his lunch over the side, "you've got an interesting shade of green going there."

The boys were part of a group of six heading to the mouth of Bridgeport Harbor to take their final SCUBA junior certification test. This cold mid-May Sunday was the culmination of a comprehensive training course that had begun with four long classroom sessions, followed by a written exam which both boys had passed with flying colors.

The local dive shop owner, Capt. Kenny Ali, a burly, bearded character who hailed from Sheepshead Bay, Brooklyn, had left no stone unturned or ego unbruised in imparting his vast knowledge of diving accumulated over the past 30 years. Again and again as the group, comprised mostly of fit men and women between the ages of 25-40, were drilled in the complexities of water pressure and breathable gas mixes, Capt. Kenny hammered home the fact that miscalculations in equipment preparations, bottom times, and ascension speed could lead to dire consequences. "You don't get second chances like topside," was his mantra.

The boys looked forward to their weekly lessons at Capt. Kenny's Dive Shop, a white cinderblock bunker plopped in the middle of a busy Bridgeport thoroughfare. The place had a certain ambience that made you just want to strap on some tanks and jump in. Up front was a

14

showroom with equipment, both new and used, for sale—everything from dive watches to knives to wetsuits, which the boys probably wouldn't be needing in Bermuda's warm June waters. Kenny's prices were fair, as far as the teens could determine. He could have charged a lot more, as his customers were primarily from wealthy nearby towns like Westport and New Canaan, but the captain's main goal, it seemed, was to not discourage newbies to the hobby with steep prices or unnecessary equipment that would make an already expensive pastime even more so.

But what really attracted them, and what caused them to hang around way after their lessons, were the thousands of shipwreck artifacts on display from Kenny's diving career, arranged on shelves and in glass museum cases. Every piece, it seemed, had a story, and the Captain reveled in each telling. The somewhat gloomy lighting and strong smell of saltwater that permeated the low-ceilinged rooms only added to the atmosphere as he spun yarns of dangerous dives to merchant ships, German U-Boats, and his personal favorite, the *Andrea Doria*, which lay about 50 miles off the coast of Nantucket in icy North Atlantic waters. He'd get this kind of faraway look and effect a reverential tone in describing his harrowing descent and penetration of the palatial Italian ocean liner which had sunk in 1957 when struck by a Swedish ship on a foggy night, causing the deaths of some 46 passengers and crew.

"See, the *Doria* lies in over 200 feet of water," he'd explained, fondling a tea cup snatched from the First Class section of the ship. "When I was ready to finally attempt a dive on her, I hooked on wit' a charter boat out of New Jersey with some of my most experienced diver pals. We'd all been diving for a while, but the *Andrea Doria* is somethin' you got to work up to. Part of it is the depth, which at the deepest is like 250 feet. But also, once you get inside it's a freakin' mess. First of all, the ship lays on its side, so everything from engine parts to machinery to furniture is trown all over the place. Then you got miles of wires and cables reaching out for you like snakes. Get snagged on that stuff and you're a goner."

"How come?" asked Bortnicker. "Don't you have a dive buddy with you?"

"Nah," said Kenny. "What you guys are learnin' is basic recreational diving, which seldom exceeds 100 feet. So the buddy system is a must. But in deep sea wreck diving, you're squeezin' through openings that are only big enough for one guy. And even if there was somebody wit' you, what happens is the guy in trouble could panic and rip off the other guy's regulator if he knows he's low on air. So now you got *two* guys in trouble.

"Another problem is, at that depth, as you two are learnin' in your dive chart study, you can't just shoot to the surface after 20 minutes of bottom time at 200 feet. You have to decompress by climbing the boat's anchor line in stages, stopping off at certain levels and hangin', so your system equalizes. If you come up too fast you suffer 'the bends', which is the buildup of gas bubbles in your system. Remember the comparison I gave you in class?"

"The seltzer bottle thing?" said T.J.

"Yeah, that's the one. Like I said, think of what happens if you quickly open a seltzer bottle. You can get a violent overflow of bubbles. Well, underwater that takes the form of an embolism in your bloodstream, which can cause blindness, a stroke, or even death.

"But if you twist the cap slowly, letting the air out a little at a time to ease the pressure, you're all right—no spill. That's what decompression stops are for, to let your body equalize. At the depth of 200 feet, you'd have to do roughly an hour of decompression on your way up; with each measured stop, the time you hang there increases, from five minutes to 25 or so.

"What's happened is, some guys get disoriented down there; they panic, lose their sense of reason, and figure they don't have enough air left to decompress. So, up they go, like a freakin' rocket, and only bad things can happen from then on.

"What's good about youse guys is that with your basic certification, you'll be good to go in shallow water, so a lot of this won't apply. But you gotta learn it, anyway. So, what is it this TV show's gonna have you do?"

"Well," said T.J., "as near as I can figure it, there was this pirate named William Tarver in the 1700s who used Bermuda as a safe harbor between trips to Jamaica and England. He later established an estate on the island that's said to be haunted, which is why we're going there. But, a year or so ago a guy with a dive shop business like yours found a wreck, mostly by accident, way out past the reefs of the South Shore—"

"And they think it's this pirate's?"

"Exactly," said Bortnicker. "According to records they uncovered in the Bermuda Maritime History archives, the ship suddenly went missing in an area near where the dive shop captain found the remnants of a wreck. So it could be the one."

"Was it sunk by another ship, scuttled on purpose, or lost in a storm?"

"They don't know," said T.J. "Kinda mysterious."

"Well," said Capt. Kenny, "not for nothing, but what light are you two greenhorns supposed to shed on this?"

"I don't think they want us to do any scientific stuff at all," said T.J. "The show's mostly about the pirate's estate house. I think they just want us to cruise by the wreck to add to the show. *Gonzo Ghost Chasers* does that all the time for like the first ten minutes of an episode. They call it 'local color'."

"Humpf," grunted Capt. Kenny. "I still think they're asking you to do too much. Just make sure you learn as much from me as you can for as long as we're here."

As T.J. and Bortnicker came to realize, there was so much that could go wrong on a dive: a leaky face mask, a tear in your buoyancy vest, running out of air, slicing your air hose on sharp coral, rip currents and sharks and barracuda and moray eels … but oh, the rewards! Capt. Kenny's thrilling diving stories had prompted the teens into watching reruns of shows like *Deep Sea Detectives*, which featured wreck dives hundreds of feet down. Bortnicker also haunted the Fairfield Public Library, bringing home armfuls of National Geographic and History Channel specials with a diving (preferably also pirate) theme which they hungrily devoured during the dreary days of March and April, when it seemed to rain as much as it had snowed in January and February.

Somehow, despite their dive fever, they had still managed to keep their grades up, and both had been chosen for the JV baseball team, T.J. as a centerfielder and Bortnicker as a statistician. But their upcoming adventure always loomed in the background.

After the written test had come some intense water training at a local college's Olympic-sized pool. To even qualify for that the boys had to swim the length of the pool six times without stopping, a gargantuan task for Bortnicker, whose hobbies of model railroading and video games hardly left him in the best of shape. Fortunately, unlike a couple of their older classmates, neither boy had panicked on their first dives to the bottom of the deep end of the pool. In fact, Capt. Kenny, who was always cognizant that the teens were in training for an Adventure Channel appearance, took special interest in technique and safety at every step.

"Don't want you guys drownin' or somethin' while America watches in horror," he cracked. Of course, he had showered the boys with every piece of equipment to which a *Capt. Kenny's Dive Shop, Bridgeport* logo could be affixed. "A little publicity couldn't hoit," he reassured.

So here they were, riding the swells and anxiously awaiting their moment of truth at the bottom of the harbor.

The test would be comprised of three basic tasks, all performed with their Divemaster, Capt. Kenny:

First, each student had to make his way to the bottom using a guide rope from the boat—roughly 25 feet—and await the Divemaster.

Upon his arrival, the trainee would have to remove his mask completely, then replace it and clear it; trade mouthpieces with the Divemaster to share their air tanks; and use a wristwatch/compass to orient himself and swim along the bottom to and back from a buoy anchor some 50 feet away.

After they'd anchored the boat, Capt. Kenny told the trainees to suit up and do a perfunctory equipment check. It was at this point that a rather attractive Asian woman, who had been the ace of the classroom sessions, declared that she couldn't possibly go through with the final part. The Captain, standing with legs spread for balance as the boat rocked, merely shrugged his blocky shoulders and said, "Your choice, ma'am. You're paid up and I shure don't wanna make you do somethin' you don't wanna do. Don't want you drownin' the both of us down there."

Slowly, the boys and their classmates pulled on their funky smelling rubber wetsuits and checked the pressure in their air tanks. T.J. tested his mouthpiece, which at first had made him gag, then spat into his facemask, spread the saliva around with his fingers, and gave it a rinse over the side. He hoped the gasoline in the water surrounding the dive boat wouldn't seep into his breathing equipment below, because the churning ocean had brought him to the edge of nausea and left him dangling.

"Okay, so who's the foist victim?" said Capt. Kenny mischievously.

"Me. I'll go first," said Bortnicker, standing wobbly on the pitching vessel. "If I don't do it now, I never will."

"Good man! Well, over the side wit' you, Bortnicker!"

T.J. watched with admiration as his friend inched his way to the stern, swung his flippered feet onto the dive platform that jutted out over the foaming waves, adjusted his mask, gave him a tentative thumbs up, and then goose-stepped into the harbor's ominous waters.

Capt. Kenny gave him a couple minutes to hopefully find the guide rope and make his way to the bottom. "Hasn't popped right back up," he announced finally. "Well, that's a good sign. I'll stay down there to wait for the rest of youse. Just follow the rope till you reach the bottom. I'll find you down there." With that, he assumed a sitting position on the inside of the gunwale then nonchalantly flipped backward into the water, leaving the remaining candidates alone with their thoughts.

Minutes passed on the rocking boat. Another diver threw up over the side, and T.J. closed his eyes, wondering how Bortnicker was doing. Then, realizing he was working himself into a panicked state, he forced his mind to go elsewhere. He thought of LouAnne and palm trees.

After an interminable wait, Bortnicker bobbed to the surface near the platform, gave a small wave, and was pulled aboard by his classmates, who eagerly awaited his report. He removed his mask, spat out the mouthpiece, and grandly announced, "Piece of cake, guys."

"I'll go next," volunteered T.J. Bortnicker escorted him to the platform with a smile, but at the last second pulled him close and whispered, "Watch it. It's dark down there." With a quick nod, T.J. stepped off.

The water wasn't as cold as he'd imagined it to be; maybe it was the sweat he'd generated, imprisoned in his wetsuit, that was keeping him warm. He found the anchor rope and started following it down, equalizing his ears every ten feet or so, telling himself, "If Bortnicker can do it, so can I." What he didn't learn until later was that, as soon as he'd gone beneath the surface, Bortnicker had quickly excused himself from the group and gone below where, locking himself in the head, he'd firmly grasped the sink with both hands until he was able to stop himself from shaking.

At the last moment, T.J. felt the sandy bottom come up to meet him. He couldn't believe, in all this inky blackness, that he was only 25 feet below the surface. Letting go of the rope, he brought himself to a standing position, looking around for Capt. Kenny. "He's just testing me," he wuffed into his mouthpiece. When Kenny tapped him on the shoulder, it was all he could manage to keep from collapsing in fright.

But Capt. Kenny was a pro who'd seen it all. He quickly calmed the teen, who much appreciated the small light attached to the top of Divemaster's mask. Then, through a series of gestures, he initiated the test exercises.

All three of the tasks were difficult for T.J., but none held as much terror as when Kenny snapped off his headlight, lifted off his student's mask, and handed it back to him. Biting back the bile rising in his throat, T.J. shakily repositioned and cleared the mask, relief washing over him when he made out Capt. Kenny giving him a thumbs up. He gained a bit more confidence with the switching of breathing apparatus exercise and then powered his way through the orienteering maneuver. It was on the swim back from the buoy anchor that he thought, *Of course I can do this. I stared down a Confederate cavalryman on the field of battle and didn't run.* He returned to where Capt. Kenny awaited by the anchor rope, received an emphatic "OK" sign and a pat on the shoulder, and then ascended to where Bortnicker and his classmates anxiously anticipated his return.

"Were you scared?" asked Bortnicker, pulling him on board after taking his flippers.

T.J. gave him a wry smile. "Not any more than you." They burst into laughter and smacked a high five.

An hour later, Capt. Kenny's mate hauled up the anchor and they headed back to Bridgeport Harbor. Only one trainee had panicked and thus failed his test, not counting the woman who'd bailed at the beginning. Overall, Capt. Kenny was pleased.

As they pulled into the boat slip T.J. could see his father, Thomas Jackson, Sr., and Bortnicker's mom, Pippa, waving from the observation deck of the Fisherman's Rest seafood shack, which boasted the best lobster roll sandwich around. Bortnicker shot them a "thumbs up" to signify they'd passed their exam, and then the boys began gathering their belongings, including a change of clothes for dinner upstairs.

They were about to exit the boat when Capt. Kenny told them to sit down. "Listen, youse two," he said seriously, "ya done real good down there, barely a hitch, so it's my pleasure to issue the both of you your own gen-u-ine PADI card. But that don't mean you're some kinda experts. In fact, in da big picture, you don't know *squat*. That's why I got my doubts about you divin' on some wreck in Bermuda, even if it is in fairly shallow water.

"A'course, if you could dive in *this* crap," he flung a hand out toward the harbor's churning waters, "youse can dive in anything. In Bermuda there's probably gonna be like unlimited visibility, and in June, the water temp is like your bathtub." Both boys broke into broad grins at the prospect.

"But you gotta promise me that, no matter what, you don't take any stoopid chances down there, and whatever else you do, *never* dive alone. Somethin' goes wrong down there, you need a buddy. Understood?"

"We gotcha," said T.J., extending his hand. "Thanks for everything, Capt. Kenny."

"Yeah, right," the old seadog replied, engulfing the boys' hands in his huge paw. "Just make sure you flash my shop's logo on camera whenever possible. That would be nice."

"I bet we can even get you a 'special thanks' in the closing credits!" chirped Bortnicker.

"That's what I'm talkin' about! Now youse two clowns get outta here and let me wash down this tub."

Chapter Four

"Lobster roll's a little too mushy—they should've eased up on the mayo," said Bortnicker, dipping a French fry into his little paper cup of ketchup.

"Well, maybe if you'd actually *chewed* it you'd have enjoyed it more," quipped T.J. "I can't believe you got your appetite back so quick after being seasick." He had only nibbled at his own sandwich and had avoided the greasy fries completely.

"What can I say?" grunted Bortnicker through a mouthful of food. "Now that I'm back on land I need nourishment!"

The sun had broken through, and the day had actually become quite pleasant. They had found a vacant picnic table with an umbrella on the deck of Fisherman's Rest, which was becoming crowded with boat people and other harbor visitors passing the late spring afternoon. The wind had died down a bit, and the harbor's waters looked less threatening than a couple hours before, when Capt. Kenny's 36' dive boat *NeverEnuf* had ferried the boys out to the mouth of Bridgeport Harbor for their SCUBA certification dive test. A slightly overweight waitress dressed in faux pirate gear dropped off a second round of iced teas.

Pippa Bortnicker, who earned a good living as a feng shui interior decorator to the well-heeled of Connecticut's "Gold Coast," smiled warmly at her son as she plucked a cherry tomato from her garden salad. "He's become quite the food critic," she commented with a wink. "I'm getting a complex about my cooking." With her 70s style peasant blouse and long, frizzy hair tied back with a pink bow, she looked like a rather

22

attractive middle-aged refugee from Woodstock. Her son could have countered that Pippa's strict vegan diet severely cramped her creations, but he chose to let it go. The day was going too well.

"I, for one, think it's great that he's picked up a hobby that's useful," said Thomas Jackson, Sr., who was decked out in his standard uniform of golf shirt and khakis. "Some girl is going to be *very* lucky."

"And model railroading isn't useful?" countered Bortnicker, referring to his first love.

"Oh surrre," said T.J., rolling his eyes for effect. "Girls really dig it."

Pippa delicately wiped her mouth with her napkin and placed it on the table. "All right, gentlemen," she began, "now that the diving exam is over, could you tell me again how this whole excursion is going to work?"

The three males looked at each other, hoping someone would take the lead. Tom Sr. ran a hand through his stylish salt-and-pepper hair and spoke first. "I've been in touch with The Adventure Channel people, as well as Mike Weinstein, the host of *Gonzo Ghost Chasers.* They have arranged for us to occupy four efficiency units at the Jobson's Cove Apartments Hotel on the South Shore. Mike and I will have our own units, the boys will share one, and T.J.'s cousin LouAnne will have the fourth. This has all been cleared with my brother-in-law, Mike Darcy."

"I really appreciate this, Tom," said Mrs. Bortnicker. "It will allow me to attend the Feng Shui workshop in New York City during that week. I signed up for it ages ago—"

"We know, Mom," interrupted Bortnicker, obviously hoping to derail a long monologue on the benefits of Feng Shui living that had become Pippa's trademark.

"Anyway," continued Tom Sr., "the boys will be allowed to take their freshman finals a week early and we'll hop a plane to Bermuda that first Friday in June. Mike Weinstein is supposed to be there already, and he's bringing all the equipment. LouAnne will be a couple days behind us because she has finals and a big track meet to close out her spring season that she refuses to skip. So, she'll fly out of Philadelphia, and we'll pick her up at the airport.

"After that we're on Mike Weinstein's schedule. Make no

mistake—although Bermuda is the ultimate vacation destination, the kids are going to have to put in a lot of hard work to finish up in their allotted time of under two weeks."

"Such as?" queried Pippa.

"Well, for starters, Mike will have to verse them on the usage of the various ghost hunting gadgets used on the show—the electronic voice phenomena stuff and whatnot. Remember, there's no film crew on site. The team does its own filming as it conducts the investigation. Mike's involvement on site will be minimal—that's the whole idea of this *Junior Gonzo* show or whatever they're going to call it."

Mrs. Bortnicker frowned and furrowed her eyebrows. "And you really believe in this stuff, Tom?"

The elder Jackson chewed on the inside of his cheek, realizing that the boys' eyes were upon him. "Pippa," he said evenly, "if you'd asked me this a year ago I'd have told you that *Gonzo Ghost Chasers* was just another schlocky paranormal show and that the idea of spirits and ghosts moving among us is a bunch of baloney.

"But last year, something happened to those kids down in Gettysburg that they all swear to. And what's more, so does my brother-in-law, whom I'd trust with my life. So, to answer your question: yes, there are a lot of ridiculous, exploitive ghost shows on TV, and *Gonzo Ghost Chasers* can be as over-the-top as any of them. But if there is a pirate's ghost in Bermuda, these kids are as qualified as anyone to prove it."

T.J. felt his chest puff out with pride at his father's words, and Bortnicker lightly kicked him under the table in agreement.

"But where does the SCUBA diving come in?" she asked worriedly. "Why is it so necessary?"

"Apparently, this William Tarver had a sloop called *The Steadfast* that may or may not have been discovered off the reefs near where he established an estate, no doubt financed by the spoils of his pirate adventures. It sits in only 25 or so feet of water. So, The Adventure Channel wants them to check it out for any clues as to its age or use."

"And they're qualified to do this?"

"Of course not!" laughed Tom Sr. "But remember, it's a ghost hunting show, not some treasure quest."

"Of course, Mom," broke in Bortnicker sweetly, "if we do find jewels and stuff, you'll get your cut."

"Very funny. I'm just worried about sharks and such."

"Well," said Tom Sr., "if it makes you feel any better, the dive shop owner who found the wreck, Jasper Goodwin, will be the guy running us out there on his boat, for which The Adventure Channel's paying him some serious money. He's supposed to be one of the top diving guys in Bermuda, and since it's he who discovered the wreck, he has exclusive rights to dive on it for a period of time. I'm sure he'll keep a close watch on the kids. And I'll be there, too, whenever I can."

"I still can't believe how you worked this out, Tom," smiled Pippa, sipping her tea. "Such fortuitous circumstances!"

"It's pretty simple, actually. Bermuda is one of my favorite places on earth, and I've been just about everywhere. While most guys were going down to Daytona Beach or Ft. Lauderdale for Spring Break, my college buddies and I preferred Bermuda. It was cleaner, safer, and a lot less crazy, though we managed to have our fun. Plus, we could play golf and swim in pristine waters. We'd rent a couple mopeds and have a blast.

"Then, when I got married, T.J.'s mom and I went there on our honeymoon, and I fell in love with the place all over again. Cheryl and I visited a couple more times, including once when T.J. was around two years old, and as an architect I hoped to someday be able to work on a project there, something that would blend perfectly with traditional Bermudian surroundings and add to an already fantastic landscape.

"Well, last fall I was contacted by this golf resort near the town of St. George's on the East End that is revamping its clubhouse and dining facilities. The manager is a guy originally from Bermuda who was one of my college buddies, and the one who actually had suggested we do Spring Break there. We've always kept in touch, so when this project came up he thought of me, because he knew I could create something that in no way would look out place.

"I took a quick trip over there in March to get the lay of the land. Since then I've been working on the design, and I'll be meeting with the resort committee and Bermudian officials during the kids' two weeks to submit my presentation. Hopefully, they'll accept my ideas."

"You know they will, Mr. J," said Bortnicker.

"Not to brag, but I'm pretty confident," Tom Sr. replied. "Anyway, to get back to the itinerary, they're figuring two or three days of diving on the wreck, and then a few more investigating the estate house. In between, the kids will have a little down time to hit the beach or whatever. And T.J. and his cousin are even supposed to participate in a road race of some sort."

"It all sounds so marvelous," gushed Pippa.

"That's what I've been trying to tell you, Mom," said Bortnicker with exasperation. "I mean, *really*. What could possibly go wrong?"

Chapter Five

"I told you I'd hit .300," said T.J., as he dropped his equipment bag on the kitchen's hardwood floor.

"Yeah, but only just," said Bortnicker, who had already cracked open the refrigerator in search of snacks. "You no hit curveball so good."

"Something to work on for next season. But jeez, cut me some slack, Bortnicker. I hadn't played in two years!"

"No problemo, Big Mon. Overall, I'd say you had a great season. I mean, when Coach Pisseri asked you to come out for the team last winter, he was just looking for guys to round out the bench. I think you were a pleasant surprise for him."

Indeed, T.J. had even surprised himself. It was true that he'd only been asked to try out for the Bridgefield High JV because the small school's talent pool was so limited, but after an early season injury had shelved the team's starting centerfielder, T.J. found himself roaming the outfield with the long, loping strides he'd cultivated during cross country season in the fall. His arm was only fair but extremely accurate, and as the team's number two hitter, he had become adept at bunting or hitting behind the runner to move his teammates into scoring position. And although the JV season had ended with a rather mediocre 12-12 record, Coach Pisseri had taken him aside after today's game and told him that, with a little hard work—namely, playing American Legion ball over the summer—he would have a good shot of starting on the varsity team by his junior year. T.J. had thanked him but reminded the coach that Cross Country was his first priority and that he'd have to make those running workouts his main focus during the summer. Pisseri, afraid to lose an athlete of his potential from a talent-depleted program, had agreed to help him work something out after the Fourth of July.

"Your dad left a note on the fridge," said Bortnicker, juggling a container of milk and two boxes of ice cream that he'd snatched from the freezer. "He'll be home for dinner. He's thinking we'll hit Pizza Palace."

"Sounds like a plan."

"And he says a package came for you this morning from The Adventure Channel. Go grab it while I whip up some milkshakes. You got any chocolate sauce?"

"In the pantry," T.J. said, opening the FedEx envelope his father had left on the butcher block-topped kitchen island. He removed a thick folder with *Junior Gonzo Ghost Chasers Pilot* embossed on the black cover. Inside was a note which he read aloud:

Dudes,
        Hope the end of the school year is going well for you. In this folder is a lot of background history on Bermuda and pirates who operated in that area. There isn't much on William Tarver—we're going to have to visit the historical society's archives over there to get a better read on this guy.
But dig this—they've had to close down his residence to the public because people are too scared to work there! So the government's losing tourist money, which is why they called us. It's common knowledge that after we visit a site their visitor rate goes way up. Of course, it would help if we actually find something!
So, read up on all this stuff before we go. I've sent a copy to your cousin in PA. This is gonna be awesome!
Catch you later,
Mike

"What do you think?" said T.J., reaching into the cupboard for some parfait glasses.

"Way cool," replied Bortnicker, scooping chocolate chip mint and rocky road ice cream into the blender. He added some milk and a squirt of chocolate sauce, popped on the top, and hit the toggle switch. "Looks like we've got homework while we study for our school finals."

"I'm not really *that* worried about our school tests," said T.J., "except maybe math. But I want to go over there prepared. We don't want to embarrass ourselves or make Mike look bad for volunteering us for this investigation. You know, last year in Gettysburg we just kinda went with it as stuff happened, but now it's all going to be captured on film. I don't want to look like an idiot."

"I don't think your fair cousin would allow that to occur," quipped Bortnicker, pouring the silky mixture into their glasses. "Tell me how it tastes."

T.J. took a gulp, creating an instant ice cream mustache. "Excellent, as always."

"Some Oreos would go great with this."

T.J. rummaged around in the pantry. "We're out. How about Chips Ahoy?"

"Just as good. Give me half the folder and let's start reading."

Chapter Six

As was usually the case, Pizza Palace was hopping this Saturday night. It wasn't the fanciest eatery in Fairfield, but the food was hearty and the portions were large, the only requirements necessary for the boys. They slid into a red leatherette booth across the table from Mr. Jackson and eyed the people at the other tables, most of whom were families with squirming children.

"So, what'll it be tonight, guys?" said Tom Sr., opening the surprisingly voluminous menu.

"We were feeling like pizza," said Bortnicker. "The Seafood Supreme, in honor of Bermuda and all."

"You want a salad with that?"

"Salad?" said T.J. with mock horror, "who needs salad?"

"Yeah," agreed Bortnicker, "it's not like my mom's here or something."

"Okay, okay," said Tom Sr., raising his hands in surrender. "I was just trying. And a pitcher of Coke to go with that?"

"Sounds good," said Bortnicker, "and could I get a wedge of lemon in mine?"

"Done."

A harried waitress came over, and Mr. Jackson put in the order for their large pie, well done. "And could you bring some breadsticks while we wait?" he added. "These two are about to start eating the napkins."

"No problem, sir." She smiled, hurrying off.

"Okay, guys," said Tom Sr., "so tell me the basic info you learned in that big old packet they sent you. Let me see if there's any stuff I didn't know already."

"Well," said Bortnicker, snatching a sesame breadstick the second the waitress put the basket on their table, "we only really got through the part about Bermuda itself. There's still all the pirate history to go over."

"Fair enough. T.J.?"

"For starters, Dad, Bermuda's not an island, really. It's a group of like 120 smaller pieces of land covering 20 or so square miles, and it's kind of shaped like a fishhook."

"Yup, it sure is," said the elder Jackson, fondly remembering Bermuda's distinctive shape as seen from the air on his many visits.

"What's cool," said Bortnicker, "is that what Bermuda really is, is the exposed tip of an extinct volcano with a layer of limestone over it. That's what kinda creates the pink sand on its beaches that everyone raves about."

"And it really is pink," said Tom Sr., munching a breadstick. "Wait till you see it. People come just to see the sand!"

"Besides the beaches," said T.J., pouring himself some soda, "it has a pretty fair climate because of where it's located, 500 or so miles east of North Carolina, in the Gulf Stream. When we get there it should be in the low 80s."

"Heavenly," sighed Bortnicker.

"The temperature?" asked T.J.

"No, that eggplant parmigiana platter the next table over. Check it out."

"Could you focus, please? Anyway, Dad, what the write-up didn't explain is why the place is so expensive, like you're always saying. What's up with that?"

"Well, after World War II the population of the place really started growing. Now it's well over double what it was. So, the government's put the brakes on people establishing residences there—"

"It's British, right?" asked Bortnicker.

"Oh, yeah, though white Anglo Saxons are in the minority. They're a lot more proper than we are here, though that's seemed to break down a little in my most recent visits. Time was, you couldn't walk around Hamilton, that's the capital, wearing a tank top or skimpy shorts. You'd get looks or even maybe a comment. But now, with cruise ships crowding in and flights around the clock, the place is flooded with tourists in the warmer months, and a lot of them—especially us Americans, I'm afraid—think they're just at the Jersey Shore or something and don't respect Bermudian culture. You kids are going to make sure you behave, TV show or no.

"Anyway, by the 80s, when your mom and I went on our honeymoon, Bermuda had ceased to export *anything*—"

"Even Bermuda onions?" questioned Bortnicker.

"Even Bermuda onions. What little produce that comes out of their small farms is bought up by the locals and the restaurants. Now, everything is shipped into Bermuda, a lot of it from the States. That's why you'll pay four bucks for a bag of chips, or why this seafood pie they just took out of the oven would run you double or triple what we're paying at good old Pizza Palace.

"What's a shame is that, getting back to the 80s, Bermuda had something like 99% employment. Everybody had a job, so everybody was relatively happy. And most of those jobs, even today, revolve around the tourist trade. But that fell off in the 90s, and today you might even see some beggars around Hamilton or St. George's, which was unheard of back then.

"You see, what made Bermuda so great then, and even now to an extent, is that it's not like some of these other islands you go to where they tell you that you shouldn't venture outside the resort area for fear of drugs or violence. But if you keep up on world news, you'll see that every once and awhile there's some Bermuda crime—usually between gangs of locals—that the government tries to play down. Because tourism is *everything* in Bermuda, and that's why I'm being brought into this golf club project. The people who go there are prepared to spend the big bucks, and what's being offered has to be of the highest standard."

The waitress set the smoking pie onto a pedestal in the middle of their table with a quick "Watch it, it's hot!" and was off to take another order. The mozzarella was still bubbling over the bed of mussels, clams, and shrimp that gave the Seafood Supreme its distinct flavor.

"So, what I'm saying," said Tom Sr., gently pulling apart the slices and distributing them to the drooling teens' plates, "is that while I want you to enjoy the friendliness of the Bermudian people and all the island has to offer, you still can't let your guard down completely. And you've got to keep an eye on LouAnne. She's an attractive girl with a mind of her own. If anything happened to her, we'd all have to answer to Uncle Mike, and that wouldn't be pretty."

The boys nodded as they chewed. Mike Darcy, who was now a park ranger at the Gettysburg National Battlefield Park, had been an all Big-10 linebacker at Michigan State in his younger days where he had come to be known as "Maddog Mike" and was still fearsome.

They made short work of the pie, stopping only to order a second pitcher of Coke. As he settled the bill, Tom Sr. asked, "So, are you guys too full for ice cream?"

"I think not," said Bortnicker confidently.

"Aw, Dad, you just want a good reason to show off your baby," quipped T.J.

Tom Sr. couldn't help but smile. A trip to the local Dairy Queen on Post Road was the perfect occasion to drive his 1993 Jaguar XJS Coupe through town. The car, which T.J. jokingly called "The Midlife Crisis Mobile," had been picked up by Tom Sr. fairly cheaply and lovingly restored to concourse-level condition. Its oyster metallic paint gleamed in the twilight as Bortnicker wedged himself into the ridiculously cramped back seat while T.J. flicked on the surround sound stereo Tom Sr. had installed. The three bachelors cruised around, in no particular hurry to reach the DQ, and took in the sights of their quaint little town.

"How are we going to get around in Bermuda?" asked Bortnicker, trying to maneuver into a position where his leg wouldn't fall asleep.

"That might present a problem," said Tom Sr. "Because the island's population is so large, and the roads are only two-lane, each family on the island is only allowed one car." He chuckled. "What's funny is, when Jaguar was marketing this very car, they shipped an XJS to Bermuda to shoot the photos for the sales brochure. But you won't see and Jags there—just compacts or minivan taxis. And the price of gas there? Astronomical, because—"

"They have to import everything!" called Bortnicker from the back seat.

"Exactly. So, most families have a moped or two to go with the car, or they take public buses. But the moped thing's another problem. See, tourists can rent them anywhere on the island, but you have to have a driver's license, which means you guys are out of luck. But even though only adults can rent them, there are accidents galore because in Bermuda, you drive on the left side of the road, which throws Americans off. Then, there are rain showers that come out of nowhere and make the pavement slick, and let's not forget the idiots who have too many beers and think they're Evel Knievel."

"So what you're saying," said T.J. glumly, "is that we'll be taking the bus a lot."

"Well, not necessarily. I'm sure The Adventure Channel has hired some transportation for you guys to get you from place to place. I'll probably rent a moped myself, and I'm sure Weinstein will, too. Shouldn't be a problem."

They pulled up to the DQ and T.J. could see the pride on his dad's face as patrons in line pointed to the XJS. "Okay," he said, "time for some Blizzards. But remember, no ice cream in the car. Find a bench out front."

"Preferably one with a good view of the Jag?" said Bortnicker, extricating himself from the back seat.

"Of course." Tom Sr. locked the car with his remote and looked wistfully around at the place he used to come every Saturday with his wife and little boy. It brought a smile to his face. "Just think, guys," he said finally, "two weeks from today you'll be in paradise."

Chapter Seven

"Ahoy, me hearties," said LouAnne through the speaker phone in Bortnicker's bedroom.

"What's that playing in the background? *Meet the Beatles*?"

"You've got it," said Bortnicker as "It Won't Be Long" bounced off the walls of his cluttered enclave. "Hey, bet you don't know what the British version was called." He raised an eyebrow, awaiting her response as he stared at the iconic album cover photo of the foursome that was taken in half shadow.

"Bet I do. It's *With the Beatles*."

"She strikes again," said T.J. "Bortnicker, why don't you just give up trying to stump her?"

"I have not yet begun to fight," he said dramatically.

"Whatever," said LouAnne dismissively. "So, one week to go before you guys head over. Have you done all your studying?"

"Yeah," said T.J. "But what kinda surprises me is, here we are going after this pirate guy and all, but Bermuda wasn't exactly a big time pirate hangout."

Bortnicker agreed. "Compared to the Spanish Main, you're right. The reefs and the small islands with their coves provided protection for pirate ships, but as a whole, Bermuda was what you'd call out of the way.

"Most of the treasure ships in pirate times were going from South America back to Europe. They'd only stop in Bermuda if it was an emergency. And if they did, there wasn't much to steal there. Once the British established Bermuda as a colony in the 1600s they pretty much had it to themselves, although Spanish explorers had actually discovered the place."

"Which brings us to how Sir William Tarver fits in," broke in T.J. "There were two main privateers on the island in the early 1700s. One guy was Henry Jennings, who attacked Spanish strongholds where they were storing salvaged treasure from sunken Spanish galleons. The other was Tarver, whose background is really sketchy.

"Anyway, the governor of Bermuda, who was no dummy, figured that if he allowed Jennings and Tarver a pardon, they would establish legitimate businesses on the island and, as a bonus, provide a little protection against anyone who might attack.

"Jennings decided to turn to supplying colonial pirates outside of Bermuda with salt or tobacco. His men, using a few smaller boats called Bermuda sloops, would also harvest sea turtles or salvage treasure from sunken ships and then distribute their goods throughout the Caribbean."

"Yes," said LouAnne, "I read all that, but all I could get about Tarver was that he established a tobacco plantation on the island in what's now known as Southampton Parish."

"Which is why we're going to have to visit their historical society after we get there. Try to get a read on his murky past," said T.J.

"I see him as one of those swashbuckling types, a real ladies' man," LouAnne observed dreamily.

"You've been watching too many Johnny Depp movies," said Bortnicker. "Most of these guys were disease-riddled lowlifes with no teeth."

"Maybe," countered LouAnne, "but he must've been doing something right because he was pals with the governor and lived past the age of 40, and pretty comfortably, by all accounts."

"So, why is he haunting this Hibiscus House?" said T.J.

"Well," said Bortnicker, "if you owned a mansion on a tropical island would *you* want to leave? Ever?"

"But that's the thing," said LouAnne. "It seems the encounters have really only kicked into gear during the past seven months or so. Something must have triggered it. Remember the deal with Major Hilliard?"

"Yeah," said T.J., "what brought him back was when the grounds crew at the Battlefield Park unearthed his bones while they were digging a storm drain near the Emmitsburg Road."

"Exactly. So my guess is he's got a reason for coming back, just like Hilliard. And it's going to be up to us to find him and figure out what the story is."

"And we've got two weeks at the most to do it," stated T.J. seriously.

"And it's gonna be on TV," added Bortnicker.

"Yikes," said LouAnne. "Hey, by the way, what are you guys bringing over there?"

"Well," said T.J., "we've got all our basic dive gear, supplied by our guy Capt. Kenny. All we have to pick up there is our tanks. And then, enough shirts, shorts, and footwear for a couple weeks."

"Don't forget your track shoes," admonished LouAnne. "We've got to fit some running in—"

"Including a 5k race."

"Uh-huh. Are you ready for it?"

T.J. winked at Bortnicker and said, "Well, I just got done with baseball here, so it'll take me a few morning runs to get back into cross country mode."

"You mean, like last year when you came down to Pennsylvania and almost died on our first run?"

"Busted!" laughed Bortnicker.

"Very funny," said T.J., as his face grew hot with embarrassment. "Don't worry, I'll be prepared. And, oh, don't forget a change of nice clothes. Mike Weinstein said we might have to go out in public a couple times, and being underdressed in Bermuda is a real no-no."

"No problem," said LouAnne, "I've got a couple cute sundresses I'm packing."

"I'll bet she does," whispered Bortnicker, and T.J. punched him in the shoulder. "And don't forget your bathing suit!" he added impishly.

"Bortnicker, *really*. How could you go to Bermuda and not bring a suit?"

"I'm just saying."

"Okay, guys," she said finally. "I've gotta go. Are you as nervous about this as I am?"

"We can handle it," said T.J. somewhat confidently. "Remember, Mike will be there to help us out."

"Maybe so," she said, "but I wouldn't get too carried away. If you remember last year, he was a mess after Hilliard spooked him on the battlefield."

Indeed, the cousins' chance encounter with the then-inebriated paranormal investigator had occurred in the deserted bar of the inn were LouAnne worked as a Civil War reenactor.

"Don't worry, luv," said Bortnicker in his best Beatle twang, "a splendid time is guaranteed for all."

"*Sergeant Pepper*," she countered. "Talk to you soon."

Chapter Eight

"We're here!" crowed Bortnicker triumphantly as he emerged from the plane into the brilliant sunshine of a Bermuda morning. He smacked high fives with T.J. and Tom Sr. as they made their way down the mobile stairway to the tarmac of Bermuda International Airport.

Overall, the trip over had gone quite smoothly. A large SUV limo had come for them at 4:00 a.m. for the ride to LaGuardia Airport in Queens, NY, and the boys had been chatting away ever since. Check-in went without a hitch, with the teens securing their dive equipment and clothes while Mr. Jackson stowed his travel set of golf clubs.

"Some of the best business deals are struck on the back nine," he was always saying—for a few rounds on the club course he hoped to be renovating. The only thing they'd have to buy in Bermuda was a golf shirt for Bortnicker, who didn't have one that fit.

T.J. had managed to doze on the flight for a little while, but he was abruptly awakened by Bortnicker punching his shoulder and pointing out the window next to his seat.

"Look at the water!" Bortnicker marveled. "It's turquoise, just like the commercials!"

T.J. nodded, remembering his long ago childhood visit where he was constantly struck by the greenish-blue shallows and pastel-colored houses that lined the shores.

They walked across the hot tarmac to the terminal, adjusting their watches to Bermuda time, which was an hour ahead of the States. Though the place was a bit nondescript and a heckuva lot smaller than the cavernous US facilities T.J. was used to, he did vaguely remember the huge portrait of Queen Elizabeth and the imposing mounted sailfish that adorned its walls.

Of course, Bortnicker had to make their customs check more interesting. When the very proper inspector was stamping his passport and asked, "Are you here on business or pleasure?" Bortnicker was quick to answer with the former, which caused the official to look up. "And what business might that be, young man?"

"Well, actually," he sniffed, speaking loudly enough for those—especially the young ladies—in their vicinity to hear, "my friend and I are here to film a television show for The Adventure Channel."

"Oh really?" answered the inspector, playing along. "Quite the celebrities, you are?"

"Well, not yet," Bortnicker shot back. "But stay tuned."

"Oh, I'll make sure to, Mr. Bootnacker."

"It's *Bortnicker*," he replied suavely, retrieving his passport while T.J. rolled his eyes in embarrassment.

They picked up their belongings at the luggage carousel and piled them on a cart, heading for the lobby. No sooner had they entered the reception area when they spied Mike Weinstein, in his trademark black cargo shorts and tight, logoed, black *Gonzo Ghost Chasers* tee shirt, signing autographs for teenaged American tourists with one hand while holding aloft a placard reading JACKSON with the other.

"Dudes, you made it!" he yelled, extricating himself from the throng. "Welcome to Bermuda!" He introduced himself to Tom Sr. with a handshake then gave each of the boys a "bro-hug". "How was the flight?"

"No problems," said T.J. "We made it in a little over two hours."

"Awesome. Let's get your stuff out to the minivan."

They lugged the cart out the glass doors to the line of taxis idling at the ready for the wave of arriving tourists. "That would be ours," he said, pointing to a jet black minivan with large stick-on *Gonzo Ghost Chasers* decals applied to the side doors. A wiry black man sporting a pink golf shirt, Bermuda shorts, and high blue socks stood nearby, waving them over. With his salt-and-pepper hair and gleaming smile, he resembled a younger Morgan Freeman. "Nigel Chapford," he said, extending his hand in friendship," but please call me Chappy."

"Tom Jackson," said T.J.'s father, shaking his hand, "and these are the supposed TV stars, my son T.J. and Bortnicker."

"My pleasure, boys," he said with a mannered nod. "Welcome to our beautiful island."

"Chappy will be our driver during our stay," said Weinstein. "He's lived here all his life and knows the island inside and out."

"Including the best places to eat?" asked Bortnicker.

Chappy laughed out loud. "Of course! But not just the most popular tourist establishments. There are some hole-in-the-wall eateries that are quite good." The men helped load their luggage into the back of the minivan, and they were off.

The minivan made its way out of the congested terminal lot, crossed a two-lane causeway that spanned Castle Harbor, and headed south. Before long they passed the famous Swizzle Inn, which even at this mid-morning hour was teeming with patrons lounging on its wraparound porches, their moped scooters parked below.

"What's a Swizzle?" asked T.J., eyeing the revelers.

"One of Bermuda's most famous drink concoctions," answered Chappy merrily. "A combination of fruit juices, grenadine, and Bermuda rum. Quite tasty, but I'm afraid unsuitable for gents your age."

"They're sneaky good," nodded Mike, who seemed to have gathered first-hand experience in the two days he'd preceded them.

"Funny story," offered Tom Sr. "When Cheryl and I were on our honeymoon we went on a glass bottomed boat night cruise. The bottom of the boat had these lights, and you could see schools of fish below, which was pretty cool. Anyway, there was an open bar, T.J., and your mom started drinking those Swizzles, which seem pretty harmless because they're so fruity. Well, by the end of the cruise she was pretty looped, and I remember her waking me up in the middle of the night, moaning, "Stop the boat, honey. Stop the boat!" Tom Sr. was smiling at the memory, but even his son could see his eyes misting over. T.J. patted his father on the knee.

Bortnicker, sensing a need to change the subject, asked Mike, who was riding up front with Chappy, what the itinerary was for the day.

"Well, I was thinking you'll want to get unpacked and have lunch somewhere. Then, I suggest you go over to the Blue Lagoon Dive Shop in Somerset. And I guess, Tom, that you and I had better get our scooter rentals squared away. Chappy can't be in three places as once, and you'll want to be able to zip over to St. George's whenever you want. We'll both get two-seater models in case someone needs a ride."

Chappy spoke up. "I'd also advise that all of you invest in a weekly bus pass. You'll find the public transportation here is quite reliable and comfortable. There goes one now," he said, pointing to a pink vehicle passing on their right, fairly full of beachgoers. "You'll see bus stops that are close together, especially along South Road. They're marked by pink or blue poles. The pink ones designate buses going toward Hamilton; the blue, away. The bus will only stop if there are passengers who are waiting to board or wanting to disembark. The only drawback is that during the high season, you might have a bit of a wait."

The minivan cruised at a leisurely pace past sherbet-colored stucco houses crowned by whitewashed, terraced roofs designed to catch fresh rainwater which was channeled to storage tanks for home use. Handmade stone walls alternated with gardens and wildflowers and small plot farms. Occasionally a moped zoomed by, usually at speeds far exceeding the posted limit of 20 mph. Chappy, who was used to the recklessness of both residents and tourists, would just shake his head and carry on. Finally, after meandering down some connecting roads with colorful names like Ducks Puddle Drive, they hit South Road, which passed through Smith's, Devonshire and Paget Parishes before entering their home base of Warwick.

"I take it the parishes here are like counties at home?" asked T.J.

"That's a fair analogy," said Chappy, "though they're much smaller than in the States. There are nine in all, and are all different, though those differences are somewhat subtle. Actually, these land packets were first known as "tribes", and you will see designated "tribal roads" here and there. The divisions have to do with how the island parcels were allocated to different English shareholders centuries ago. Some of the parishes are even named for these men.

"You'll notice differences in population and even architecture as you go from place to place. Some parishes are quieter and more residential, while others, like Hamilton, are on the urban side. Southampton, where we are headed, is decidedly touristy, which is not to say that it isn't remarkably beautiful. It's just that its shoreline contains a number of the island's most stunning beaches, some of them backed by towering cliffs. Quite impressive." Chappy was obviously very proud of his homeland and seemed as delighted to share information with the boys as he probably had with thousands of other tourists.

They passed by resorts with names like Coco Reef, Harmony Club, and Elbow Beach, each entranceway spewing forth tourists on mopeds.

"So, Chappy," said Mike, "what's the story with Hibiscus House and Sir William Tarver? It's why we're here, after all."

T.J. just happened to be glancing into the minivan's rearview mirror and could see an almost imperceptible cloud settle over the driver's face. "Ah, yes, Sir William," he said evenly. "Interesting man. Made his fortune through piracy, they say … then was given the estate by the governor. But I would imagine you know as much."

"Was he a bad guy or something?" asked T.J.

"Well, that depends, young sir, upon what you categorize as 'bad'. I think that it would be in your best interest to do your research here and come to your own conclusions." From the polite, yet firm tone of his voice the Americans could tell they should pursue the subject no further. An awkward moment or two passed, and then Chappy said, "Ah, here we are." He turned into a narrow entrance road framed with bougainvillea and palm trees. "Gentlemen, I give you the Jobson's Cove Apartments."

The beachside hideaway consisted of about twelve units in an L-shaped, two-story structure overlooking a moderately-sized, kidney shaped pool. Nestled into a hillside, the surrounding dense vegetation and tropical flowers gave it a secluded feeling. A few guests lounged by the pool while an elderly couple sat on the deck chairs in the Bermuda grass, contentedly reading. As Chappy helped the travelers unload their bags, a matronly woman with long gray hair tied back in a ponytail swept out of the hotel office, her pink caftan flapping in the light ocean breeze.

"So nice to meet you!" she chirped in a lilting British voice. "I'm Virginia Maltby, the proprietor. Sorry to say, my husband Morris is visiting our daughter in England, so I'll be your go-to person for whatever you might need. Mr. Weinstein has told me all about your exciting adventure! I'm so glad you chose Jobson's Cove, and we'll try to make your stay as pleasant as possible.

"As I told Michael the other day, I've put your four rooms together on the second floor because, that way, you'll avoid any poolside noise, or people coming and going at all hours. It will be a bit of an effort lugging your bags up the stairs, but you'll see that it's well worth it. From your balconies you'll just be able to peek over the treetops of Astwood Park and view the ocean in all its glory.

"As you can see, we have a delightful pool, and there are also barbeque grills under the palm trees over there in case you'd want to eat in.

"There's a bus stop a stone's throw from the entrance, but I can see that you've hired one of our best drivers for your stay." She shot Chappy a wink; they were obviously old acquaintances, veterans of the tourist trade.

"Where's the beach, ma'am?" asked Bortnicker, slinging his carry-on over his shoulder.

"It's quite simple, really. Cross the road from our main entrance and you will be in Astwood Park. Follow the path through the trees down to the cliffs. From there you'll see walkways to the beach. Jobson's Cove, from which we draw our name, is tucked away behind some massive boulders to the right, forming a kind of shallow lagoon. It's quite picturesque."

The party thanked Virginia as she handed them the keys to their rooms. "Ta-ta!" she trilled, scurrying off to check on the other patrons.

"Well, let's get all this stuff upstairs," said Mike. "Like Virginia said, the view from up there will make it all worthwhile."

"Would you want me to stick around a bit?" asked Chappy, cleaning some squashed bugs off the minivan's windshield.

"That would be great," said Tom Sr. "We'll drop off our bags, and then maybe you can bring me to that market up the road so I can stock up on necessities for myself and the boys."

"I'll need to pick up some stuff, too," added Mike. "The only thing in my fridge is some beer and tuna fish from yesterday."

"No worries. And then I suppose you'll want me to drop you at the cycle rental place?"

"That makes sense," said Mike. "Then you can pick up the boys, grab some lunch, and run them over to the Blue Lagoon Dive Shop to check on their rentals."

"You aren't diving?" asked Bortnicker.

"Nah, not my thing," said Mike. "I'll be on the charter boat with you, but it's your show. You'll be doing all the diving and the filming. I've got all the equipment for land and sea in my apartment. If you're not too tired tonight, we'll meet there and go over how to use it all. Then you can explain it to LouAnne when she gets here."

"Sounds like a plan!" said T.J. enthusiastically.

The boys opened the door to their room and were greeted with walls of a warm yellow and cushy twin beds. There was a rather large beach-scene painting on the wall, a comfy couch, and a teak and rattan dinette set. Off to the side was a kitchenette with a sink, some cabinets, and a refrigerator. A microwave oven sat on the Formica countertop.

"All the comforts of home!" sighed Bortnicker, flopping onto the closest bed.

"Yeah," said T.J., "and we've got a big overhead fan in case the sea breeze cuts out." He slid open the glass balcony door and stepped outside. "Nice," he said to himself as the wind carried the scent of flowers from Astwood Park.

"Hey," said Bortnicker, "why don't we get unpacked and check out the beach while Mike and your dad are running their errands?"

"Sounds good." He went next door and encountered Tom Sr., who was dropping shirts into a bureau drawer in his nearly identical room. "Hey Dad, Bortnicker and I are going down to the beach. Make sure you buy a lot of food so we can grill a couple times. Some snacks, too. And some breakfast cereal. And—"

"T.J.," said Tom Sr. patiently, "I know how to stock a refrigerator. And although all this is on The Adventure Channel's dime, I don't want us to overdo it. And another thing…" He closed the door to the apartment. "I want you to keep in mind that although I'm sure Mike is a responsible adult, he is only in his late 20s, and he, understandably, likes to have a good time. Bermuda, especially Hamilton, has a pretty lively nightclub scene, and as you can see, he enjoys his celebrity. So, while I'm sure he'll be all business when you guys are doing the show, don't be surprised if we lose him once in a while. I'm counting on you guys to take care of yourselves and LouAnne when we're not around. I know you guys aren't drinkers or anything—"

"Dad, I gotcha," answered T.J. "We won't do anything dumb. I promise."

"Okay," said Tom Sr. He gave T.J. an unexpected hug. "This is such a great opportunity for you guys, and this place is wonderful, but it feels so weird—"

"Being here without Mom?"

"Yeah. Bermuda was our special place." He broke away gently and wiped his eyes. "Sorry."

"Hey, Dad, no problem. Maybe you'll meet somebody here. You never know."

"What? Like Wendy? No, thank you," he said, referring to the previous summer when he'd run off to Paris with a much younger—albeit gorgeous—woman while T.J. stayed in Gettysburg. The trip had ended in disaster, with the flirtatious Wendy leaving him for a suave Parisian waiter.

"Well," said T.J., "whatever you choose to do, I want you to know I'm okay with it. I was a little selfish last year, giving you a hard time about leaving me at Uncle Mike's. I mean, if you didn't go, I never would've helped solve the ghost mystery or got to know LouAnne. So, it all worked out, on my end anyway."

"You like her, don't you?" his father said, fixing him with a serious look.

"Well, of course, Dad, she's my cousin—"

"You know what I mean, son. I realize she's only related to you by adoption—"

"Aw, jeez, Dad," the boy said, feeling his face redden.

"Just be very, very careful with people's feelings, T.J. You've always had a good heart, but sometimes your heart gets ahead of your brain."

Mercifully, there was a knock on the door, and Mike Weinstein poked his head in. "Dude, Chappy's waiting downstairs with the car," he said brightly. "Let's get motoring!"

"Right behind you," called out Tom Sr. Father and son walked out together into the noonday sun.

Chapter Nine

"Can you believe this?" said T.J. as the boys sat atop the majestic limestone cliffs and watched foaming waves crash upon the beach below. The refreshing spray of the ocean, filled with salt and seaweed, reached all the way to their perch at the edge of Astwood Park. Below them, birds called longtails peeked in and out of the pockmarked headland. Clouds scudded across an azure sky, and the water seemed to go on forever.

"Makes you forget why we're actually here," said Bortnicker. "Hey, did you notice how Chappy clammed up when Mike mentioned William Tarver?"

"Yeah," said T.J., "like the subject was too touchy."

"Hmm. By the way, what were you and your dad doing all that time in his room? Is everything all right?"

"Yeah, we were just talking."

"About what?"

"Stuff."

"Such as?"

"Nothing important. He just wants us to behave ourselves over here, that's all. Bermuda's special to him, and he doesn't want us screwing up."

"Oh. Does this have to do with your mom?"

"Yeah, I guess. He gets pretty emotional about it sometimes, and then it makes me feel bad, too."

"I know, Big Mon. But, hey, you've got me, and by tomorrow

afternoon, LouAnn'll be joining the party!"

T.J. brightened. "Let's go check out that pink sand, man," he said, pushing up from his seat. "These rocks are killing my butt."

They clambered down to a narrow path and sprinted toward the water's edge, where the foaming surf hissed as the waves pulled back with a powerful undertow.

"Look!" cried Bortnicker, standing calf-deep in the surging current. "There's a school of fish swimming in the waves!" Indeed, a swirling mass was apparent each time a wave crested. "Too cool!"

They followed the shoreline to Jobson's Cove, climbing over the sheltering rocks that formed the lagoon. It was no more than 50 feet across or a few feet deep, but it contained a host of tropical fish that had squeezed through the boulders looking for food or calmer waters. A few tourists lay on the small beach while their children snorkeled in the crystal clear pool. "It's like seeing one picture postcard after another," said T.J.

"No question. Hey, shouldn't we be getting back to the hotel? I don't know about you, but I'm getting hungry, and Chappy's supposed to know all the good spots."

"Let's do it."

They found the personable driver stretched out on a reclining chair near the pool. "Ah, there you are," he said, rising. "Michael and Tom Sr. have already dropped off your provisions and are, as we speak, renting their scooters. What did you have in mind for lunch?"

"Is there a place near the dive shop where we can eat something Bermudian?"

"Well, that's encouraging," said Chappy. "Most Yanks just want to know where they can find a good cheeseburger."

"Bortnicker's like Joe Gourmet," explained T.J. "So let's start off with something local."

"As they say in the States, 'I like how you guys roll'. Hop in and let's go."

T.J. grabbed the front seat while Bortnicker stretched out in the back.

"Is there any particular music you gents like to listen to?" asked Chappy as he cautiously pulled out of the hotel's entrance.

"Bortnicker's really into the Beatles right now," said T.J. "I'll listen to just about anything except hip-hop."

"The Beatles, eh?" said Chappy, turning right on South Road toward Somerset. "I have most of their CDs at home. Got interested in them after I drove John Lennon around."

"*What*?" blurted Bortnicker, nearly springing out of the back seat.

"Oh, yes indeed. Mr. Lennon came here a couple times in 1980, before his untimely death. Sailed over the first time, actually. Had his young son with him. I was assigned to him quite by chance that first time, and we more or less hit it off. When he came back for a more secretive, solitary weekend, he actually requested me. Alas, a few weeks after that second trip he was killed."

"That's incredible!" gushed Bortnicker. "What did you talk about? Was he a nice guy?"

"Well, he was quite pleasant to *me*. But old John was always quick with a quip or a remark. We discussed music, mostly, with the both of us being musicians and all."

"You're a musician?" said T.J.

"Well, it's my second career, though it's my first love. Helped me put my son through school. He's entering his junior year at Georgetown University in the States, majoring in finance. Hopes to come back here and find a position with the Bank of Bermuda."

"Wow, so you're a rocker, Chappy?" asked Bortnicker.

"No, no," he chuckled. "I'm actually a member of a well-known group over here. We call ourselves the Beachcombers, and our specialties are Caribbean and Reggae. I play a fairly good steel drum, I'm told."

"And here we have the famous Nigel Chapford, driver by day and musical artist by night," said Bortnicker, channeling his inner Beatle.

"That's quite good," laughed Chappy. "You actually sounded a bit like him."

"Chappy," said T.J., "don't encourage him, unless you want to hear it all the time."

"I'll take your advice, T.J." Chappy replied. "Keep practicing, Mr. B, you'll get it eventually." He smiled, flashing a thumbs-up in the rearview mirror.

Paul Ferrante

Undeterred, Bortnicker nodded with satisfaction. "Can we come see you perform sometime?"

"Well, if your schedule allows, our band has a standing gig at the Elbow Beach Resort on Thursday nights. They stage a rather extravagant seafood buffet on their patio, and we provide the ambience."

"We're there!" exclaimed Bortnicker. "I'm sure Mike'll give us a couple nights off. Wait'll I tell LouAnne that you knew John Lennon!"

"That would be the final member of your party whom we're fetching from the airport tomorrow afternoon?"

"Yeah," said T.J. "She's my cousin. You'll like her."

"I'm sure I will," Chappy answered graciously.

"Which reminds me," said T.J., "we're taking part in the 5k Teen Run a week from tomorrow, and I'm trying to figure out the best place for us to run in the morning so we can prepare."

Chappy pursed his lips and tapped on the steering wheel, thinking hard. "Well, if you want the scenic route, you need do nothing more than take a right out of your hotel onto South Road. If you run with the traffic, meaning on the left, of course, you will at times be able to look down on the shoreline and the ocean. Wonderful vistas and all that. However, in the mornings you'll be sharing the road with what constitutes our rush hour traffic. Throw in some crazy tourists on scooters, and you have a potentially dangerous situation. I recommend instead the Bermuda Railway Trail—"

"You have your own *railroad*?" said Bortnicker eagerly.

T.J. frowned. "You've got to excuse Bortnicker, Chappy," he said. "He's like a model train fanatic. Anytime he hears 'railroad' he goes wild. But still, I would think Bermuda's too small to have trains."

"Well, it is," said Chappy, "but that didn't stop the government from giving it a try in the 1920s. Caused a lot of controversy, but by the 30s it ran pretty much the length of the island. Until the end of World War II, it was the island's primary source of transportation. But, given the amount of use, especially during the War, and the climate and salt causing corrosion on the bridges and trestles, it was deemed impractical to maintain. Then, in 1946 we introduced buses here, and by the following year, the rail system was shut down and the trains sold off to the British colony in Guyana. By the time Bermuda allowed private motor vehicles to be imported in '48, nobody even cared the trains were gone.

"But the Railway Trail where the tracks were formerly was left for hikers, bikers—but no mopeds—and runners, like yourself. There are some interruptions, but it follows most of the former track, and you'll be treated to ever-changing scenery as you run. Farms, fields, some thick jungle, even some glimpses of the ocean—it's all there."

"Cool," said T.J. "How do I get there from the hotel?"

"You're in luck," he said. "Take a left out onto South Road, and your first left on the Tribal Road about 100 feet away. You'll climb up a hill and, shortly, see the entrance for the Railway Trail. If you take a left onto the trail and go west, it will take you all the way across Southampton Parish and beyond. It's quiet, and you'll catch shady areas here and there. Joggers also like it because it provides a softer surface than the pavement of South Road."

"Are there any snakes in there?" asked T.J., remembering vaguely how his cousin had once expressed a fear of the creatures.

"Bermuda has no snakes, T.J.," he said. "Lizards, yes; snakes, no."

"Looks like you've got a training course," said Bortnicker.

"Seems like it. I'm gonna try it tomorrow morning so I can tell LouAnne about it when we pick her up."

"You'll enjoy the road race, T.J.," said Chappy. "It begins on the western tip near the Royal Naval Dockyard and ends in Hamilton. So, in the end, you will get to run on South Road, except that the police will ensure your safety. Perhaps your father and Mike will want to follow you on their scooters? It's a pleasant ride. They are renting extra helmets and double-seater bikes, by the way.

"Which reminds me," he said, snapping his fingers, "I have a note for you from Mike." He fished around in his pants pocket and pulled out a piece of stationery from the hotel.

T.J. read it aloud:

Dudes,

When you get to the Blue Lagoon Dive Shop, make sure our reservation for Tuesday's dive is squared away. Rent all the equipment you still need. The Adventure Channel has been handling this so far, and the guy who's taking us there, Jasper Goodwin, is the one who discovered the wreck you'll be diving on, which we hope is Tarver's. If he's out on a charter you're to ask for Ronnie Goodwin. Any problems, call me on my cell.

See you later,
Mike

"Sounds good," said Bortnicker. "But we're eating first, right?"

"No sooner said than done," answered Chappy, as he turned into a crushed shell parking lot near a pink building that could barely be classified as a shack. There was a small deck on the side with tiny umbrellaed tables and a couple men, who looked to be locals, taking a break from the sun to enjoy a beer. "I give you Dora's Corners, your first real Bermudian dining experience. All I can tell you is, it's where the natives eat."

They went inside, the screen door slapping shut behind them. "Well, well," said a huge black woman mopping her brow as she wiped a counter that had seen better days. "To what do we owe the honor of a visit by Nigel Chapford himself?"

"Ah, Dora, pleasant as always," cooed Chappy, leaning across the counter to plant a kiss on the proprietor's sweaty cheek. "Allow me to introduce my two friends, T.J. and Bortnicker. They're here from the States to film a TV show."

"You don't say," she remarked, quickly wiping grease off her hand before shaking with the teens. "We're honored. Not too many visitors from the U.S. find their way here."

"Well," said T.J., ever the diplomat, "we asked Chappy—uh, Mr. Chapford—where we could get the most authentic Bermuda food in Somerset, and he brought us to you."

"Did he now? What a righteous gentleman."

T.J. was starting to pick up a kind of accent from the natives. It was hard to put your finger on, kind of a switching of V's and W's, and a J sound when you had a vowel following a D. So "Bermudian" came out "Bermewjan".

"Let's see," said Dora, opening the refrigerator behind her to pull out a couple bottles of fruit juice. "How does Hoppin' John and my Smokin' Bean Soup sound?"

The boys looked to Chappy, who nodded.

"Great," said T.J.

"All right, then," said Dora, "it will take a few minutes, as you can't rush perfection. Have a seat here at the counter and enjoy your drink. Mr. Chapford, a cold Red Stripe for your efforts?"

"No thanks, not at the moment," he said as Dora placed the sweating bottle of beer back in the refrigerator. "I'm still on duty. But I could stop in later—"

"You're on," she smiled, throwing a dishtowel over her shoulder as she waddled over to the stove. "I'll count the hours."

"If you don't mind, boys, I'd like to go put petrol in the minivan. If you finish before I return, the dive shop is only a couple hundred feet up the road. I'll pick you up there."

"No problem," said Bortnicker. "Take your time."

Chappy waved goodbye and was off.

"You boys must be living well," said Dora over her shoulder. "Hiring out one of the island's best drivers for the day?"

"It might be more like two weeks," said T.J., sipping his mango juice, which was tangy and sweet at the same time.

"Do tell," said Dora. "And with petrol over eight dollars a gallon. Are your producers footing the bill for this?"

"Yeah," said Bortnicker, draining his bottle. "A pretty sweet deal. May I have another juice?"

"Yes, you may," said Dora, mixing some vegetables and meat in a skillet. "So what's the show about? Travel do's and don'ts, that sort of thing?"

"No, not really," T.J. began. "We're—"

"We're part of a ghost hunting expedition!" said Bortnicker grandly, making T.J. wince.

Dora slid another juice across the counter to Bortnicker. For the first time T.J. noticed two other people in the room who were eating at a corner table. From their appearance, they seemed to be laborers. And they were paying attention. "And whose ghost would you be hunting, darlin'?" she asked dubiously.

"Sir William Tarver," said T.J. "Ever heard of him?" He watched as the formerly effervescent woman adopted the same eerie veil of impassivity that had come over Chappy earlier.

She turned back to the stove as if his question had never occurred and busied herself with stirring a cast iron pot of soup. T.J. and Bortnicker looked at each other with raised eyebrows.

At that point, the two men at the corner table got up to leave. One of them, a towering guy with dreadlocks and a full black beard, placed a few dollars on the counter. Before heading for the door, he turned to the boys. "I'd stay away from Hibiscus House," he whispered deeply, so it was almost a growl. "A bad place. You don't know what you be messin' with." He clomped out.

Suddenly, Dora was before them, returned to her earlier cheerful self, with two steaming plates of food. "All right," she said to T.J., "for you we have Hoppin' John and paw paw Montespan, which feature black-eyed peas and ground beef made with tomatoes and paw paw, with some rice. And for your friend there's our tangy Portuguese red bean soup, with a hunk of my homemade brown bread. Feel free to share with each other." She started to turn away, then thought better of it and again faced the boys. "That man that spoke to you—Willie B.—he's not completely right in the head. Pay him no mind." Dora went back into her kitchen area, where the boys could hear the *whap-whap-whap* of her chopping vegetables.

The pair chewed robotically; though the food was savory and exotic, its taste barely registered. They finished, paid their tab, which included a generous tip, thanked Dora, and walked out. If they were expecting a "hope to see you again," it wasn't forthcoming.

"What was *that* all about?" said Bortnicker, squinting in the sunlight.

"Don't know," said T.J. "It's like if we mention Tarver, everyone goes zombie. We gotta mention this to Mike."

"So, on to the dive shop?"

"Yeah, it's gotta be friendlier than Dora's Corners."

Chapter Ten

The Blue Lagoon Dive Shop was a low-slung, pale blue stucco building near a canal spanned by a charming mini drawbridge. Behind it lay a cove where pleasure boats bobbed at their shallow moorings. A dock out back provided slips for the business's two charter boats, *Reef Seeker I* and *II*. From the tiny bridge the boys could see that one of the boats was absent.

They entered the shop and were immediately struck by the differences between this place and Capt. Kenny's back home. The decorations were decidedly more upscale; there was no musty sea smell, either. The prices on the equipment were definitely more geared to tourists with a lot of disposable income. Blue Lagoon also sported a few display cases, but unlike Capt. Kenny's they were filled with wondrous shells and pieces of coral. No historical artifacts whatsoever. Soothing Caribbean music drifted down from ceiling speakers. T.J. wondered if this was the right place to hire out a boat for a wreck dive; then he remembered that its owner was the man who had discovered their wreck in the first place. "Hello?" he called out in the deserted showroom. "Anyone here?"

The boys heard a rustling behind the front counter and made their way over. "Mr. Goodwin?" said Bortnicker, unable to ascertain the source of the sounds.

"Not here," was the muffled reply.

"We were told to ask for Ronnie if Mr. Goodwin was out," he said impatiently.

"You found her," said the girl as she rose up, a dust cloth in her hand. She stood at around the boys' height of 5'6", with shoulder length hair that projected in tight corkscrews and framed her face. But what gave Ronnie Goodwin her stunning good looks was the way her milk chocolate-colored skin was set off by turquoise eyes that mirrored the Bermudian waters surrounding the island.

T.J. was taken aback, mostly because he'd been expecting a guy to be working in the dive shop, but Bortnicker was positively mesmerized. T.J. had seen that look before, and it was always a cause for concern. If his friend ever came face to face with a pretty female he tended to gawk and invariably say something stupid. Just this past year a girl named Giulia DeCarlo had, on a dare from her mean-girl cronies, asked Bortnicker to dance at their school's Valentine's Day social. Now, Giulia was fairly attractive (though the three pounds of makeup she applied daily went a long way into producing the final effect), but Bortnicker was completely unprepared to deal with a girl who was quite clearly out of his league, so he had mumbled some kind of excuse and escaped to the safety of the boys' restroom as DeCarlo's gang howled. And of course, he'd acted like an idiot with LouAnne, with whom he'd decided a courtly kiss of the hand was appropriate when he'd first met her in Gettysburg, vexing T.J. to no end.

But this ... this was scary.

"Well, my full name's Veronique," she said with that soft Bermudian lilt, "but to everyone else I'm just Ronnie." She extended her hand, and T.J. cut his eyes sideways to see if Bortnicker would take it. When he froze, T.J. stepped in and shook with her.

"I'm T.J. Jackson," he said politely, "and this strange person with me is my friend, Bortnicker. We're here about a charter trip that The Adventure Channel's arranged?"

Ronnie fixed her gaze on Bortnicker, and a wry smile creased her full lips. "I've heard so much about you guys," she said pleasantly, extending her hand again to Bortnicker, who managed to shake it while smiling crookedly. Of course. Mike had been here already; it was all a setup. T.J. smiled to himself. *Well played, Weinstein,* he thought.

"Let me show you around the shop," said Ronnie, moving from behind the counter gracefully. She was wearing a Bob Marley tee shirt knotted at her midriff and a pair of faded cutoffs. The girl wasn't what

T.J. would call voluptuous, but Ronnie Goodwin wasn't too far off.

They followed her around as she described the equipment and how Blue Lagoon conducted their rentals. From what T.J. could tell, she was quite knowledgeable. As if reading his mind, she said, "I've been working here for ten years now. Started tagging along with Dad when I was four or five."

Finally, Bortnicker spoke. "Get a lot of tourists here, I guess."

"That's *all* we get, actually. The majority are friendly, but some are fairly demanding. We're booked most days of the week, sometimes twice a day. My dad has an assistant who either serves as first mate on the bigger boat or takes people out on the *Reef Seeker II* if we're double booked."

"How's business?" asked Bortnicker, struggling to make conversation.

"Oh, we do all right," she said with a wink. "My dad's owned the business since the late 90s, when he bought out the original owner, who was retiring. This was one of the first certified dive shops on the island. Dad spent a lot of years here, working his way up to first mate, and scraping together enough money to someday own his own place. Mr. Osgood gave Dad a pretty good deal because he'd been such a loyal employee."

"Well said, young lady!" applauded an athletic, dark skinned man who had slipped in the rear door. "You're making me sound quite the hero."

Embarrassed, Ronnie skipped over and kissed him on the cheek. "Oh, Daddy, you know you're the best Divemaster in Bermuda. You're just too modest to admit it."

"Shh, child," he whispered, giving her a quick hug. "I take it these are our American TV stars?"

"Uh-huh. This one with the Paul McCartney eyes is T.J. And this man of few words is Bortnicker."

Jasper Goodwin shook hands with the pair as Bortnicker went a pinkish red. "Great to have you here, boys. Let's have a seat and chat." He pulled a few cane chairs over to a card table littered with brochures featuring different Bermuda attractions. Ronnie took a seat next to Bortnicker, raising his already high level of self-consciousness.

When they were all settled, Jasper unrolled a detailed chart that said *Sites of Bermuda Shipwrecks*. "Right," he began. "Now, look at this map, boys. As you probably noticed on your flight in, Bermuda is ringed with coral reefs. In fact, the first British colony started here in 1609 came about because a ship called the *Sea Venture* that was bound for Virginia hit the rocks here. Salvaging the contents of wrecked ships in our relatively shallow and clear waters became a major industry for the settlers and was later sanctioned by Governor Nathaniel Butler. Bermudian salvagers of one stripe or another would continue this practice even after World War II."

"So there are lots of wrecks around the island?" asked T.J.

"Well," said Goodwin, rubbing his grey-flecked black goatee, "look for yourself. This chart alone features 30 or so wrecks that have been identified. Overall, there have been reports of over 250 sunken vessels at various depths, ranging from the 1600s to the present. Oops—please excuse me for a moment."

The passengers from *Reef Seeker I* had by now gathered their gear and come inside, escorted by a whipcord-thin white man in a Blue Lagoon Dive Shop golf shirt and white cargo shorts. Jasper approached each and every client, inquired as to whether they'd enjoyed themselves—they most certainly had—and pointed out the various tee shirts, tank tops and hats bearing the Blue Lagoon logo that they might want to purchase as a keepsake of their underwater adventure. Ronnie hustled over to the cash register to run them up, and the white man handed out certificates to the clients to commemorate the dive. When they'd all been seen to, Jasper and his daughter rejoined the boys, who were still pouring over the chart.

"Sorry, gentlemen, business and all that," said Jasper.

"No problem," said T.J. "Seems like they had a great dive."

"Oh, yes. Today we had optimum conditions—water temperature 80 degrees and around 100 feet visibility. So, we checked out some marine life and then dove on the wreck of the *Constellation*, an American schooner that sank in 1943. Perfect for recreational divers."

"I'll go wash down the boat," called the white man, who had finished lugging the air tank inside for refilling.

"Brilliant, Skeeter. I'll join you in a bit." Jasper traced a calloused finger along the South Shore, which was sprinkled with ship icons and names. "All right, boys. What I'm pointing to here is the Gibbs Hill Lighthouse, the oldest cast-iron lighthouse in the world, located in Southampton Parish. I believe you're staying nearby at the Jobson's Cove Apartments?"

"Right," said T.J.

"Okay, well you must realize that the lighthouse didn't go up until the mid-1800s, not that shipwrecks didn't occur way after that and even today. But back in the 1700s it was quite difficult to see at night, even in clear weather under a bright moon.

"A few months ago I took a small party out to a wreck called the *Mary Celeste*—"

"I saw that ship on *Deep Sea Detectives!*" broke in Bortnicker.

"I thought you said he was quiet," Jasper said playfully to his daughter.

"Well, TV people *can* be rather dramatic, Daddy," she replied, rubbing Bortnicker's shoulder supportively.

"I suppose. Anyway, I got everyone in the water and then decided to have a dip myself, maybe catch a lobster or spear a hogfish for dinner. And the most extraordinary thing occurred."

The boys inched closer on their seats like they used to with Capt. Kenny.

"I was swimming along, hugging the bottom, when I topped a rise and then looked down. Now, we had a couple hurricanes blow through during the fall, and it must've disrupted the landscape down there dramatically, because I came upon the remains of the timbers of a very old ship."

"Cool!" said T.J. "And no one had ever seen it before?"

"Apparently not. It was like Neptune had pulled back a curtain for me or something.

"Of course, it's not like you see in cartoons or whatever—an intact ship sitting upright on the ocean bottom. As I said, I found the outline of the ship's ribs and some ballast stones. There were even a few coral-encrusted cannon lying about."

"Any treasure?" said T.J.

Jasper Goodwin gave a hearty laugh. "No, boys, no pieces of eight, or emeralds winking at me from the ocean floor. The ship—which appears to be what we call a Bermuda Sloop—lies in less than 30 feet of water, so I would imagine most of whatever it held was salvaged years ago. That doesn't mean there's nothing left there, however."

"Why do they call it a Bermuda Sloop?" asked Bortnicker.

"Well, basically because the design was conceived on the island, a fore-and-aft rigged vessel with anywhere from one to three sails. It was sleek and highly maneuverable, which was essential to pirates who wanted to surprise the more unwieldy treasure galleons you see in those fanciful Johnny Depp movies—"

"I think he's cute, actually," Ronnie whispered in Bortnicker's ear, her warm breath making his eyes widen.

"—and then escape quickly around the reefs and small islands both here and throughout the Caribbean. Later the vessels were used in the merchant trade, but the sturdy construction of Bermudian cedar was highly rot-resistant, and the low density of the wood made the ships lighter, faster, and more durable. What little wood I found was cedar."

"But how could you possibly connect it to William Tarver?" asked T.J.

"Good question. Well, it was no secret that Sir William had made his fortune through privateering, though he remains a somewhat shadowy figure in Bermudian history. If your investigation team is going to truly prepare for this enterprise, I can't stress enough the importance of a trip to our Maritime Museum to speak with a Bermuda historian. But there's long been a rumor that somehow, Tarver's ship—a Bermuda Sloop called the *Steadfast*, sank off the southern coast of the island. How and why is equally mysterious, and so far any information that might be known by the historical authorities has not been freely shared.

"That doesn't mean they won't cooperate with your group. In fact, it must have been the National Heritage Trust that contacted The Adventure Channel in the first place. And I suppose that someone mentioned my claim to your people as well, because here you are."

"Your claim?" asked Bortnicker.

"Oh, yes, let me explain. To be brief, our government enacted in the 1960s a series of strict laws to restrict the removal of any artifacts—including those classified as treasure—from wrecks in our local waters.

If someone such as myself discovers a wreck and they want to dig on it, they must, for a nominal fee, file an exclusivity claim with the island's Curator of Wrecks. Then, they must turn over all that is found to the government."

"So there must be a lot of guys out there with salvage permits," said T.J.

"Actually, no. Most discoveries go unreported, because the finder wouldn't want to turn over those wonderful doubloons and silver bars, would he? So they are dived upon illegally, and whatever is found gets sold through back channels."

"So, why did you apply for a permit, then?"

Goodwin sighed as his daughter shook her head slowly in disappointment. "I figured that most of what was of any value was long gone—"

"And you're disgustingly honest!" cut in Ronnie, before Jasper silenced her with a stern look.

"I'm looking at this from a purely historical perspective. That's why I welcomed the opportunity to have you boys join me here."

"But we're not exactly crack archaeologists," said Bortnicker. "Besides, our schedule will give us only a couple diving days, max."

"Well, I'll take all the help I can get. If we can find just one artifact that is linked to Sir William or the *Steadfast*, it would be incredible."

"Like what?"

"Oh, a monogrammed piece of silver or china. Or, of course, the ship's bell. I was able to make out the inscription of the year on one of the cannon, and it fits the period, so we are, as you Yanks like to say, 'in the ballpark'."

"So, when do we dive?" asked T.J. eagerly.

"Well, I have scheduled us for Tuesday and Thursday of this week. Let's start with that and see how much time you've got to give it. You've brought your certification credentials, I hope?"

The boys immediately fished the PADI cards Capt. Kenny had awarded them from their wallets and flashed them proudly.

"Splendid. So many of our clients are new to the sport and most just want to poke about the reefs and look at tropical fish, so it's refreshing to meet people your age with an interest in history—"

"And in a great man," said Ronnie with a definitive air.

"You think so?" asked T.J., happy to at last hear from someone who was willing to even discuss Sir William Tarver.

"I *know* so. Okay, he was a pirate. So were a lot of other men of the time. What's important is that he helped build Bermuda and was willing to protect her from attack."

"I'd tone that down a bit, young lady," said her father gently. "There's a lot about him we still don't know."

"But that's why the guys are here!" she said strongly. "To bring light to our country's past." She turned in her seat and looked Bortnicker square in the eye. "If there's any way I can help you learn more about Bermuda on this trip, just say the word."

Bortnicker, clearly in a state of panic, had barely opened his mouth to speak when she said, "What about tomorrow? I'll take you guys on a tour of our first capital, St. George's. Is it okay, Daddy?"

"Well," he said, "I'm sure The Adventure Channel wants the biggest bang for their buck, as they say. But I'll need you until noon in the shop. I've got a charter in the morning."

"Shouldn't be a problem," said T.J. smoothly. "We're picking up my cousin around that time at the airport. We can get her unpacked at the hotel and be here by around two, if that works."

At that moment Chappy came through the shop's front door, smiling as always. "I see you've met my friends," he said to Jasper, shaking his hand.

"Indeed, Chappy. In fact, Veronique has volunteered to be their tour guide on a trip to St. George's tomorrow."

"Marvelous. Well, boys, have you completed your business here?"

They looked to Jasper, who nodded. "We're all set for our first dive, bright and early on Tuesday."

"Fine. Ah, boys, I just got a call from T.J.'s dad. He and Mike are throwing some steaks on the grill back at the hotel and your presence is requested."

T.J. looked at his watch and was amazed. "Five o'clock already? Let's get moving!"

Ronnie walked the boys to the door. "We'll have a great time tomorrow," she assured them. "Lots to see, and it isn't a terribly big place." Again she rubbed her hand on Bortnicker's upper arm, and T.J. knew it was all his friend could do to keep from melting. "See you then!" She turned on her heel and followed her father through the shop and out the back to help secure the boats for the night.

"Spirited one, that," observed Chappy as they climbed into the minivan.

"She's ... beautiful," managed Bortnicker, in a dreamy daze.

"That, too," agreed Chappy. "By the way, Mr. B, I stopped off at home and brought you a little music. What say you to a little *Abbey Road*?"

Bortnicker turned to T.J., his crooked grin never wider. "My day just keeps getting better," he said as "Come Together" began to play.

Chapter Eleven

"You sure you don't want to join us, Chappy?" said Tom Sr., holding aloft a sizzling steak on his cooking fork. "We've got plenty."

"No, no, thanks, anyway," the driver said with a wave of his hand. "The missus will be upset with me if I come in late. I think she's fixing up one of her special cod dishes, and I don't want to miss that. You men enjoy your steaks. I'll be 'round at eleven tomorrow morning to get you to the airport." He climbed into the minivan, flashed them a thumbs-up, and was off.

"Couple more minutes, guys," said Tom Sr. "We had a minor setback when the charcoal wouldn't light—must be the humidity in the air. Mike had to motor over to the market to pick up some more."

"Let's see the bikes, Mike!" said T.J.

"Okay, follow me," Mike replied, heading for the covered scooter park near the back of the hotel. "Ta-da!" he said, pointing to a fairly new pair of black G-Max 150cc bikes, both of which had seats built for two riders. For mopeds they looked pretty sporty, despite the baskets that were attached to the back.

"How do you start it?" asked Bortnicker.

"Allow me to demonstrate," Mike answered, hopping on the nearest one. The boys watched intently as he fired up the machine, revving the motor with his right hand grip until the machine purred. "So, who wants the first ride?" He pointed to a metal chest Virginia's husband had provided upon which HELMETS was stenciled in bright yellow paint. T.J. removed three of them and tossed one each to Mike and Bortnicker.

"Don't mind if I do," said Bortnicker, easing onto the black vinyl seat behind Weinstein.

"Hold onto the sides of the seat bottom and keep your feet on the passenger pedals," Mike warned, and they cautiously inched out of the parking area and down the paved path to South Road.

T.J. leaned against the limestone wall of the pool enclosure as he waited for their return. The sun was still bright, though it had begun its slow descent. The first tree frogs had begun to chirp, a sound that brought back bits of memories from his early childhood visit. He thought of his mother, and how happy this place had made her, and he smiled. Even this far from the ocean, he could hear the waves pounding the beach of Astwood Park. The smoky smell of steak and charcoal filled the air. And yes, those palm trees were swaying overhead. "I *still* can't believe I'm here," he said aloud.

Mike and Bortnicker pulled into the lot and abruptly stopped in front of him. T.J. snapped on his helmet as Bortnicker climbed off. "Hold on tight—he drives like a madman!" Bortnicker warned, and T.J. laughed. He climbed onto the seat, tapped Mike on the shoulder, and held on for dear life.

Out on South Road the traffic was light, but steady. As Mike zoomed along, T.J. could understand how a rain shower or a patch of oil could wreak havoc on scooters. They went around a bend, and T.J. could spy the ocean and a bit of the shoreline. Mike then ducked the vehicle into a scenic vista area and U-turned for home.

"Dude, these bikes are cool!" Mike cried aloud as he shut the motor off. "I'm gonna buy me one when I get back to the States!" With the success of *Gonzo Ghost Chasers*, he could afford a fleet of them.

"Soup's on!" sang out Tom Sr., who was loading the steaks and tinfoil-covered baked potatoes onto a large tray.

"Let's eat in my room so we can hear about your day," Mike said. "Then we can go over the equipment." Tom Sr. went to his refrigerator and grabbed sodas for the boys as they helped Weinstein set their Spartan dinner table. He popped open beers for himself and Tom Sr., and the famished foursome dug in.

"Great steaks," grunted Bortnicker as he chewed away. "Were they expensive?"

"Dude, you don't want to know," said Mike, forking some butter onto his potato. "Thank you, Adventure Channel!"

"You must be away from home a lot," said Tom Sr.

"Yeah, about half the year, all told. We film all over the place in the States, and we've been down to Puerto Rico and South America, too. But none of the four of us is married, and we all get along pretty well.

"We started doing this in college at Fresno State just for a goof, but then we began having experiences—weird stuff that made us want to learn more and push the envelope. Along the way, we've tried to use every bit of technology available to stay ahead of some of those dull paranormal shows.

"The show itself started by accident. One of our team members, Caroline—"

"She's *really* hot!" cut in Bortnicker.

Mike laughed and continued, "Her brother had a connection at The Adventure Channel. So, we went to this deserted prison in Nevada and filmed the pilot for the show, and incredibly, they liked it! So here we are, a couple seasons later and going strong." He put his knife and fork down and looked directly at T.J.

"But in all the investigations we've done, and all the crazy evidence we've picked up on audio and video, *nothing* compares to what happened to me last year in Gettysburg. I was talking to a real, honest-to-God ghost, and I blew the chance to document it. That's what keeps me going—the quest to, beyond a doubt, prove to America that the spirit world really exists. That's why I admire you dudes so much, and your cousin, too. When it was crunch time, you showed more guts than I ever did."

"I'm sure the opportunity will present itself to you again," assured Tom Sr. "You're too passionate about it to not achieve your goal."

"Well, I'm hopin'. But, hey, life is good. We've all made a lot of money on the series, and there's no end in sight. So, when they asked me last year about a possible spinoff, I said, 'How about kids?' and they said, 'Why not? Let's give it a try!' You have no idea how many letters we get from young people all over the *world* who have either formed their own teams or want to. So, if this project is successful, it could open the door for lots of other dudes like yourselves."

"Gee, no pressure *there*," said T.J. to Bortnicker.

"Don't worry," said Mike, sipping his beer, "I have a feeling you guys are gonna do great. Now, fill me in about today."

"Well, it was kinda mixed," said T.J. "First, Chappy took us to this restaurant near the dive shop that's owned by one of his friends, a lady named Dora. Real authentic Bermuda food, so we were pretty psyched. But when we mentioned that we're here to investigate Sir William Tarver we got the silent treatment, kinda like the reaction from Chappy on the way back from the airport."

"Interesting," said Mike, chewing on the last of his steak.

"But that's not all," said Bortnicker. "There were these two local guys there, pretty tough looking dudes in overalls, who must've been listening in because one of them came over to us and said that we should leave it alone."

Tom Sr., concerned, asked if the boys felt threatened in any way.

"Not exactly," said T.J. "But it was a little awkward."

"That's why our meeting with this Mrs. Tilbury over at the National Heritage Trust Museum on Monday is so important," said Mike. "There's got to be something going on with Tarver that's being kept on the DL—"

"But then, why publicize him in the first place?" said Tom Sr. "You know the show will draw attention to Hibiscus House."

Mike frowned. "All I can think of is that, with the economy as weak as it is over here, there's a lot of competition for the American tourist dollar. And Bermuda's a very expensive place to visit. But, believe me, you mention the word "haunted" and interest picks up. Maybe the people in charge over there just don't know what they're dealing with, if there's anything at all. You know, we've been called in to investigate places based on some pretty wild claims by the local government or whoever runs the facility, and they turned out to be total duds. I mean, we can spice up the investigation here and there, though not to the point of fabricating our results to fit the reports we were handed. But like you said, whether the place is a hot spot or not, there's instant publicity generated, which means mucho dinero for the owners of the property."

"Please tell me things went better at the dive shop."

"Oh, yeah, no problem there," said T.J., pushing his plate away. "We met the owner, Mr. Goodwin—"

"And his daughter also?" cut in Mike, a mischievous grin on his face.

"And Ronnie," said T.J. "I think Bortnicker's in love."

"Well, she did seem to take a shine to me," Bortnicker said proudly as he polished his glasses with his Red Sox tee shirt.

"Whatever," continued T.J. "Mr. Goodwin showed us a map of all the wrecks around the island, and where we'd be going to dive. It's not too far off the coast around here, in the area of the Gibbs Hill lighthouse, which we passed on South Road on the way to Somerset. We're scheduled for two dives, on Tuesday and Thursday. It's a long shot, but he's hoping we can find out if the wreck is Tarver's ship."

"And what happened when Tarver's name came up with Goodwin?" asked Tom Sr.

"Mr. Goodwin didn't react one way or the other," said Bortnicker, "but his daughter went off on how he was a great Bermudian, blah blah blah. She seems pretty patriotic, among other things."

"The people here are very proud of their country," said Tom Sr. "Take it from me. You ask them a question about their culture and they'll bend your ear, which is all part of them being so accommodating. But Bermuda, as great as it is, has dark parts in its history like any other country. You might be dealing with one; who knows?"

Mike looked at his watch. "Wow, 8:00 already. Do you guys think you can give me another hour to show you the equipment you'll be using during the investigation?"

"I'm pretty beat," said T.J. "but I think we can make it through another hour."

"I'm in, too," said Bortnicker.

"Well, I've got some calls to make," said Tom Sr. "My process begins tomorrow at 8:00 a.m. on the first tee of the Coral Bay Golf Club. I'm playing with my buddy and a couple guys from the government. Then, hopefully, our conversations will continue over lunch and drinks, so you won't be seeing me for most of the day. And if tomorrow goes well, you won't be seeing much of me at all, which I guess is okay because I'd only be in the way."

"No problem, Tom," assured Mike. "I'll keep an eye on things, and Chappy will be a help, too."

"So, tomorrow it's okay if we take a trip to St. George's in the afternoon?" asked T.J. hopefully. "Ronnie Goodwin promised to take us around, show us the sights."

"*Lots* of sights," added Bortnicker with a devilish wink.

Mike laughed out loud. "You dudes are too much. Of course you can go to St. George's. It's part of picking up on the local history of the investigation site. And it's a Sunday anyway; not everything's open.

"Listen, when *Gonzo Ghost Chasers* does an investigation, we spend anywhere from three to five days in the area of the place we're checking out. But I convinced the suits at The Adventure Channel that if they wanted you to do a thorough job they'd have to make it worth your while. So, we're booked here for up to two weeks if we need it. I *want* you to have some down time, because if you're rushed, the final product will show it. Understood?"

"Great," said T.J. "So I was thinking that tomorrow morning I'll go for a run, then maybe me and Bortnicker could hit the pool for a little bit before we go pick up LouAnne at the airport. Then, Chappy could take us to Blue Lagoon and we can pick up Ronnie and go to St. George's."

"He's very organized," explained Bortnicker.

"Okay, whatever," said Mike. "I've been invited to go charter boat fishing tomorrow by a young lady I met in Hamilton the other night. Since you guys seem to have your plans under control, I think I'll take her up on it. Maybe bring home some fresh fish to grill.

"Now let's talk tech."

* * * *

The men of Jobson's Cove were just sitting down to their succulent steak dinner when Nigel Chapford entered Dora's Corners for the second time that day. She was bent over the stove, stirring three pots simultaneously for the dozen patrons seated at her tables. He slid onto a stool at the counter and said, "And here I am, back again in search of the beer a certain lady promised me this afternoon."

Dora cut him a look over her broad shoulder that signaled her displeasure.

"Have I done something wrong?" he wondered aloud.

She stopped stirring and strode to the counter, leaning her elbows on the chipped wood until her moist face was only inches from his. "I don't like this thing you've got going with those boys," she hissed. "Stickin' their noses where they don't belong."

"I take it they mentioned William Tarver," he sighed.

"Of course," she said. "The odd one with the glasses was making like the town crier, for goodness sake."

Chappy frowned, tracing an old water ring stain with his finger. "They're good boys," he said patiently, "and it's understandable they're all caught up in this TV thing. Wouldn't you be, at their age? It's a big adventure in the tropics for them."

"At whose expense?" she retorted. Then she dropped her voice a few octaves. "Nigel, you know quite well the rumors about what went on in that house—"

"Never substantiated—"

"Says you."

"And you honestly expect a group of teenagers to uncover a mystery that's been locked away from the public for over 250 years? I'm surprised at you, Dora."

"You listen here. I realize that to most of the people on this island you are Mr. Nigel Chapford, chauffer to the stars, but don't forget where you came from, *Chappy*—the Back of Town, just like me. Just like your wife. Don't you *ever* let me see you putting outsiders before your own people. I don't care how nice they are or how much they pay you!"

Chapford was actually afraid that Dora, who was never the greatest specimen of health, was on the verge of a major coronary attack. He reached out and laid a tentative soothing hand on her muscled forearm.

"Dora, my love, I will do everything in my power to keep things under control," he assured, his teeth gleaming white. "So please calm yourself. Believe me, it will all work out. Now, about that beer?"

Chapter Twelve

"Okay, here goes," said T.J., completing his preliminary leg stretches on the concrete deck of the deserted pool. It was barely 7:00 a.m., but the sun had broken through an early morning cloud cover to beat down on Bermuda and evaporate the morning dew. He'd tiptoed past the snoring Bortnicker, pulled on his Bridgefield High Cross Country tee and shorts, and carried his New Balance 1226 sneakers outside. Now, as his cousin would say, it was time to rock. The fact that she would be here in a few hours only heightened his excitement. Following Chappy's directions, he headed left out of the driveway, then found the Tribal Road that went uphill to the Railway Trail, which was clearly marked. He hung a left and began padding on the mat of dirt and fallen leaves that formed the floor. Overreaching trees shielded him from the sun, and although there was no breeze to be had, it was quite pleasant under the canopy. Nothing like his first run with LouAnne last summer on the wide open, blazing battlefield when he almost killed himself attempting to keep up with her. He chuckled at the memory of his foolishness in trying to impress her. Instead of cannon and regimental markers and statues, T.J. was treated to a colorful riot of Bermuda flora, most of which had been imported from other countries to thrive in the island's warm climate and ample rainfall. Bamboo and orchids, bougainvillea and begonia, Poinciana and hibiscus and scarlet cordial— they all swirled together around him as he clipped along.

Running always gave T.J. quiet time to think; rarely did he use an iPod to make it go faster. This fine morning many things crossed his

71

mind. The previous day's events flew by like a flipbook: the plane flight, the cliffs of Astwood Park, the strange man at Dora's and the intriguing girl at the dive shop.

And Bortnicker. Jeez, was he going to make a fool of himself again? Okay, this Ronnie was a bit of a flirt, but wasn't that the byproduct of accommodating the tourists day after day? Bortnicker was probably so stunned that a girl had even noticed him that he'd misread a little innocent byplay. Of course, he reasoned, this wasn't necessarily a bad thing. Perhaps, he thought selfishly, it would divert his friend's thoughts from LouAnne.

Ah, LouAnne. The failure of them to meet up during the school year vacations had only elevated the anticipation of this trip. He knew, deep down, how he felt about her, adopted cousin or no. How *she* felt was another story altogether. T.J. had gotten what he believed were mixed messages last summer. However, he feared that what little knowledge he had about females and their ways, and the way he had built her up in his imagination into some kind of teenaged goddess, had left him as off base—and hopeless—as Bortnicker was with Ronnie Goodwin.

Suddenly he slowed and looked up. Through the canopy of palms and lush vegetation he could make out a towering pink hotel.

What? He thought. *Can I have gone this far?* He stepped into a small clearing; sure enough, he'd reached the Southampton Princess resort, which they'd passed way down along South Road the previous day. T.J. checked his watch. Yup, he'd been running for a half hour, lost in his reverie. He chuckled at himself, then turned around and hit it for home.

After a breakfast of cold cereal, the boys lounged in the pool. Bortnicker, who'd slathered his fair skin with sunscreen, floated around on a rubber tube, his Ray Ban sunglasses pointed to the sky. T.J., tired from his run, just sat up to his neck in the shallow end.

"How'd the run feel?" Bortnicker said, his hands behind his head.

"Not bad at all," T.J. answered. "I'm glad I started training last week at home. I'll be ready for her."

Bortnicker checked his watch. "Touch down in an hour and forty minutes. We have to grab a shower soon, Big Mon."

"A few more minutes," said T.J. contentedly.

"Hey, what did you think of the tech session last night? Think we'll be able to actually use all that equipment?"

"I have my doubts. Listen, I understand what Mike said about the TV audience liking gadgets, but I don't know if we'll get to use all the stuff, and if it really works at all. I mean, there's the night vision camcorders with the infrared lenses, full spectrum still cameras that we have to set up, thermal imaging cameras and digital EVP recorders—"

"And don't forget the underwater movie camera LouAnne's gonna have to shoot from the surface, probably lying on a float or something. It's incredible that she'll be able to zoom down to where we are. That is, if we have a crystal clear day."

"Modern technology, man. Anyway, Mike said we don't need that much underwater footage."

"And Mike said his main job is to help us get set up and then review the audio and video at the end of each investigation, right?"

"Yeah, so I wouldn't sweat it. We use camcorders and stuff all the time when we do projects at school." T.J. rose up from the water and grabbed his beach towel. "I'll get in the shower first, wash this chlorine off."

"Make yourself look nice, now!" called Bortnicker behind him.

T.J. showered quickly, then gave his hair a thorough toweling. He had what the girls at school called "perfect hair", which these days constituted a Justin Bieber (actually, a Beatle) cut that fell across his forehead and brushed his ears. Kate, the girl who cut the Jackson men's hair at her Fairfield salon for free (Dad had designed the salon at a bargain price because she'd been a friend of his mom's) never failed to compliment how enjoyable giving him a haircut was. Bortnicker, on the other hand, presented a challenge. There wasn't a hairstylist alive who could get his unruly mop under control. It was all he could do to keep his locks from obscuring the Coke-bottle glasses through which he observed the world.

"Well, don't we look rather suave!" chided Bortnicker as he entered the apartment to find T.J. primping in front of a hallway mirror and sporting a dark blue golf shirt to go with his khaki cargo shorts.

"What'd you expect me to wear, my *Gonzo Ghost Chasers* shirt? It's bad enough we have to have our logo plastered all over Chappy's minivan."

"Ah, you love it," his friend said dismissively. "Be out in a second." And, as was his MO, Bortnicker emerged dripping wet some scant minutes later, shook the water out of his hair, threw on a clean tee shirt and shorts, and was good to go.

A car horn sounded down below. "That's Chappy," said T.J. "Let's get to the airport."

It was Bortnicker's turn to ride up in front, and he immediately inserted *Rubber Soul* into the CD player. "And how are you men this fine day?" asked the driver.

"Can't complain," said T.J. as the appropriate first track, "Drive My Car", began to play. "Another beautiful morning."

"You'll get the odd shower here and there this time of year, but no worries," said Chappy, tapping the steering wheel to Ringo Starr's backbeat. "It may be raining on one side of the island and not the other. In any event, the downpours are brief and dry up quickly. It's late July through October you have to be careful of."

"How come?" asked Bortnicker.

"Hurricane season. We've had a few howlers over the past five years. Caused a lot of heartaches."

"Including your house?"

"I've been lucky. Minimal damage every time. But many have had to rebuild from nothing. The price you pay for living on an island in the middle of the Atlantic Ocean."

"Where *do* you live, exactly?" asked T.J.

"It's an area called 'Back of Town', just outside Hamilton," Chappy said. T.J. thought he detected a slight grimace as he uttered the words. "Not the nicest area, I'm afraid. We have our share of crime there, unfortunately. It's the part of the island you never see in the tourism adverts. I hope someday to purchase a small cottage in Somerset or perhaps Flatts Village, near the aquarium. But it's rather pricey here, and I am putting a child through college. So the cottage will have to wait."

It was fairly silent after that, the boys taking in the sights as they wound their way through the island, retracing the route they'd traversed the previous day. No mention was made by either party of Sir William Tarver or the events at Dora's Corners.

Finally they reached the airport, which, as usual, was hopping.

Chappy parked the minivan and they made their way to the Arrivals Terminal. They weren't there long when Flight 622 from Philadelphia landed.

And then, there she was, wearing a sundress adorned with yellow and light blue flowers, oversized sunglasses perched on her flowing mane of blonde hair. LouAnne Darcy was even more beautiful than T.J. remembered her; obviously, she'd filled out a bit more while maintaining her athletic runner's build. Her blue eyes twinkled as she caught sight of them and gave a little wave with her free hand.

"Ho-ly moly," was all T.J. could muster. He started moving toward her.

"And this is his cousin?" Chappy asked Bortnicker with a raised eyebrow.

"By adoption," he answered in a sideways whisper.

"Ahh."

LouAnne dropped her carry-on, and the two embraced for more than a few seconds. Her perfume was intoxicating. "Missed you, Cuz," she whispered in his ear.

"Yo, what about me?" cried Bortnicker, throwing his arms open for a theatrical hug that she happily returned.

"LouAnne, this is Chappy, our driver," said T.J. as the black man stepped forward.

"Our *driver*?" she marveled, shaking his hand daintily. "You can't be serious."

"Oh, yes we can, m'lady," said Bortnicker, slinging her carry-on over his bony shoulder. "The Adventure Channel is giving us the VIP treatment."

"So nice to meet you, Chappy," she said, batting her eyelashes.

"And you," he replied. "The boys have been anticipating your arrival."

"Well, I'm glad to be here. Not a big terminal," she observed.

"The easier to find your luggage!" said Bortnicker. "Let's go get it and take you to the hotel. Wait'll you see it!"

They plucked her oversized suitcase from the carousel, clicked open the pull handle, and made their way outside. "Palm trees!" the girl cried. "All right!"

"Cuz, it's not any hotter than Gettysburg," noted T.J. "And we have a pool and a beach right across the street!"

"Wow. Can't wait." She shook her head in wonder at the sight of the *GGC* logo emblazoned on the minivan. They climbed in and Bortnicker reinserted *Rubber Soul* in the CD player. "In your honor," he proclaimed gallantly.

"How was the flight?" asked T.J., sharing the back seat with his cousin.

"Not bad. It's been a hectic few days," she replied. "I had to finish up with finals, and Thursday was the last track meet of the season, County Championships."

"How did you do?"

"I took third in the mile. Not bad for a sophomore. You been running?"

"Yup, and Chappy showed me a neat route for us to train on for the race next week."

"Used to be a railroad bed," said Bortnicker. "Way cool."

"Well," she said brightly, "I turned in early last night and even slept on the plane coming over, so I'm ready for anything you guys have planned for today."

"How about a sightseeing trip to St. George's?" asked her cousin.

"That's on the Eastern end, right?"

"Uh-huh."

"Sounds great!"

The boys were really getting a kick out of watching LouAnne gawk at the passing scenery. It was as if she wanted to lock every palm tree or pastel-colored house in her mind forever. They both realized that unlike their parents, the Darcys didn't have much disposable income (LouAnne worked two jobs at home, including nights at a Civil War-era inn where she was a civilian reenactor for the hordes of tourists who flocked to Gettysburg from May through October) and though she never mentioned it, they wondered if she'd ever been anywhere farther from home than Philly. It was ironic to see a person from one of the most touristy places on earth be so taken with another travel mecca.

They arrived at the Jobson's Cove Apartments and were warmly greeted by Virginia Maltby, who handed LouAnne a flower for her hair.

"Well, now, this completes our party!" she trilled. "And you're every bit the beauty that Michael Weinstein described."

LouAnne blushed.

"Take care of that precious skin in the sun today!" she sang. "I'm off to the market!"

"Is everyone here so friendly?" LouAnne asked.

"'Fraid so, miss," answered Chappy, removing her luggage from the minivan. "I'll let the boys show you to your room. What say we meet back here in a half hour for our day trip?"

"That'd be super," said Bortnicker. They hefted LouAnne's bags and climbed the stairs to the second floor balcony, where she stopped to take in the view.

"How ... romantic," she said dreamily as the boys lugged her stuff inside.

"Ya think?" laughed Bortnicker, setting down her suitcase with a thunk.

LouAnne was amazed to find her kitchenette refrigerator stocked with all the necessities her father had rattled off to her Uncle Tom, including nonfat milk, protein bars, and Gatorade. She was equally impressed with the queen-sized bed she'd be sleeping on.

"So, how did yesterday go?" she asked, unzipping her larger suitcase and hanging stuff in the bedroom closet.

T.J. gave her a full rundown of the incident at Dora's Corners and their meeting with Jasper Goodwin. He made sure to accentuate their encounter with Ronnie. "I think she has the hots for Bortnicker," he joked, causing his friend to go a bright red.

"And why not?" countered LouAnne, shooting him down. "I think he's a definite hottie, don't you?"

"Oh, yeah, of course," said T.J. playfully.

"So when do I get to meet Miss Bermuda?"

"Actually," said Bortnicker, "in about 40 minutes. We're picking her up before we go to St. George's."

"*Really*. Well, this should be interesting. Now, you two get out of here for a few minutes so I can change into something more touristy. Shoo!"

They retreated outside to the balcony and could hear LouAnne humming gaily as she got dressed. Minutes later, wearing her Beatles *Sgt. Pepper* tee shirt, capris, and sandals, she joined them. "Hey, where are Mike Weinstein and your dad, T.J.?" she asked, adjusting her sunglasses.

"Mike's out big game fishing, and Dad's meeting the golf club officials he's gonna sell his plan to."

"How's Mike been? Is he still as crazy as last year?"

"Nah. I think we just caught him at a bad time. Plus, he probably just hams it up a lot for the show. He's actually been pretty serious."

"Yeah," said Bortnicker, "this whole project is on him, and he wants it to succeed."

"So, from what you're telling me, people around here are kinda weirded out about Sir William Tarver?"

"Well, Chappy and that lady Dora were, not to mention that guy who got in our face. I wouldn't talk about it in the car today."

"Gotcha."

As always, Chappy was patiently waiting by the minivan and opened the front passenger door for LouAnne. The boys slid open the side door and jumped into the back seat.

"I'm glad you could get some time off," T.J. said to his cousin as Chappy pointed the minivan toward Somerset. "Gettysburg must be filling up."

"Oh, yeah. But it just so happens that the owner's niece is visiting for a couple weeks and agreed to stand in for me. I kind of coached her, and she came a couple nights to observe me doing my shtick. I think she'll handle it okay."

"What about that lady you babysit for during the day?"

"Mrs. Spath? Her family's actually doing the family road trip thing the next week or so, visiting relatives in Florida. So it all worked out. I'll just pick it back up when I return. *Some* of us have to work all summer. Right, Chappy?"

The driver smiled. "Right-o, Miss Lou."

"I almost forgot!" blurted Bortnicker. "Chappy, tell LouAnne about how you knew John Lennon!"

"No way," she said. "Really?"

The driver patiently retold the story, with LouAnne hanging on every word. "That must've been some experience," she said finally.

"To tell the truth, Miss Lou, it was no more or less than any others I've had over the years. I just enjoy meeting people and learning about them. And since most of them are happy to be here and in a good mood, it makes for a pleasant experience. It's just regrettable that he came to such a tragic end."

"But the music lives on," said John Lennon/Bortnicker, causing the other teens to roll their eyes. "Here's a good question for all you fans of ours: which of our hit songs did we also record in German? There were two, but you only have to name one."

"Too easy, John," said LouAnne. "'I Want to Hold Your Hand'; which was, I believe, on the *Something New* album."

"I *told* you to give it up, Bortnicker," laughed T.J.

They pulled in to the Blue Lagoon Dive Shop parking lot as the last of the morning charter clients were mounting their mopeds and heading back to their hotels. Some had placed their own masks, snorkels, and flippers in their moped carry baskets. "They look like a bunch of happy campers," observed LouAnne.

"Yeah," said T.J. as they got out of the car. "Are you sure—"

"Yes, I'm sure I will not be doing anything below the water's surface," she snapped, cutting him off.

"Oh, well, he had to try," cracked Bortnicker.

They approached the counter, where Ronnie was ringing up a *Dive Bermuda* ball cap for a middle-aged customer. "Thanks so much for diving with us, sir," she purred. "Please come visit again!" Ronnie bagged the hat and he left, smiling at the entering teens.

"Hi, Ronnie," said T.J., "this is my cousin LouAnne from Pennsylvania."

"She just got here this morning," added Bortnicker, making an effort to join the conversation.

The two girls eyed each other warily. T.J. had often noted this kind of interaction at school, especially between females who were obviously attractive.

"Hi," the black girl said finally. "Welcome to our dive shop."

"Thanks."

"I hope you're as excited about our dive trips as these guys are. It should be fun."

"I don't dive."

"Oh."

"But I am looking forward to a couple days out on that beautiful water."

"It is beautiful."

T.J. gave Bortnicker a sideways look as if to say *What the heck is going on here?* But his friend was too busy staring at Ronnie to notice him. "Well," T.J. said uncertainly, "is everybody ready to go to St. George's?"

"Brilliant!" said Ronnie, brightening. "Let me just run out back a moment and tell my dad we're off. I'll meet you out front."

T.J., Bortnicker, and LouAnne exited and walked toward the minivan. "Everything ok, Cuz?" he asked nervously.

"Sure, why not?" she answered sweetly. Chappy again held the front door open for LouAnne, and the boys hopped in the back. Ronnie came bouncing out of the shop and slid in next to Bortnicker. "Hi, Mr. Chapford, wonderful day," she said in greeting.

"That it is, Miss Ronnie. On to St. George's." He fired up the engine.

Ronnie turned to Bortnicker, who was being very careful to stay in his own space. "Did you sleep well last night, Bortnicker?" she said amiably. "Those tree frogs can take some getting used to."

"No, I, uh, I mean I really slept pretty well," he managed. "I actually kinda like the sound. It's, ah … soothing, you know?"

From his seat in the back T.J. could see LouAnne's face in the rearview mirror. She was trying not to laugh at Bortnicker's obvious discomfort.

But it was Chappy who came to the young man's rescue. "Miss Ronnie," he said, "why don't you tell our guests about where we'll be visiting today?"

She smiled, aware of the driver's obvious diversion tactic. "Well now, where to begin," she said. "Let's see…

"St. George's is one of the oldest Northern European cities in the Western Hemisphere. It was actually the capital until the early 1800s, when Hamilton took over.

"Many of its old stone buildings still stand today, and they were based on English designs. A lot of the houses and properties have been passed down through families over the generations. You'll find, though, that the majority of residents are African-Bermudian, not European.

"What's so cool about St. George's is that it still has those narrow streets and lanes from the old days, when all you had was horses and carriages. And a lot of those streets have old-timey, funky names."

"If I may add some information, Miss Ronnie," said Chappy. "You'll notice a cruise ship or two in St. George's Harbor, so there should be many tourists about. I'd say you'll need a few hours to really see the sights, which is best done on foot. But Miss Ronnie should serve as an excellent tour guide. I'll come round about 4:30 to pick you up. Will you be all right for lunch?"

"I know a few places, Chappy," assured Ronnie.

"Of course you do."

They filled the rest of the ride with idle chatter, mostly about school and the cost of living on the island. A couple times while making a point, Ronnie laid her hand on Bortnicker's thigh, inducing a mild panic in the boy. LouAnne seemed to doze for a few minutes in the front seat, but by the time they reached King's Square at the waterfront, the group was raring to go.

Chappy handed T.J. his business card with cell phone number and said to call if they were done earlier than agreed upon. "Meantime, I might try to squeeze in a few airport pickups, if you don't mind."

"No problem, Chappy," said T.J. As the driver pulled away in the minivan, T.J. remarked aloud, "A nice guy."

"My dad's known Mr. Chapford a long time," said Ronnie. "They grew up together in the Back of Town. He's good people."

"Your family doesn't live there anymore?" asked Bortnicker.

"No, we moved closer to the dive shop in Somerset. It's a small cottage, but we call it home."

"You have any brothers or sisters?" asked T.J.

"No, it's just me, Dad, and my mum. Maybe you'll get to meet her during your stay."

"That would be nice," said Bortnicker with what seemed like hopefulness.

"Would you guys want to eat first or explore a bit?" she asked.

"Let's walk a little," said LouAnne. "I've been sitting on my butt all day."

"Fair enough," Ronnie said, grabbing Bortnicker's hand. "Follow me!" she took off at a brisk clip, and Bortnicker looked back at T.J. and LouAnne as if to say "Help!"

They started off with the *Deliverance*, a full scale model of the ship which Sir George Somers rebuilt after his ship *Sea Venture* was wrecked on the island in 1609. From there it was on to the Bermuda World Heritage Center. The boys, who'd had their fair share of museum-hopping the previous summer in Gettysburg, were interested in the provided overview of the town, its heritage, and historical background. Bortnicker especially enjoyed the dioramas of 1600s city life because they reminded him of the elaborate train setups he'd created back home.

From there the teens began winding their way through those charming lanes and alleys with names like Aunt Peggy's, Featherbed, One Gun, and Needle & Thread. They popped into shops both quaint and touristy. Whenever Ronnie took a break from addressing the group as a whole, she chit-chatted to Bortnicker, who seemed to be stuck somewhere between terror and rapture. Her corkscrew curls bounced as she animatedly pointed here or there. Though the town was flooded with tourists, many of the locals greeted her by name.

"She seems pretty popular," said T.J. to his cousin.

"Ya think? I just wonder what she's whispering to Bortnicker all the time."

"Me, too."

"You think she's pretty, Cuz?"

T.J. hesitated, wondering what his cousin's intention was in asking such a loaded question.

"The truth?" he said, finally.

"Yeah."

"She's a knockout."

LouAnne nodded. "I was thinking the same thing."

They stopped for a bite at the George and Dragon in King's Square, where Bortnicker and Ronnie ordered crab sandwiches while T.J. and LouAnne shared a Shepherd's Pie.

Then it was back outside and over to St. Peter's church, the oldest Anglican church in the Western Hemisphere. T.J. was taken by the many memorials to Bermuda's seafarers sprinkled throughout the place of worship.

"You'll also want to visit Fort St. Catherine on the east end of the island, which Sir William helped design, by the way, but that's a couple miles walk from here, and I think we're all a little tired," said Ronnie finally. "We can hit a few more shops and work our way back to King's Square."

They were clowning around at the ducking pool and prisoner stocks when Chappy pulled up, precisely on time. "Have fun, people?" he asked as the overheated teens luxuriated in the minivan's air conditioning.

"It was great," said Bortnicker. "Ronnie sure knows her way around."

"Glad you enjoyed it," she replied, flashing a winning smile.

"Has Mike said anything about our schedule for tomorrow, Chappy?" asked T.J.

"Actually, yes. The three of you have a morning meeting with a representative from the National Heritage Trust regarding the house investigation you'll be doing … fact finding and all that. Then, you'll have the afternoon to yourselves before your first dive on Tuesday."

"You know what would be cool?" ventured Ronnie.

"What?" replied Bortnicker, hanging on her every word.

"How about going snorkeling near Somerset? I know the perfect shallow-water cove. My dad and I call it Treasure Beach."

"How come?"

"Well, because of the currents, it seems like a lot of stuff collects there—"

"Like what?" asked T.J.

"Old bottles, china, sea glass. You can see it from the surface and actually dive down ten or twelve feet to get it. With all the storms we had over the winter, I bet some interesting things have rolled in."

"Cool!" cried Bortnicker. "You guys want to go?"

"I don't know," LouAnne began uncertainly.

"Oh, you could just paddle about on the surface or sit on the small beach," Ronnie said with a wave of her hand. "Or just enjoy the scenery."

T.J. could sense his cousin doing a slow burn and tried to beg off, but his friend was having none of it.

"C'mon, guys, it'll be fun!" he pleaded. "Besides, T.J., we'll be able to get used to our masks and flippers again before the big dive on Tuesday."

LouAnne realized that she was the only thing standing in their way and reluctantly agreed to go. "All right," she relented, "I've gotta start working on my tan anyway."

Chappy dropped off the three Americans at the hotel and then pushed on toward Somerset with Ronnie.

"So, what'd you think?" said Bortnicker as the minivan drove off.

"About what?" said LouAnne.

"Ronnie."

"A little pushy," was her reply, and his face fell.

"Hey, is that LouAnne?" called Tom Sr. from the balcony. "Welcome, my dear! How was the flight?"

"Great!" she said waving. "And Bermuda's fantastic."

Mike, back from his fishing trip, wandered out of his room. "All right!" he said, clapping. "The *Junior Gonzo Ghost Chasers* are complete!"

"Catch any fish, Mike?" called T.J.

"Couple nice tuna. We're gonna have tuna steaks tomorrow night. I know just how to grill 'em. But tonight, to celebrate LouAnne's arrival, we're going all out—there's this British place up the road called King Henry VIII. Good English food and the waitresses all dress like wenches. You'll love it! But it's a little dressy. So, why don't we meet at the pool at seven and I'll call a cab, give Chappy the night off."

"Sounds cool," said T.J., and they retired to their rooms after some welcoming hugs for LouAnne.

Once the door to their room was shut, Bortnicker turned on T.J. "What's up with your cousin?" he asked, an edge to his voice.

"What?"

"You know what. *Ronnie*. She doesn't like her?"

"You know how girls are, man."

"Exactly. Maybe you should tell her to be nice. The girl's just being a good host."

"I know, I know," said T.J. tiredly. "It's just like school. You can't figure girls out."

"Yeah, well I don't want your cousin to ruin it for me."

"Ruin *what*?"

"Well, I don't know if you noticed, but I think Ronnie kinda likes me."

"Bortnicker, we've only been here like one day. Don't go jumping to con—"

"Are you saying it's impossible for a girl to like me?"

"No, that's not what I—"

"It's easy for you, T.J. Lots of girls at school want you to go out with them."

"Not as many as you'd think."

"Yeah, right. The only reason you weren't booked every weekend back home was LouAnne."

"Bortnicker—"

"As if I can't see you have the hots for her."

"Could we not talk about this?"

"But I'm really surprised at her. Couldn't she just be happy for me?"

"I'm sure she … will be. But c'mon man, give her a break. She just got here, and she's probably dead tired. Cut her some slack, okay?"

"Will you talk to her, please?"

"And say what?"

"To be *nice*! Can you do *that* for me, at least?"

T.J. closed his eyes and pinched the bridge of his nose like he always did when he was collecting his thoughts or calming himself down. "Tell you what," he offered. "I'll try to talk to her after dinner. But you've gotta leave us alone for a while."

"No problem."

"All right, then. Could we please get dressed and go out for a fun dinner?"

Bortnicker brightened. "Of course, Big Mon. I was just starting to get hungry again anyway."

* * * *

85

King Henry VIII provided the Jackson party of five with an evening of atmosphere and hearty food. True to its reputation, the restaurant had a Middle Ages theme, with waitresses and barmaids in low cut peasant outfits—which Mike Weinstein found especially appealing—and the male staff in blousy shirts and breeches.

After Mike and Tom Sr. enjoyed a pre-dinner cocktail called a Dark and Stormy, comprised of ginger beer, lime, and dark Bermuda rum, the group compared notes on their day. Mike was still beaming over the tuna he'd brought home and was looking forward to seeing again the young lady whose father owned the boat. Tom Sr. lamented the sorry state of his golf game but couldn't get over the gorgeous vistas from many of the tees; he said that the preliminary vibes from the government officials were promising. T.J., Bortnicker, and LouAnne then regaled the adults with their descriptions of picturesque St. George's.

Dinner began with a round of the classic island dish, Bermuda fish chowder, to which the Americans were advised to add a few drops of rum and sherry peppers that was provided in a stylish glass decanter. Then it was on to various British forms of meat and potatoes, though everyone gave a nod to good health by ordering a garden salad.

While a wandering minstrel entertained the patrons with English folk songs and Bermudian standards, Mike got down to business. "Okay, team," he said, while dousing his steak and kidney pie with black pepper, "tomorrow the investigation begins. Chappy will drive the four of us to the National Trust Headquarters in St. George's where you'll interview one of the government people who oversee Hibiscus House. Take a camcorder along. We'll see what you can get out of her about the background of Sir William Tarver. If we need it, we've also been granted a follow-up visit to the National Trust archives later this week."

"Think they'll tell us anything juicy?" asked Bortnicker.

"You never know. These people, as you've noticed, tend to be reserved. But then again, they're the ones who contacted *us*, so I hope they'll divulge some good stuff about Tarver. Be polite, but firm."

"Gotcha," said T.J.

"Now, Tuesday morning's dive is all set for 10:00 a.m.. Chappy will pick the four of us up at 9:00. LouAnne, are you okay with using the underwater camcorder?"

"Sure, as long as you have something for me to float on," she answered firmly.

"That's been taken care of. Jasper Goodwin has an inflatable he's bringing. You can stay on the surface and zoom in because the depth of the wreck is so shallow. Hey, we're only talking about a five minute segment of the show here, so don't think it has to be a National Geographic documentary or anything."

They passed on dessert, paid the tab, and had the front desk call a cab for the ride back to the hotel.

"I'm bushed," said Tom Sr. with a yawn as he held the door open for LouAnne upon their return. "Sweetheart, I'll call your dad and tell him all is well."

"Thanks, Uncle Tom. Tell him and Mom I miss them, and I'll speak to them soon or shoot them an email tonight."

"Will do. Then I'm going to take a hot shower and turn in. I'm due back on the golf course at 8:00 a.m. tomorrow."

"Two days in a row?" said Bortnicker.

"It's a tough job, but *somebody's* gotta do it," Tom Sr. joked.

"I'll phone Chappy to pick us up around 9:30," said Mike. "That should give you guys time enough to—"

"Go for a run," finished LouAnne.

"And eat and shower, I hope!" joked Bortnicker.

"What should we wear to meet this lady?" asked T.J.

"Well, I think it's time to break out the team shirts. Since we're in Bermuda I got you guys both tees and golf shirts. I'd go with the collared shirts and clean shorts. You'll have to be on your best behavior."

Everyone's gazes drifted toward Bortnicker.

"What?" he said defensively.

"Oh, nothing," said LouAnne airily.

"Hey, Cuz," said T.J., "we've still got some daylight left. Want to see the cliffs across the street?"

"Sounds great. Bortnicker, you coming?"

"Nah," he said tiredly, "I'm gonna go online for a bit. You two go on ahead." He gave T.J. a quick look and then went upstairs.

The cousins crossed South Road and cut through Astwood Park. "Hear the waves?" said T.J. "Just watch your step on the rocks."

They reached the crest of the cliffs and gingerly sat down, their legs hanging over the edge. "I can't believe how beautiful this is," said LouAnne, the wind fluffing her hair.

"Bortnicker and I checked out the beach before," said T.J. "The sand really is pink."

"Cool." She looked sideways at her cousin. "Okay, so what's up?" she said.

"With what?"

"I saw that look Bortnicker gave you. You have to talk to me about something?"

"Well, yeah, actually. He wants you to lighten up on Ronnie."

"Oh, really? Was I that much of a witch today?"

"No, nothing like that. He's just sensitive, that's all."

"Listen, T.J.," she said, looking out to sea, "I care about you guys a lot. I know what you've had to go through to be his friend, and I admire you for it. But it doesn't take much to turn his head, and this girl has absolutely steamrolled him. Unfortunately, in two weeks we'll all be home, and this place will just be a memory. This girl must meet hundreds of guys who are just passing through. I don't want our friend to get hurt."

"I won't let that happen," said T.J. earnestly.

LouAnne shivered involuntarily. "Getting a little chilly up here."

"Want to go?"

"Nah," she said. "Just put your arm around me."

They sat awhile longer.

Chapter Thirteen

"You were right, Cuz," panted LouAnne as they clipped along The Railway Trail. "It's as beautiful as you described it." Tropical birds sang gaily in the dense foliage as another glorious Bermuda morning got underway.

The cousins had met poolside for their 6:45 pre-stretch and were on the running path by 7:00. As they ran they went through their athletic accomplishments of the past year. Overall, LouAnne had the more notable results, but T.J. had lettered in two completely different sports, which was impressive.

"So, what do you know about this race on Saturday?" she said, her blonde ponytail swishing behind her.

"Well, it's open to athletes on the island, of course, but there are a few visitors like us who've entered, too. Could be over a hundred runners total."

"Cool. And we're running on South Road?"

"Yeah, and it follows the water most of the way, so it's pretty scenic."

"I'll concentrate on the scenery some other time. My goal is to win the thing."

T.J. smiled. His cousin was a real competitor, and he knew she'd go all out to win. He'd have to work hard to stay with her.

"How was Bortnicker when you got back last night?" she asked, knowing full well he'd begged off so T.J. could talk to her about Ronnie.

"Okay. He'd just gotten done texting back and forth with his mom. She's at some Feng Shui expo in New York or something. He just wants

89

you to give the girl a chance."

"Okay, okay. I won't mess up whatever wonderful things he's imagined for himself. By the way, I had a good time last night, just talking."

"Me, too."

"Race you back!" she called out over her shoulder, breaking into a sprint. T.J. took off behind her but never closed to within ten yards the whole way back. This girl was *serious*!

* * * *

"I fixed you some cereal and O.J.," said Bortnicker, who emerged from the steamy bathroom with a towel around his skinny waist. "How was your run?"

"She kicked my butt," confessed T.J. "I think she's gonna be tough on Saturday."

"I don't know, I've got a feeling you're gonna surprise yourself."

"Really?"

"Yup. Oh, by the way, Mike dropped off our shirts. Very classy." He held up one of the black golf shirts with *JGGC* embroidered on the left breast. The tee shirts, also black, were a little more ornate, with the *Gonzo Ghost Chasers* logo of a running Casper-like being on the back.

T.J. hopped in the shower and then dressed while mixing in bites of his cereal. "No gourmet breakfasts on this trip, I guess," he lamented, remembering the feasts Bortnicker and Aunt Terri had whipped up the previous summer in Gettysburg.

"No ingredients, no gourmet breakfasts," answered Bortnicker. "Hey, I'm glad your dad bought us as much food as he did. Have you seen the prices on the cereal boxes and granola bars? Mucho expensivo, Big Mon."

They finished dressing and met LouAnne, who'd chosen khaki capris to go with her golf shirt. "This is scary," she said. "I never pictured the three of us with identical outfits."

"That's show biz!" thundered Mike, bursting out of his room. "Is my team ready to start the investigation or what?"

"Can't wait!" said T.J.

"I've got the camcorder right here," said LouAnne, patting the camera.

"Great. How do I look?" he said, sporting a larger-sized golf shirt and black slacks.

"Like an overgrown *Junior Gonzo*," said Bortnicker playfully.

"Perfect! Let's get downstairs. I'm sure Chappy's waiting for us."

And he was. "Beautiful day, folks!" he beamed. "We're off to the National Trust Museum in St. George's, correct?"

"That's it," said Mike, slipping into the front seat. "My team here is ready to grill a Mrs. Tilbury. Ever heard of her?"

"That would be Constance Tilbury," said Chappy, nodding. "Been with the National Trust forever. A rawther proper one, is Mrs. Tilbury," he added, rolling his r's for effect. "I'd mind my manners around her. She's considered one of the foremost authorities on Bermudian history pre-1900. Always being interviewed on TV and all that. Make sure you've worked out your questions ahead of time; I don't think she'd suffer unprepared interviewers gladly, even if they are young people."

At that, Bortnicker whipped out a small notebook he'd been preparing for the trip, and they all contributed ideas for the list, Mike included. Before they knew it, they were again in St. George's. Chappy pulled up in front of an old stone building.

"Here we are, my friends. The Bermuda National Trust Museum, built around 1700 by Governor Samuel Day. Good luck with Mrs. Tilbury. I'll go for a cup of tea and meet you back here."

As they approached the museum's entrance, Mike stopped them and looked around. "Okay, guys, now I have to do my part. For this show, I'm going to introduce each segment, since I'm acting as the technical advisor. Then, you can expect to be doing a lot of sound bites before, during, and after each part of the investigation, explaining the use of different equipment, or stuff you might have seen or heard.

"We're going to end up with loads of footage. Then I'll send it off to the production people in LA, and they splice it all together into an hour TV show. But I will have some say into the final cut. So let's film this first intro. LouAnne, you want to handle it? Just give me a 3-2-1."

"Sure thing," she said, shouldering the camcorder. She counted down, and Mike began his monologue:

"We begin our investigation of the strange goings-on at Hibiscus

House in Bermuda with a visit to the National Trust Museum, where the team will be meeting with Mrs. Constance Tilbury, chairman of the National Trust. Perhaps she will be able to shed some light on the exploits of the pirate William Tarver and why he has apparently decided to come back and terrorize the visitors and staff at his former residence."

"Got it," said LouAnne, clicking off.

The foursome walked through the front door and gave their name at the desk. The receptionist pointed toward a large mahogany door at the end of the hallway. "Through there," she said in a businesslike manner. "Mrs. Tilbury is expecting you."

Mike gave the door a soft knock, and they entered Constance Tilbury's domain. The walls were lined with cedar shelves filled with books, some of which appeared to go back centuries. The wood floor was polished to a high sheen, and her mahogany desk gleamed. T.J. noticed that it was probably the most neatly ordered desk he'd ever seen.

"Come in, please," said the petite woman with snow white hair. She had been reading at her desk, and her granny glasses were pushed far down on her nose. By the time she came around the desk to shake their hands they had been removed.

"Please sit," she offered, pointing to four rather uncomfortable straight-backed chairs that had been arranged facing her desk. She returned to her seat behind the imposing piece of furniture and sat back, tenting her fingers in front of her pink blouse.

"Quite a room," said Mike, breaking the ice.

"Yes, well, it was Governor Day's library originally. We use it as our office."

"Fantastic. Mrs. Tilbury, I'm Michael Weinstein, we spoke on the phone—"

"Yes, I remember. Pleased to meet you finally."

"And these are my colleagues for the project: Mr. Jackson, Mr. Bortnicker, and Miss Darcy."

"Charmed. And aren't you the pretty one, Miss Darcy."

"Thank you, Ma'am," said LouAnne, blushing. "Is it all right if I film our conversation? For the television show?"

"By all means, my dear. Now, what do you want to know?" she said primly as LouAnne hefted the camcorder and pressed RECORD.

"To begin," said T.J. nervously, "what exactly is the Bermuda National Trust?"

"It's a charity, actually, established in 1970 to preserve our natural, architectural, and historic treasures, and to encourage the public's appreciation of them. The purpose of our programs and activities is to ensure that Bermuda's unique heritage remains protected for future generations.

"To that end, we oversee some 70 properties throughout the country that include a number of different historic houses, islands, gardens, cemeteries, nature reserves, and the like.

"The Trust also runs three museums displaying a collection of artifacts owned and made by Bermudians, as well as an education program that focuses on the island's history and what it means to our future."

"And Hibiscus House is one of those properties?" asked Bortnicker.

"One of our finest," she answered proudly. "Sir William Tarver played a prominent role in Bermuda history of the 1700s, and his home is a testament to his influence."

"Except that nobody wants to work there," said Bortnicker pointedly.

"There have been ... issues," Mrs. Tilbury said, a bit of a squint in her eye.

"Do you think the house is haunted?" asked T.J. gently.

"Good heavens, no," she answered smartly.

Bortnicker and T.J. looked at each other with concern. "Well," ventured T.J., "then what are we doing here, Mrs. Tilbury?"

The woman seemed taken aback by the question, though it was a fair one. She gathered herself and leaned forward on her desk. "Please don't be offended," she said tactfully, "but this whole enterprise was most certainly *not* my idea. The fact of the matter is that we have a committee that makes such decisions. As you can see, I was outvoted." She didn't seem too happy about it.

"But, wouldn't you want someone to come in here and hopefully determine that the site is fine?" asked Weinstein.

Mrs. Tilbury turned to Mike and fixed him with a disapproving look. "I have seen your television program, Mr. Weinstein," she began, her voice becoming edgy. "A lot of idiotic raving and playacting, if you ask me. And that includes the ridiculous contraptions you pass off as paranormal investigation equipment. You will be allowed access to the house, but you will *not* turn the investigation of a National Trust site into a circus. Am I making myself clear?"

"Yes, very," answered Mike.

"May I ask you a question, Mrs. Tilbury?" said T.J., attempting to change the tone of the interview. He gave his most charming smile, and she actually attempted one in return.

"Surely, Mr. Jackson."

"Sir William Tarver, according to our research, was a pirate—"

"A *privateer*, Mr. Jackson," she corrected. "You are aware of the difference?"

"A pirate was out for himself," said Bortnicker, "while a privateer was under contract, usually by a government or a governor of some kind."

"Well done, Mr. Bortnicker. Sir William had begun as a full-fledged pirate, capturing ships of any flag and keeping the plunder for himself and his crew. But then, the governor of Bermuda convinced him that he could still make money—and save his neck, as they were hanging pirates in England—by attacking Spanish merchant ships in the name of England by way of Bermuda."

"And he made enough money to finance that huge house and plantation just from working for the governor?"

Mrs. Tilbury paused for just a second, which T.J. thought was strange, before replying, "It would appear." She looked up at the mahogany encased grandfather clock in the corner, a signal that their interview was nearly over. "Of course, he also served as a military advisor to the governor, as many forts and other defensive installations were being built at the time."

"Are there any in particular he had a hand in designing?"

"Yes. Fort St. Catherine here in St. George's Parish, and Fort Hamilton in Pembroke Parish."

Bortnicker scribbled the names in his notebook.

"You've been rather quiet through all this, Miss Darcy," said the woman.

"Busy filming, I guess," said LouAnne. "But I did have one question."

"And what would that be?"

"Well, it's customary on the show to speak to employees or visitors of the site in question who have experienced paranormal occurrences, or what they believed to be such. Will we have that opportunity?"

Mrs. Tilbury took a measured breath, probably berating herself internally for giving the girl an opening.

"Miss Darcy, it is against everything I believe in to base an investigation on hearsay or the fanciful claims of those who might desire their so-called fifteen minutes of fame."

"But," pressed LouAnne, "the house has remained closed to the public for going on six months because you can't find anyone to work there, isn't that correct?" True to her nature, she wasn't backing down one inch. Tilbury glared at her.

"Ladies and gentlemen, here is what's going to happen. You will conduct your investigation of Hibiscus House on our agreed date, with the option for a second visit. I am completely confident that your visit, or visits, will reveal that this building is no more than an interesting historical site that will forever entice visitors based on its sheer beauty … and nothing more."

"But can we still have access to the historical archives?" said Bortnicker.

"That is what was agreed upon," she answered through slightly clenched teeth.

T.J., who noticed a vein that had been pulsing on the side of Mrs. Tilbury's forehead, went into his finest suave mode, rising to shake her hand. "Mrs. Tilbury," he said sincerely, "we thank you so much for your time and expertise, and promise that we will produce a show that you will be proud of, one that will help promote your beautiful island."

"Why, thank you, Mr. Jackson," she said, taking his hand while the others rose. "I'm sure that under *your* guidance, Hibiscus House will be accorded the respect it deserves. Good day."

They walked out of the office and through the building. Once outside, Mike said, "So, what do you think, dudes?"

"She's lying," said Bortnicker.

"No doubt," agreed LouAnne. "If she could snap her finger and make us disappear, we'd be history."

"Sir William Tarver had a secret," said T.J. "And it's gonna be up to us to find out what it is, which will explain why he's hanging around all of a sudden. And I think it all starts tomorrow on our wreck dive."

"Which reminds me," said Bortnicker. "We're supposed to be going snorkeling at this Treasure Beach this afternoon. Is it okay if we pick up Ronnie on the way?"

T.J. and his cousin looked at each other. "Sure, why not," said LouAnne casually. "The more the merrier."

"Besides, she'll know where to find the cool stuff she mentioned," added T.J.

"You dudes won't mind taking the bus there?" asked Mike as Chappy pulled up in front of the museum. "This really isn't on the itinerary for Chappy."

"No big deal," said T.J. "We're just bringing our dive bag with our masks and snorkels and stuff. Dad got us all weekly bus passes, so we might as well use them."

They got into the minivan. "How did it go, my friends?" said Chappy nonchalantly.

"Not good," said Bortnicker. "Mrs. Tilbury was okay and all, but I don't think she wants us poking around Hibiscus House."

"And she won't let us talk to anyone who's quit working there," said T.J. "I don't know what that means exactly.""It means you have a mystery to solve," said Chappy matter-of-factly. He slid a

CD into the player. "What say to a little *Magical Mystery Tour*?"

Chapter Fourteen

It was hot at the bus stop. The boys, at Ronnie's suggestion, had worn a floppy tee shirt over their baggy bathing suits because it was possible to get sunburn on your back if you were snorkeling on the water's surface for an extended period. Besides, it was bad form in Bermuda to go shirtless in public, even if you were on your way to the beach.

LouAnne had thrown a flowered cover-up over her one piece that matched her red Phillies baseball cap. "Gotta get used to these new flip-flops," she muttered. "Not too many beaches in Gettysburg, if you know what I mean."

"What, no bikini?" said Bortnicker mischievously, eyeing the outline of her bathing suit under her cover-up.

"Tell you what, Bortnicker," she shot back, "I'll buy a bikini here if you wear a Speedo."

They looked over at T.J. "I'm staying out of this," he laughed.

Soon a pink bus labeled "Dockyard" came by. The teens hefted their dive equipment bags and towels and climbed aboard, showing their passes to the bus driver, a young black man in a crisp uniform. "Afternoon, folks," he smiled. "Looks like a snorkeling expedition here."

"You know it," said Bortnicker.

"Well, move to the back and find a seat. This bus will fill up like a sardine can by the time we reach the Royal Dockyard."

The boys sat together and piled their bags on the seat next to LouAnne, who sat across the aisle. Sure enough, with every stop along the South Road beaches, more people, mostly tourists, came aboard,

97

most of them happily exhausted from riding the ocean waves. Before long the boys had given up their seats to an elderly couple and stood, gripping the handles on the corners of every seatback.

"Mike didn't want to come, huh?" asked Bortnicker.

"Nah," said T.J., swaying slightly as the bus negotiated a curve, "he's trying out the underwater camera in the hotel pool, and then it's off to Hamilton for a little free time with that girl he met."

"Not bad."

"The perks of being a TV star, man."

"Do you guys know where this beach is?" asked LouAnne from her window seat.

"Ronnie says it's near this bridge when you're almost at the Dockyard. It's like a cove, so we won't get the waves like at the beaches along the coast here."

They passed through Somerset and stopped just past Dora's Corners, where Ronnie Goodwin stood talking to an older woman. She helped the lady aboard, then made her way to the trio of Americans in the back. And though she was wearing a tie-dyed long tee-shirt on top, it was clear that Ronnie Goodwin had no such inhibitions about wearing a bikini. Bortnicker cut his eyes sideways at T.J., a smirk on his face, then noticed LouAnne frowning at him.

"Hi, guys!" said Ronnie, squeezing in beside the boys in the now jammed vehicle. A couple more people came in behind her, so that she was practically glued to Bortnicker. "Sorry," she said. "We're pretty packed in, aren't we?"

"Yeah," said Bortnicker, who didn't seem to mind at all.

LouAnne just shook her head.

"We'll be at Treasure Beach in ten minutes, max," she assured. "Then it's just a minute's walk from the bus stop." True to her word, they arrived shortly thereafter.

There was actually a little picnic area under some palm trees that sat on a bluff overlooking the small beach. The waves barely rippled, and the shallow water gleamed green. The group staked out a picnic table just short of the protective rock jetty and took in the scenery.

"Gorgeous," said LouAnne, peeling off her cover-up. "Hope I put enough sunscreen on."

A second later Ronnie had shucked her tee shirt and was sticking a toe in the water. "Like a bath," she reported. "So, are we snorkeling?"

The boys, doing their best to avoid staring at her curves, began rooting through their dive bags and laid their equipment on a beach towel. Ronnie, who'd brought her own mask, snorkel and flippers from Blue Lagoon, was set. In a matter of seconds she and Bortnicker, hand in hand, were negotiating the jetty down to the spit of sand that constituted Treasure Beach. Which left T.J. and LouAnne, who was settling in on a picnic bench with a paperback and a bottled water.

"Cuz, I, uh, brought an extra set of stuff for you," offered T.J. "Courtesy of Capt. Kenny."

She looked at him over her sunglasses. "I don't think so," she said.

"Just do this much for me," he said. "We'll walk in up to our knees, and you can float there to see what it's like. I'll stand right next to you, I promise."

"T.J., I—"

"I'll take care of you," he said with sincerity so deep that she couldn't say no.

"Okay, I'll give it a shot," she said nervously. "But if I don't like it—"

"We'll come right out, and you can go back to your book. Deal?"

"Deal," she sighed.

They sat at the water's edge and put on their flippers. T.J. helped his cousin adjust her mask and attach the snorkel by means of a rubber ring. He taught her how to spit on the inside of the glass, smear it around, and then rinse before putting the mask on. "Then you just take nice, easy breaths and float along, gently kicking your flippers. That's all there is to it," he said confidently.

"Let me try," she said. "Stand right here next to me, okay?"

"Yup."

She first knelt down in the sand, then slowly got horizontal and actually floated next to him, her arms at her side. Suddenly she popped up and tore off her mask.

"What's the matter?" T.J. cried in alarm.

"A fish! I saw a little itty-bitty fish, and it was … gold and black! Swimming right below me!"

"Pretty cool, huh?" he laughed with relief.

"Yeah."

"Take my hand," he said, seizing the moment. "We'll swim together. I won't let go. I promise."

She readjusted her mask, nodded her head, and tentatively offered her hand. They waded in a bit farther and then they were floating, kicking as one, gazing down at the plethora of fish, rocks, and coral that inhabited the cove's waters. T.J. felt a joy that was hard to describe—he didn't know if it was from the pride he had in knowing his cousin trusted him with her life, or of sharing in her wonder as a whole new world opened up to her. Soon they were skimming along where the water was ten feet deep or more, but neither seemed to care. It was perfect.

After what seemed like hours they turned back toward shore, but they hadn't gone far when LouAnne stopped abruptly and pointed below. T.J. followed her finger to the bottom where a small octagonal bottle lay. It was of a purple hue and looked to be quite old. He gave her a signal to stay put, then jackknifed downward and plucked the bottle from the seabed in a graceful swoop. T.J. kicked hard for the surface, cleared his snorkel with a sharp toot, then took his cousin's hand again to resume their trip to shore.

When they reached the shallows, T.J. and LouAnne sat, masks tipped back on their heads, examining their find. "Looks like 1800s, maybe earlier," he said. "And the glass stopper's still in it! Incredible!"

"I think it's handmade," said LouAnne. "See how uneven it is? Wow."

"What are you gonna put in it?" asked T.J.

"You want me to have it?"

"Of course. Why'd you think I dove down for it?" He smiled at her, his eyes crinkling in the sunlight.

She leaned over and kissed him on the cheek. "Know what I'm gonna call this? My wish bottle. Whenever I wish, I'm gonna say it into the bottle and then put in the stopper to keep my wish safe."

Suddenly T.J. was overcome; by what, he didn't quite know. "Sounds good to me," he managed, trying to play it off. "I hope you'll at least wash it out first."

"Of course, silly!" she said. "Let's go find Bortnicker and Ronnie and show them our treasure!"

As it turned out, Bortnicker and his diving mate had found their own collection of odds and ends on the sandy bottom, including some nearly complete china tea cups and most of a dinner plate.

"Where does all this stuff come from?" asked T.J.

"Who knows?" said Ronnie. "There are shipwrecks all over the place around here, T.J. The different currents just drag this stuff around, and it ends up here. Makes you feel quite the explorer, doesn't it? But I must say, LouAnne, that bottle you brought up is quite a find."

"T.J. got it for me, actually," she replied, beaming at her cousin.

"How'd you like snorkeling, LouAnne?" asked Bortnicker. "Was it cool?"

"Better than that," she replied, holding the purple bottle to the sunlight.

"Enough to make you learn SCUBA?"

"Let's not get carried away."

"Well, what now?" asked T.J. "We were in the water over an hour."

"Guys, I have an idea," said Ronnie. "Why don't we towel off, pack up and take the next bus the rest of the way to the Royal Dockyard? There are lots of cool shops and such, and we could catch a late lunch at this pub called The Frog and Onion. Sound good?"

"We're on it!" piped Bortnicker enthusiastically. "To the Royal Dockyard we go!"

The boys put on some dry tee shirts they'd brought, and the foursome made their way back to the bus stop, where another pink vehicle came along shortly. Fortunately for them, this bus wasn't as packed as the last one. Bortnicker and Ronnie sat together, as did the cousins.

"So, why is this place called the Royal Dockyard?" asked Bortnicker.

"Well," said Ronnie, "after England was defeated in your War for Independence, they needed an Atlantic naval outpost, so this was built in the early 1800s. They shipped in convicts from England to help build it. It continued to serve the Royal Navy until after World War II. Then it wasn't used for a while, but in the 1990s the government started revitalizing it and making it acceptable for docking cruise ships.

"The main fort has become the Bermuda Maritime Museum, which we can check out if you like, but there are some other attractions as well. We can nip in to a few if you don't mind a bit of walking."

"Sounds cool," said T.J. "I'll text Mike and Dad and tell them not to wait dinner for us. Mike's supposed to be grilling some tuna steaks."

The bus pulled up near the clock tower at King's Wharf and disgorged its excited passengers. All four of the teens took turns lugging the snorkeling equipment as they wandered about in the Maritime Museum, where artifacts and interactive displays guided them through the island's history. There was even mention here and there of Sir William Tarver. Ronnie, who'd obviously been paying attention during history class, was eager to add her commentary, which was understandably pro-Bermudian. Then it was on to the Dolphin Quest, where people could have the opportunity to feed and swim with dolphins, and the Bermuda Clay Works, an art center where they watched the crafting of pottery and other art objects.

After a pub lunch at The Frog and Onion in the Old Cooperage Building, it was on to the Clocktower Shopping Mall, where tourists milled about in search of items ranging from fine china and Irish crystal to Scottish woolens and all manner of craftwork.

By five, they'd all had it and returned to the bus stop for the return trip to Southampton. LouAnne nudged T.J. and discretely pointed over to where Ronnie was dozing, her mop of curls resting comfortably on Bortnicker's shoulder.

As she rose to disembark at her Somerset stop, Ronnie reminded the Americans to be at the dive shop by ten the next day. "We've got a pirate wreck to explore tomorrow!" She bounced down the aisle and off the bus, her energy magically restored.

Back at the hotel, the teens quickly showered and joined Mike and Tom Sr., who were plowing through their tuna steaks. "You've gotta try this, guys," said Tom Sr. "Mike made this marinade that's a killer."

"Don't mind if we do," said Bortnicker, pulling a couple of clean plates out of the kitchenette cupboard.

"None for me, thanks," said LouAnne. "I'm still full from The Frog and Onion."

The boys, who could seemingly eat around the clock, forked hunks of tuna steak onto their plates and dug in. "We had a great time today," said T.J. "We visited a really cool spot for snorkeling and found some neat stuff. Want to see?"

"Sure," said Tom Sr., sipping his iced tea.

LouAnne produced the china pieces that Bortnicker and Ronnie had brought up then proudly showed off her perfume bottle.

"Cool!" said Mike. "This is like a perfect warm-up for tomorrow. Who knows what you'll find on that wreck site?"

Bortnicker then went on to describe their exploration of the Royal Naval Dockyard with Ronnie Goodwin.

"This girl sounds pretty interesting," said Tom Sr. "Will she be on the boat with you guys tomorrow?"

"She usually handles the shop when her dad has a charter out on the water," said Bortnicker, "but I wouldn't be surprised if she ends up with us."

"Really?" said Mike. "Any particular reason, Bortnicker?"

He blushed and quipped, "The girl has an obvious fascination with history."

They all had a laugh at that one.

"Well," said Tom Sr., "I guess this is as good a time as any to tell you that the committee has accepted my proposal for the renovations at the golf club. So, for the next few days I'll be putting together the team that will be doing the actual building and interviewing local contractors. Lots to do. I'll get away when I can."

"Right," said Mike. "So let's meet downstairs at 9:00 a.m. sharp tomorrow. Make sure you have all your diving stuff, and I'll pack the cameras. I tried out the underwater camcorder in the pool, and it works great. You'll be filming, LouAnne?"

"No problem. I even went snorkeling today, thanks to T.J."

"Then, that's it for today," said Mike with a yawn. "Rest up. Tomorrow, the adventure *really* begins!"

Chapter Fifteen

"You've definitely improved since last year, Cuz," said LouAnne as they approached the halfway point on the Railway Trail. "You're running much more free and easy."

"Thanks," said T.J., who was matching her stride for stride. "It wasn't as hard to get back into it after baseball ended as I thought."

"I think we'll try to get one more practice run in on Thursday, then rest our legs on Friday so we're fresh for the race."

"Sounds like a plan." Above the runners a slight breeze caused droplets of rainwater from an overnight shower to pepper them with refreshing moisture. "Hey, did you enjoy your afternoon at the Royal Dockyard?"

"Yeah. It's cool how they turned that fort into shops and all. And the Maritime Museum was interesting. I guess there's only one place left to check out, and that's Hamilton."

"Well, on Wednesdays they have this thing called Harbour Night. Supposed to be like this big outdoor festival on Front Street where the cruise ships dock. Dad said something about going into Hamilton for dinner at an Italian place he knows and then checking out Harbour Night."

"Sounds great, but don't you sometimes get the feeling we're kinda losing focus on why we're here?"

"Huh?"

"I mean, I've only been on the island a day or so and I feel like I'm on vacation, instead of a ghost hunting expedition."

"Well, today's dive should get everybody focused. Not that we're

104

really gonna find anything major—"

"You don't think so?"

"Cuz, even Mike said that the dive segment is just a part of the 'local color' deal. I bet if the TV show airs it'll be less than five minutes. But it'll give me and Bortnicker a chance to do some real diving in clear water, and I've been looking forward to that since we started the course with Capt. Kenny."

"Speaking of Bortnicker, could he be any more into Ronnie? He follows her around like a puppy dog."

"Excuse me for saying this, Cuz, but she's pretty easy to follow. Besides, she pays a lot of attention to him, which, believe me, has never happened since I've known him."

"Yeah, I guess you're right. Is she coming along on the boat today?"

"I wouldn't bet against it. Race you to the end?"

"Let's do it!" she said, and they sprinted off together.

* * * *

Chappy turned into the Jobson's Cove Apartments driveway to find Mike and his team ready to go, their dive equipment neatly bagged. The teens were sporting their flashy *JGGC* tee shirts, which they would be wearing in the water.

In the car, Mike turned from the passenger seat and told his team that he was looking for some exciting footage. "We're not here to look at coral and fish, guys," he reminded. "Anything and everything that could give us a clue as to the ship's identity is what we want.

"I spoke to Jasper Goodwin this morning, and he's actually going to give you dudes a kind of handheld metal detector that you can wave around over anything you think isn't natural. Who knows what you might find?"

"Cool!" said Bortnicker. "I wouldn't mind some doubloons or pieces of eight."

"Keep dreaming," cautioned T.J. "That wreck had to have been picked over centuries ago."

"Don't be so negative, Cuz," scolded LouAnne. "The least you could do is show me something exciting while I'm filming."

"Okay, okay," said T.J. "But jeez, don't get too hopeful about all this."

"Hey, uh, Mike," said Bortnicker, "did Mr. Goodwin mention whether his daughter was coming?"

"As a matter of fact, dude, she is," said Mike with a sly grin. "Apparently, she asked onto the trip, so her dad's got some part-time employee watching the shop. Is that okay with all of you?"

"Uh-huh," said LouAnne.

"Fine with me," said T.J.

"As long as she doesn't get in the way," offered Bortnicker, trying to hide his excitement.

"Hey, Chappy," said T.J., "you ever go diving?"

"No, not for me, T.J.," he answered. "I'm like Miss LouAnne back there. I'd rather be on top of the water looking down than on the bottom looking up."

"Gotcha."

"But I have to say," he added, "that I have a strange feeling about today. In a good way, that is. I think you're going to find something interesting."

"See?" said LouAnne, elbowing her cousin in the ribs. "Positive thinking!"

They arrived at Blue Lagoon and carried their bags around back where Jasper Goodwin, Ronnie, and Skeeter were securing the dive tanks to their holders along the inner sides of the gunwales. Ronnie took a second from her work to shoot them a quick wave.

The team handed their bags down to Skeeter and then stepped aboard. It was a perfect day to dive; there was hardly a cloud in the sky and only the slightest hint of breeze, which would help decrease the amount of chop on the water.

"Welcome to *Reef Seeker II*," said Jasper, shaking hands first with Weinstein before greeting the teens. "And you will be our film photographer?" he asked LouAnne with a brilliant smile.

"That's me—the scaredy-cat," she answered.

"Well, I've got a great float for you to use that I've rigged a tow line to, so you'll be able to have both hands free to maneuver your camera."

LouAnne, relieved, gave the captain a thumbs-up.

"A few more minutes, folks, and we'll be underway. We're going to have a bit of a trip ahead of us to get to our destination because we're on the other side of the island. So, we'll leave this cove and push on to that bridge near where you went snorkeling yesterday, then take a left and follow the coast to a point a few miles off Gibbs Hill Lighthouse, where I found the wreck. Don't worry, I have the coordinates locked into my GPS, so we'll be over the exact spot in about an hour.

"I've also taken the liberty of packing some sandwiches and bottled water for you. I figure we'll be good for two dives today, about 45 minutes each. Conditions seem to be optimal, though that could change out there. Let's get cracking, then!" He clapped his hands for emphasis as Skeeter fired up the twin inboard engines that shattered the quiet air with a sense of purpose.

They threw off the mooring lines and slowly crept away from the dock, observing the 5 mph wake rule that was posted on a buoy nearby. As LouAnne and Mike lounged on seats near the stern, Ronnie helped the boys check out their BCD vests and other equipment. She fitted them with weighted belts and pointed out the tanks they'd be using. The boys grew more excited with anticipation as the *Reef Seeker II* left the cove, and Skeeter opened her up, speeding for the bridge where they could shortcut to the South Shore.

They passed Treasure Beach and turned left, skirting the shore, maneuvering in and out of the reefs. Here and there another boat passed and they waved, but little was said, each member of the party alone with his thoughts. T.J. and Bortnicker went through Capt. Kenny's safety checklist while LouAnne prayed she wouldn't foul up the filming.

Finally the Gibbs Hill Lighthouse came into view, and the *Reef Seeker II* began to slow as Jasper and Skeeter picked their way through the reefs, some of which were barely submerged. Skeeter then went to the front of the bow and gave Jasper hand signals to go left or right. The boat was now crawling, heightening the team's tension.

Finally they came to a clearing, and Skeeter flashed the stop sign. Jasper checked his GPS coordinates. "Brilliant!" he called out. "We're right over it!" LouAnne, who was sitting next to her cousin, gave his thigh a quick supportive squeeze.

Jasper flicked off the ignition and immediately sent the remotely controlled anchor spinning downward. After a few seconds the chain line went slack; Skeeter set the anchor, and gave Jasper a thumbs-up.

"Okay, boys," said the captain, pulling up a deck chair. "Let's make sure of our hand signals, shall we?" As he called them out, T.J. and Bortnicker showed him Distress, Danger, Okay, Out of Air, and other gestures they'd been taught in Connecticut. Satisfied with their responses, he gave them the dive plan as Mike stood nearby. "All righty then. You'll be doing two dives today, each approximately 45 minutes in length. The first, for which I'll accompany you as a precaution, is solely for the purpose of becoming acclimated with your equipment and surroundings.

"You'll notice the outline of a few timbers, if you look closely, and also a somewhat scattered pile of ballast stones. There are also a couple cannon. Of course, everything's going to be encrusted with marine growth; that's to be expected. Believe me, it takes a trained eye to make out anything of note, so don't get frustrated if nothing jumps out at you, so to speak.

"Now, you'll be diving in relatively shallow water, so if you find yourself in any sort of trouble give us a signal and ascend. There are some reefs about, but we'd rather you stay off them unless absolutely necessary, for two reasons. First, stepping on them can damage the marine life. Second, some species of coral are extremely sharp and will slice right through a flipper or your diving gloves. Okay so far?"

The boys nodded intently, and T.J. could feel his stomach knotting the same way it had before his training dive in Bridgeport Harbor.

"Right. Just one more thing. The water has been rather warm lately, so I wouldn't expect any unwelcome visitors in the area, though a few barracuda might pass by, which you'll do best to steer clear of and calmly ignore. But Skeeter will keep a close watch on the surrounding area for any signs of sharks. If he sees something, even off in the distance, his signal to us will be to start the boat's engine. Even underwater, the sound will be unmistakably clear. But again, I wouldn't worry about that. So, are we ready?"

"You know it," said Bortnicker, putting on his brave face for Ronnie, who stood to the side with her arms crossed.

"Brilliant. Then get your BCD vests on and check your regulators. I'd like to be in the water in a few."

Ronnie and LouAnne assisted as the boys rigged up, giving the thumbs-up as they took a few breaths through their regulators. Jasper helped fit on their tanks, and they spat in their masks before swishing some saltwater around. Goodwin adjusted his own kit quickly and then toppled backward off the gunwale into the water after a quick thumbs up.

"What time you got?" said T.J., checking his Capt. Kenny dive watch.

"Eleven-thirty," answered Bortnicker.

"Okay, so we've got till 12:15, max."

"I'm going to have LouAnne film my sound bite as you guys jump in," said Mike. "Then I'll help her over the side with the float, and it's showtime."

"Good luck, guys," said Ronnie, who quickly leaned over and gave Bortnicker a peck on the cheek. LouAnne opted for a fist bump with each boy. And then, one at a time, they copied Jasper's backward tumble into the turquoise water.

T.J. effected a slow drift down, adjusting his BCD to counteract his weighted belt. After clearing his ears at about twelve feet, it was an easy descent to the bottom.

Capt. Kenny, you were so right, he thought as a palette of nature's colors bloomed around him. One hundred percent visibility. He glanced over at Bortnicker, who gave him a clenched-fist "Yeah!" signal. It was all he could do to slow his breathing so as not to gulp oxygen. While Jasper Goodwin swam about on the fringes, probably looking for a spiny lobster or two, the boys glided along a couple feet off the bottom, trying to make out the shapes Goodwin had mentioned on the boat. *This isn't as easy as it looks on TV*, thought T.J.

But then, ten minutes or so into the dive, he saw Bortnicker pointing to a mound of some sort. Swimming over, he realized that it was a pile of three cannon, each about six feet long, heavily encrusted with coral and fuzzy sea growth. They looked like the Lincoln Logs he'd played with as a boy.

Their next discovery was a ragged hill of ballast stones, each roughly the size of a peewee football. They were making progress.

Soon a splash was felt overhead, and a dark shape sent a shadow over the bottom. Momentarily panicked, the divers peered up to see it was only LouAnne positioning her float over the wreck site. Bortnicker looked at T.J. and patted his chest as if to say, "She almost gave me a heart attack!" T.J. nodded, then relaxed. He inflated his BCD a bit to get a view from higher up of the site, hoping that some other shapes would reveal themselves. This proved fruitful, as he was able to somewhat identify the ghostly remainders of the ship's timbers below. As Jasper had told them that first day at Blue Lagoon, it was a sloop, not a full-blown Spanish galleon. He motioned to Bortnicker to join him, and pointed out the faint outlines of the timbers. Bortnicker nodded and gave him a thumbs-up of recognition.

Just then a couple barracuda drifted by them, their razor sharp teeth evident as they flashed a slightly menacing smile. But nothing could deter T.J. or his friend. They were having the time of their lives.

The boys made a couple more passes, then spied Goodwin giving them the sign to ascend. Locating the anchor rope, they found their way back to the *Reef Seeker II* with no problem. Mike helped them aboard, where Ronnie was ready to help unhook their tanks.

"Awesome!" blurted Bortnicker the second his mask was off.

"Really, really cool," agreed T.J. "It was worth all the lessons."

"Any sunken treasure, dudes?" asked Mike eagerly.

"Nada," answered Bortnicker, accepting a bottled water from LouAnne, "but we saw a few cannon-"

"And we can tell the front of the ship from the back. It's not all that big, really. But the scenery down there's incredible," added T.J. He turned to his cousin. "Got any good footage?"

"Won't know till we look at it later," she said, "but it was cool when you guys pointed stuff out and got all worked up."

"Didja see the barracuda swimming around us?" asked T.J. as he shucked his BCD vest.

"Yeah, and about a million other fish," she answered. "Very photogenic."

By this time, Goodwin had removed all of his gear and had downed a couple bottles of water. "Great dive, boys," he said, wiping his mouth. "You've obviously been trained well. Now, have a sandwich and relax a little, and I'll speak to you before our second dive."

Ronnie broke out some turkey and ham sandwiches and potato chips, and the teens sat together eating while Mike asked Goodwin about the boat; he was thinking of buying one back in LA. Then they stretched out on the forward deck, and the *Junior Gonzo Ghost Chasers* removed their black tee shirts to get some sun.

T.J. and Bortnicker were semi-dozing, the boat's gentle rocking almost lulling them to sleep, when Goodwin called everyone together on the stern where he'd laid out an odd assemblage of equipment.

"All right, boys," he said with mild excitement, "here's what I have in mind. Before you are some tools you might find interesting. First, these wand-like thingies are handheld metal detectors. Wave them over anything you think looks promising, and we'll see if you're lucky. There will be an audible beep if you pass over metal, I assure you. Then, we have a simple ping-pong paddle which you can use to fan the sand away once you get a hit. We use these to avoid breaking any delicate items which might lie beneath. And, of course, we have for each of you a mesh 'goody bag' in which you can secure any small items."

"What do we use to dig with?" asked Bortnicker.

"Your hands, naturally," answered Goodwin.

"Gotcha."

"Now, if there's something that's confusing you, or the wand goes haywire, wave me over," said Jasper. "If not, I'll just putter around and pick up some lobsters for my dinner tonight. I think I found some rather promising hidey holes on our first dive."

"Can we suit up?" asked T.J.

"Let's have at it."

The boys and LouAnne donned their still-clammy black tee shirts and geared up again, this time with less trepidation. As before, Goodwin went over the side first. "One treasure chest, coming up!" said Bortnicker with a wink at Ronnie, and then they were again falling to the wreck.

T.J. stuck the ping pong paddle inside his BCD and started wanding. He was excited to get a couple hits, but just as deflated when his waving/digging turned up ancient handmade nails and nothing more. Bortnicker was having as little luck as his friend, finding only broken glass and pottery shards.

But then, almost 30 minutes into the dive, T.J. got a clear *ping* as he passed the wand over a small bump in the sand. He quickly took the paddle and began fanning the mound, carefully scraping with the other hand. Gradually, a circular outline came into focus, then a hard edge of something at least a good foot across. He motioned Bortnicker over and pantomimed an eating motion. Had he found a pewter plate, perhaps? He glanced above to where LouAnne was looking down and realized that she was on it, whatever it was.

Gently, T.J. started scooping handfuls of sand from the center of the circle as Bortnicker pulled sand from around the outside of the edge. T.J.'s hand went deeper. This was no dinner plate. Realizing that time was now running out on their second dive, he frantically gave Goodwin, who was back on the bottom after bringing up a few spiny lobsters, the "come here" signal. The Divemaster swam hard to the boys, his flippers fluttering. When he reached them he stopped cold, and T.J. could see his eyes widen in amazement.

Now all three of them scooped for all they were worth, their excitement building with every palm full of sand.

It was an inverted bell, encrusted with various types of coral and other growths, and a few shells attached to boot. Goodwin stopped and shook his head slowly, still not completely accepting what he was seeing. Then, he gave the boys a signal to wait a minute and kicked hard for the surface. They continued excavating until they felt him re-enter the water, dragging with him a metal basket attached to a rope. Once on the bottom, the three divers managed to rock the bell enough that it broke free from the sands which had covered it for centuries. Goodwin tipped the basket, and the boys managed to push/roll the bell inside. Making sure it was securely in place, he gave the rope a couple yanks and motioned the boys to move back.

Almost immediately the rope went taut, and the basket began a slow climb to the surface. Goodwin, after exchanging slow motion high fives with the teens, tapped his watch and then gave the signal to ascend.

"Are you kidding me, dude?" yelled Mike as they broke the water. He was helping Skeeter, who'd used a winch to retrieve the basket, to ease the bell down onto the deck. Ronnie was jumping up and down excitedly, and LouAnne was paddling hard back to the boat.

"I got it all on film!" she cried triumphantly. "The whole thing!"

The divers quickly shed their equipment, then sat around the basket in awe. "This is … quite extraordinary," said Goodwin finally.

"Ya *think*?" answered LouAnne.

"The ship's bell," Weinstein marveled. "What are the odds?"

"Astronomical," said Jasper. "I simply cannot believe we found this. Boys, I'm … flabbergasted."

"Are there any markings?" asked Ronnie, hosing some sand off the bell's outer surface.

"Well, there's moderate encrustation," answered her father, "which is to be expected. But if we can chip some of this lighter stuff away, I think we can get to the brass fairly easily. This must've spent a lot of time totally buried."

Skeeter, who had momentarily disappeared, suddenly produced a hammer and chisel-like instrument.

"Oh, I don't know about this," said Goodwin doubtfully. "Wouldn't want to cause any damage. I'm a diver, hardly an archaeologist—"

"Oh Daddy, *please!*" exhorted Ronnie. "You're not going to leave the discovery to someone else, are you?"

The captain looked at all the hopeful faces, frowned, then sighed. "It appears I'm outnumbered," he observed with a slight grin. "Miss Darcy, you might want to grab that camera again. Skeeter, hand me those things and let's have a go. But I warn you now, if it doesn't work fairly easily I'm going to stop before I ruin the surface. Agreed?"

"Agreed," the team said in unison.

"Whenever you're ready, Mr. Goodwin," piped LouAnne, clicking on RECORD.

And so, very gingerly, Jasper Goodwin began chipping away at the bottom third of the bell. At first, only the tiniest bits of coral flaked off, but he gradually became bolder, and after one particularly solid tap, a chunk of matter dropped off. "Oops," he said quietly.

"Keep going, Daddy! I see something!" urged Ronnie.

Another tap; another flying piece of crust. Then another.

"Stop!" cried T.J. suddenly. "Look!"

There, inside a band which most certainly circled the base of the bell, were etched the letters DFA. All of them were breathing heavily now.

"One more letter," said Goodwin, and gave the chisel another rap.

Winking in the Bermuda sunlight were the letters ST. They'd found the *Steadfast*.

"Incredible," said Goodwin, by now drenched in sweat, as the others danced around in glee. Weinstein was so overcome he roared a loud "Woohoo!" and cannonballed off the *Reef Seeker II* into the crystal blue water.

T.J. stood, frozen in amazement, until his cousin put down the camcorder and gave him a bear hug. "Proud of you," she whispered amid the joyous din.

"Thanks," he mumbled, unable to hug her back.

After a few minutes of whooping and hollering, Jasper Goodwin assembled his crew, including a dripping Mike Weinstein, on the stern. "Right," he said evenly. "It appears we've surpassed our wildest expectations here, and that's all well and good. The question is, what next?"

"What do you mean?" asked Mike, toweling off.

"Well, the fact of the matter is that you've only just begun your investigation," he answered, picking a snail shell off the bell. "You still have to visit Hibiscus House, and I reckon another dive this week is in order, now that we know it's actually the *Steadfast*. If we go ahead and announce our find, it will be front page news on this island, and none of us will have a moment's peace."

"So we keep it quiet?" asked Bortnicker.

"For the time being. It will give me some time to really work on the bell and for you to continue your activities. Agreed?"

"Mum's the word," said Skeeter, the first thing he'd uttered all day. The group burst into laughter.

"So we're agreed," said Jasper. "Good. But though we're keeping this amongst us, I think a celebration is in order, don't you? I fetched us a few good-sized lobsters while you archaeologists were at work, and I wouldn't be averse to cooking them up for a proper feast. Your thoughts?"

"Sounds great," said T.J.

"If it's not too much trouble," added LouAnne.

"No trouble at all. Veronique, ring up your mum on the cell and tell her to meet us at the Blue Lagoon in an hour or so with all we'll need to whip up a serious lobster boil."

"I'll call T.J.'s dad and tell him to take the scooter over and join us after I call Chappy to pick us up later than planned," said Weinstein. "Jasper, should I tell Tom to bring anything?"

"I should think a couple bottles of champagne would be appropriate," he replied with a broad smile.

Chapter Sixteen

It took a while to dock the *Reef Seeker II* and wash her down, but everyone was on such a high that nobody cared. By the time T.J. and the other divers had rinsed off in the Blue Lagoon's outdoor shower stall and thrown on a change of clothes, Jasper Goodwin and his wife had transformed the back patio into a waterfront café, complete with umbrellaed picnic table and chairs.

Upon meeting Claudette Goodwin, T.J. and Bortnicker immediately determined how Ronnie had gotten her looks. She had the same stunning eyes and smooth skin and seemed to glide as she walked. "I'm thinking Halle Berry," whispered Bortnicker as T.J. stepped into his flip-flops.

"With a little Beyoncé thrown in," T.J. quipped.

But whereas Ronnie was demonstrative and outgoing, Claudette was more like her husband—all Bermudian politeness and reserve. "So pleased to meet you," she said with a feminine handshake. "Veronique has told me so much about you. I hope you're enjoying your stay."

"It's been great so far," answered Bortnicker.

"And you must be LouAnne," said the woman, taking her hand warmly. "You're as beautiful as my daughter described you."

"Thanks," LouAnne said, coloring. "I still feel kind of sticky and salty—"

"Nonsense. You look just fine. Would you like to help Veronique and I prepare the cassava pie?"

"Actually, Mrs. Goodwin," said Bortnicker, stepping forward, "that's kind of my specialty. I'd be glad to pitch in!"

"Well, fine then," she smiled. Claudette put her arm in his and led him to a corner of the patio where her husband had set up a grill, which Ronnie was lighting.

"I think he's in heaven," said T.J. to his cousin.

"Oh yeah," agreed LouAnne. "They've got him surrounded."

T.J. looked around uncertainly. "Want to go for a walk?" he offered.

"I'd like that," she smiled. "Get my land legs back." They wandered off just as Tom Sr. pulled in on his moped.

"So what happened?" he asked Jasper while handing the champagne bottles off to Mike.

"The boys actually found the *Steadfast*'s bell. Come look." He led Tom Sr. to a back room where the bell sat submerged in a tub of saltwater. The telltale letters were even more visible now, as Jasper had been chipping away at more of the encrustation.

"Wow," said Tom Sr. "Things like this don't normally happen, right?"

Goodwin shook his head. "Mr. Jackson, things like this *never* happen. Not to amateur divers, anyway. It was like a magnet drew them to the bell. Rather spooky, actually."

"What now?"

"Well, we've agreed to, you might say, 'sit on it' for a bit while the kids conduct their investigations of the house. But I have strongly suggested another dive day on Thursday to see what else we might find."

"Such as?"

"Well," said Goodwin, "Sir William was, after all, a pirate. There could be some valuable items under that sand, or there could be nothing. I just want the kids to have the opportunity to find it first because, quite frankly, secrets don't last long on an island as small as Bermuda. If we could keep the news of our find quiet for just another week, I'd be pleased—and amazed."

"Understood." Tom Sr. reached into the tub and felt the outer shell of encrustation on the bell. "The kids must be sky-high over this," he marveled.

"Oh, yes. And no matter what happens from here on, when word of this discovery gets out the boys will be instant celebrities."

"But it's also good for your dive shop, isn't it?"

Goodwin smiled. "Let's say it won't hurt business a bit," he replied, clapping Jackson on the shoulder. "Let's get outside. The lobsters should be about done."

While Bortnicker and the Goodwin women cooked and Tom Sr. was perusing the bell with Jasper, T.J. strolled with his cousin along the small beach of the cove. The sun was just beginning its slow descent, and the Blue Lagoon party's laughter carried across the water.

"Everyone's so happy," observed LouAnne as she looked back toward the dock.

"Well, it was a pretty amazing day," said T.J. "I still can't believe we found that bell."

"Mr. Goodwin wants us to dive the wreck again on Thursday. If we already know the wreck is the *Steadfast*, what's the point?"

"Maybe there's like millions of gold doubloons and stuff we could find. Who knows?"

"Yeah, but didn't Mr. Goodwin tell you that, by law, anything we find that's valuable has to be turned over to the government?"

"That's what he said. But, I'll tell you what. Any gold baubles, I'll smuggle them out of the country for you."

"Deal," she said, laughing. LouAnne stooped to pick up a flat stone, then skipped it across the Lagoon's gentle waves.

"Something wrong?" asked T.J.

"I'm worried about your buddy," she said.

"Again with this? C'mon, Cuz, he's having the time of his life. A girl—who by the way is gorgeous—is actually paying attention to him."

"I'm just so frightened for him," said LouAnne. "He seems so clueless at times when it comes to girls, and Ronnie, in my humble opinion, is anything but clueless."

"I get you," said T.J., who wasn't exactly a lady-killer himself at Bridgefield High School, despite his good looks. "Jeez, when I think of some of the disasters he's had over the past couple years—"

"Well, last summer you told me about that one girl he asked to a dance, remember? Bought her flowers, the whole bit?"

"Yeah, and she blew him off," he said, shaking his head. "And then there was Madison Blitstein."

"Are you serious? There's actually a girl at your school named Madison Blitstein?"

"Well, there was, back in the seventh grade. She's at some toney all-girls prep school now."

"So what happened?"

"A typical Bortnicker train wreck. Lots of the Jewish kids in our school were having their Bar or Bat Mitzvahs that year, and this girl Madison's parents are loaded. They threw this huge party at the most exclusive country club in Fairfield County, something like 400 people. I mean, it was a bigger production than most weddings I've been to with my dad.

"Anyway, Madison—who believe me, was never gonna win any beauty contests herself—invited like every kid in the seventh grade—"

"Except Bortnicker."

"Yup. Jewish kids, Catholics, Protestants ... didn't matter. The more the merrier. As long as you weren't Bortnicker."

"What a witch!"

"Yeah. So, like always, I went to her and said, like, 'C'mon Maddie, can't you have just one more person? You've got around half the population of Connecticut coming already."

"What did she say?"

"She said, and I quote: 'Bortnicker? Ew!' Which about describes her level of intelligence."

"Did you go?"

"Nah. I told her if he isn't invited, neither am I. So I personally handed her back the invitation. It felt kind of good, actually. We ended up spending the night of Blitstein's Bat Mitzvah at his house, working on his model train layout. And he kept saying, 'You didn't have to do this, Big Mon,' over and over, but I knew I did. Want to know what's funny about the whole thing?"

"What?"

"On the kids buffet menu they had these buffalo chicken wings that everyone was scarfing down. Well, the country club had left them standing around too long before they got cooked, and almost everyone got food poisoning."

"No way!"

"Oh yeah. The next day was a Monday, and Bortnicker and I were like the entire seventh grade!"

LouAnne chuckled, and her eyes got filmy. "That's why I love ya, Cuz," she said and gave him a hug, which he didn't mind at all.

"So, is that all that's bothering you?"

"Kind of. T.J., did you ever get the feeling that something's too good to be true?"

"Sometimes. What's the matter?"

"I don't know. It's just that ... here we are in this magical place, having a great time, making this incredible find ... maybe I'm just too pessimistic."

"Nah," he said, lightly resting his hand on her shoulder. "To tell you the truth, I was having the same feeling on the boat on the way back. But, hey, why shouldn't this happen to us? We're all good people, right?"

He looked into her eyes, and for a moment, time seemed to stand still.

Suddenly a piercing "Oww!" broke over the water. Bortnicker must've burned himself or something.

"Guess we'd better get back," said LouAnne.

Reluctantly, they turned toward the Blue Lagoon.

* * * *

Over succulent boiled lobsters dripping in butter, the divers recounted the day's exploits for Tom Sr. and Claudette, who seemed to have somewhat different reactions. T.J.'s dad was brimming with pride, and kept high-fiving Mike and the kids with each round of champagne. Mrs. Goodwin, however, seemed a bit more reserved. When Ronnie picked up on her reticence she simply shrugged and explained, "It's just a bell, after all."

"Just a bell?" exploded Jasper good naturedly. "And I suppose Buckingham Palace is just a house?"

"You know what I mean, Jasper," she answered quietly. "The discovery itself is remarkable, I'll give you that. I just don't know what this will lead to. Maybe that bell was never meant to be uncovered."

"Aw, c'mon, Mum, you can't mean that," said Ronnie. "Think of what this will mean to our business! Dad will have to beat back the customers!"

"I suppose," she said with a half-smile. "Still, I think our lives were rather fulfilling to begin with. I hope things stay positive."

"Of course they will, my dear," said Jasper, taking her hand.

"So, one more dive on Thursday?" said Mike, draining his plastic champagne cup.

"I'd like to give it a go," said Jasper. "Boys? LouAnne?"

"We're in," said T.J.

"In that case," said Jasper, solemnly rising from his seat, "I must propose a toast. First, to the three cooks who produced this marvelous feast—"

"Hear, hear!" sang out a slightly tipsy Mike Weinstein, as the others gave Claudette, Ronnie, and Bortnicker a round of applause.

"…and more importantly, a toast to what may prove to be one of the most significant historic finds in Bermudian history!"

With that, the congregation broke into cheers and the teens high-fived each other with bone-jarring smacks.

* * * *

"Now did you hear that, Hogfish?" whispered Willie B. "I knew something was going on with those kids. The question is, how did Jasper Goodwin get involved, and what did they find?"

Hogfish, an overweight black man with a bowling ball head and a lazy eye that gave him the appearance of the creature he was named after, replied quietly, "I don't know for sure, but if you figure this is about Black Bill Tarver, my guess is that there's gold or silver involved."

"Like a pirate treasure?"

"Uh-huh."

"Hmm," hissed Willie B., his dreadlocked head now glistening with sweat. "It's time I did a little detective work, see what I can find out."

"Who are you going to talk to? Nigel Chapford? He's their driver, right?"

"No, no," said Willie B. with a devilish smile. "I can get even closer than that. Let's get out of here." With that, the two men slithered out of their hiding place in the tropical undergrowth and made it to the road where they caught a late bus to Hamilton.

* * * *

121

"So, how was dinner, folks?" said Chappy as the Americans piled into the minivan.

"Great," said Mike as he waved to Tom Sr., who pulled onto the road ahead of them on the scooter. "We ate like kings. Jasper found us some spiny lobsters and his wife made—what was it?"

"Cassava pie and candied sweet potatoes," reported Bortnicker proudly.

"My goodness, Bermuda classics all. Well, Claudette Goodwin is rather famous around here for her cooking. And how was your day of diving?"

Silence fell over the vehicle, leaving only the sound of the Beatles' "Here, There, and Everywhere" from the *Revolver* album. The Americans looked at each other with concern.

"Have I said something wrong?" asked Chappy.

"No, no," replied Mike. "It's just that … okay, Chappy, we'll level with you, but you've gotta keep this quiet—"

"You have my word, Mr. Weinstein."

"That's good enough for me, so I'll just cut to the chase. The boys found the bell to Tarver's pirate ship."

Exuding calm, their driver smoothly pulled over to the side of the road and put on his flashers. "You're quite serious?"

"No doubt, Chappy," said T.J. "We could read the letters and everything."

Chapford let out a low whistle. "The *Steadfast*. Remarkable. They've been searching for it for years. All I can say is congratulations. And when do you intend to make this discovery public?"

"Not 'til the show's done filming," said Bortnicker. "Mr. Goodwin thinks it'll turn into a circus if we tell the press at this point."

"He's quite right, Mr. B.," said Chappy, easing the car back onto the road. "So, what next? This is becoming quite the adventure."

"Mr. Goodwin wants us to do another dive on Thursday when he's got the whole day clear," said T.J. "I say that since we've got a free day tomorrow we really hit those archives at the National Trust Museum. I feel like we're missing a key bit of information somewhere."

"Me too," agreed LouAnne. "We've got to tie the ship to the house, or vice versa. Hopefully, that nasty Mrs. Tilbury won't give us a hard time."

"Don't worry," said Bortnicker, "T.J.'s managed to charm her already. It'll be a breeze."

"I'm not so sure," said T.J. "Chappy, could you pick us up around 9:00 a.m. tomorrow morning?"

"Not a problem."

"Oh," said Mike, "and we'll be going to Harbour Night in Hamilton as well."

"Quite a full day," said Chappy, "and you'll probably have time to squeeze in a swim in the afternoon."

"Any suggestions for dinner?" said Bortnicker, as food was never far from his mind.

"Hmm … well, if you fancy some Italian fare, La Trattoria is reasonably priced, and the food is good. I'd give that a go."

"Great!" said T.J. "That's the same place my dad's been raving about."

A short time later they pulled into the car park of Jobson's Cove Apartments, and the exhausted ghost hunters lugged their equipment upstairs, said goodnight, and retired to their rooms.

But as bone weary as they were, neither of the boys could fall asleep immediately, as the day's events kept playing in their heads like a movie marathon. Finally, Bortnicker broke the silence in the darkness. "Didja like the food?" he asked.

"Are you kidding? I couldn't stop eating it. You're learning a whole new bunch of recipes."

"Yeah. Ronnie's mom is really nice. A lot like Aunt Terri in Gettysburg."

"Ronnie isn't so bad herself," said T.J., fishing for a response.

"You think she's out of my league?"

"I wouldn't say that. Don't underestimate yourself."

"C'mon, Big Mon. You know that if she went to Bridgefield High the guys would be all over her."

"So?"

"So, why's she paying so much attention to *me*?"

"Must be your cooking."

"*Seriously.*"

"I don't know, man. Girls are just funny. Haven't you figured that out yet?"

"I guess. Well, my plan is just to enjoy it as long as it lasts."

"Sounds like a good plan."

"And don't think we all didn't notice you and your lovely cousin steal away for a romantic promenade on the beach."

"Bortnicker, please."

"It's okay, Big Mon," he said. "If you can't be romantic in Bermuda, you might as well pack it in."

"Uh-huh," T.J. replied, thinking that maybe he wasn't giving his nerdy friend anywhere near enough credit.

Chapter Seventeen

"If you guys don't mind, I'm going to take the scooter into Hamilton this morning and try to find some backup batteries for the video cameras," said Mike to the boys as they wolfed down their morning cereal. "In the past we've had situations where an entity has drained the batteries as it tried to manifest itself, and I don't want to be caught short if it happens here."

"Good idea," said T.J. "Now, where will you be while we're searching the house?"

"I'm going to set up a command center in the foyer area near the front door. From there I'll be able to monitor the DVRs we'll position in the various rooms and stay in contact with you guys via walkie-talkies."

"How many nights did they say they were giving us?" asked Bortnicker, wiping milk off his lips.

"We have two filming ops if we need it. Judging by what's happened so far, it seems like a given. You dudes finding that bell make the whole project a lot more interesting. I can't wait to see what you'll bring up on the second dive tomorrow."

"Me neither," said Bortnicker. "Some gold ingots and silver bars would be nice. Maybe the government will give us a cut, like they do in Florida."

"I wouldn't count on it," said T.J., rinsing his cereal bowl in the sink. "These people seem pretty possessive about their belongings." He paused a second. "Hey, Mike, I don't mind that you're not coming with us to the museum this morning, but do you think they'll give us a hard time about checking out the archives without you there?"

"They shouldn't. It's all in the agreement they signed with The Adventure Channel. We're supposed to have total access, no matter what that grump Tilbury says. If it gets dicey, you have my cell number. Call me and I'll contact the proper higher-ups. I'll see you back here this afternoon."

"I betcha he has a date," mused Bortnicker as Mike started up the scooter down below.

"Well, we shouldn't need him all the time anyway," said T.J. "And we won't see my dad till tonight, so we're kinda on our own." They checked their look in the mirror—Bortnicker especially seemed to be doing more of that lately—and met up with LouAnne on the balcony. As usual, she was radiant in her black *JGGC* tee shirt and matching ponytail scrunchy. "Man, did I ever sleep last night," she declared. "Even the tree frogs didn't bother me. Good thing we took today off from running."

"No doubt," agreed T.J., whose arms were still sore from digging out that bell the previous day.

They strolled downstairs just as Chappy was pulling in. "And how is the team today?" he asked, holding a door open for LouAnne.

"Relaxed and ready for some research!" said LouAnne pertly.

"Got any music for us today, Chappy?" asked Bortnicker as he buckled up.

"Why don't you choose, Mr. B?" he replied, handing Bortnicker a travel case of CD's.

"Hmm," the boy said, shuffling through the pile. "I think we'll go with *Abbey Road*." As "Come Together" came on the kids chatted about their upcoming night on the town in Hamilton.

"So, Chappy," said T.J., "this Harbour Night thing is supposed to be pretty cool, right?"

"Oh yes. They hold it every Wednesday because, by then, the weekly cruise ships are docked on Front Street. All the shops stay open later, and there are all kinds of vendors on the sidewalk selling everything from snacks to jewelry. And they have face painting and whatnot for the little ones. It's more or less a huge street festival. My favorite, however, would be the Gombay Dancers."

"What's that?" asked Bortnicker.

"Well," said the driver, "Gombay is a kind of traditional folk music

126

that mixes British, West African, and other cultures. The dancers, usually male, wear masquerade costumes with bright colors and tall, crazy hats that give the effect of tropical birds."

"What kind of instruments do they use?" asked Bortnicker.

"The drumbeat is key," answered Chappy. "They employ both the snare and kettle drum; occasionally a fife is added."

"Sounds like us last year," quipped T.J.

"How so?"

"Chappy," volunteered LouAnne, "you should've seen these guys last summer in Gettysburg. Since T.J. and Bortnicker played the kettle drum in their school orchestra, my dad recruited them as drummer boys for his Civil War reenactment unit. They were playing the snare drum during the battle reenactment!"

"Well," he answered, "having seen a few Civil War movies, I can tell you that Gombay is a bit more energetic and can get pretty wild, depending upon how much the performers and spectators are into it."

"So what you're saying," said Beatle Bortnicker, "is that not even our Ringo would be a suitable Gombay."

"Something like that."

LouAnne turned to her cousin, a sneaky smile on her face. "Hey, T.J., you been noticing how Bortnicker's inner Beatle never seems to come out around Ronnie?"

"Yeah," said the boy. "I wonder why that is?"

"Ah, she wouldn't get it," he explained embarrassedly. "Besides, it's kind of *our* thing."

The cousins let his words settle for a few seconds and then burst into laughter.

"You guys are brutal," acknowledged Bortnicker with his trademark crooked smile.

"So," said Chappy, coming to his rescue, "what time do you anticipate being finished at the museum?"

"I'd give us a couple hours," estimated T.J. "Maybe a little more if we want to grab a quick lunch afterwards."

Despite their earlier bravado with Mike, the junior ghost hunters approached the museum with an air of trepidation. LouAnne had brought the camcorder in case anything turned up during their research.

"Here we go," said T.J., opening the front door for his colleagues.

A young man was at the front desk today, smartly dressed in a blue sport jacket and tie. "May I help you?" he inquired politely.

"Ah, we're here from The Adventure Channel show to look in the archives," said T.J., trying to be as suave as possible. "Mrs. Tilbury said it would be no problem?"

"Yes, of course, the *Junior Gonzo Ghost Chasers*," the clerk said with what T.J. interpreted as a hint of derision. "Our archives room is down the hall opposite Mrs. Tilbury's office. I hope you don't need to see her because she's out sick today."

"No, that's okay," T.J. said, inwardly pleased that the old woman wouldn't be hovering over them.

"Fine, then. Mrs. Rayburn, our archivist, will be happy to assist you." He smiled faintly and went back to doing busywork in his ledger.

"Hope it's not another old battle axe," LouAnne whispered as they entered the door marked ARCHIVES—NO ADMITTANCE WITHOUT PERMISSION.

"Well, hello there!" called a matronly black woman who was on a rickety ladder replacing a book.

Bortnicker immediately ran over and steadied the ladder, which seemed to be wobbling under the woman's weight.

"You're so kind!" she called down, somewhat relieved at the boy's assistance. "I'm Violet Rayburn, National Trust Archivist. You must be those ghost chasers!"

"That's us," said T.J.

The woman gingerly eased her way down, the ladder creaking with every step. Introductions were made all around, and the teens were pleased to have been greeted warmly. "Mrs. Tilbury told me to expect you. I take it you'll want to see our materials dealing with Sir William Tarver?"

"Yes, ma'am," said LouAnne respectfully.

"Well, have a seat at that small table over there and I'll get the files. You'll find a box of white cotton gloves on the table. Please put them on so as to not damage the papers. Some of them are quite fragile. Would you like a cup of tea? I was about to put on a kettle in the back room."

"No, thanks," said T.J., flashing his most ingratiating smile. "We

128

just appreciate you helping us."

"It's a pleasure to assist our friends from the States," she said. "And TV personalities at that! I'll be right back." She hustled off, leaving the kids to seat themselves and pull on the cotton gloves.

"Must be really old stuff," said Bortnicker. "At least this lady is nice. Remember the woman in Charleston who helped us out last year?"

"Yeah," said T.J. "What was her name? Thibodeaux, that was it. From the Museum of the Confederacy. We got some really good background stuff on Major Hilliard that helped us figure out his situation."

"All right, here she comes," said LouAnne hopefully. Mrs. Rayburn approached the table a little hesitantly and put a large archival box down. As Bortnicker went to open it, T.J. could sense a look of distress on her face. He removed the cover, then looked up quizzically, his long bangs drooping over his glasses. "That's *it*?" he said with a mixture of disappointment and surprise.

The only contents of the rather substantial box were a couple of dusty ledgers. T.J. wondered why they would be stored in such a roomy container. Mrs. Rayburn seemed just as confused. "Well, ah, it appears that, ah—"

"Something's been removed?" said LouAnne impatiently.

"It would appear so, yes," she said quietly, perspiration forming on her forehead.

"Well," said T.J., "let's at least go through what's here. Can we have you photocopy things, Mrs. Rayburn?"

"Oh yes, Mr. Jackson, that shouldn't be a problem. I'll, ah, leave you three alone to work. Call me if you need me." She disappeared into the stacks, and the teens looked at each other blankly.

"Something stinks here," said Bortnicker.

"No duh," said LouAnne, "but did you notice that even Rayburn was surprised?"

"And embarrassed," added T.J. "Well, we might as well look through what's here."

There wasn't much. The most notable document was the deed for the acreage upon which Hibiscus House and the surrounding plantation were created. Dated 1722, it looked very official, with a lot of whereases and heretofores in flowing calligraphy. The fragile parchment was signed by the governor and featured a wax seal with his official crest.

There was also a commendation, again with the governor's seal, recognizing Sir William Tarver for his assistance in the construction of Fort St. Catherine. Rounding out the file were some period newspaper articles that mentioned Tarver, usually for such mundane things as his hosting of a gala ball at Hibiscus House or his participation in boundary dispute hearings and such. Nothing pertaining to piracy, the *Steadfast*, or his death could be found.

"I don't know if there's anything here that's even worth copying," said T.J. dejectedly. "All this stuff reflects is that the guy was a wealthy, respected citizen of the island."

"That's why it's still in the file," said Bortnicker. "What a waste of time."

"Maybe not," said LouAnne. "I think it's obvious that somebody doesn't want us to know what this guy was really about. Somehow, we're going to have to piece it together from tomorrow's dive and the house investigation."

"Or *he* could just tell us," joked Bortnicker.

"That's not so far out," she replied. "If you remember, once we got Major Hilliard talking, it was hard to shut him up."

"That is, until you ticked him off," chided T.J.

"Hey, how was I to know he considered battle reenactments insulting? Jeez, guys—"

"I'm just breaking 'em on you," said T.J. "But, Cuz, don't you think we're kinda taking it for granted that Tarver's going to show up while we're there? I mean, I've been watching *Gonzo Ghost Chasers* since it came on, and the most they've ever had happen was shadow figures and a few words here and there on the EVP recorders."

"That's been worrying me, too," admitted LouAnne. "If you remember, last year on the battlefield Hilliard's voice didn't come out on the audio tape for either Mike or us, although he was there plain as day. I wouldn't count on video of Tarver, either, even if we do have a gazillion DVRs positioned all over the house. We've just gotta see what turns up … we can't do any more than that."

"Especially not knowing anything about him," said Bortnicker in a raised voice he hoped Mrs. Rayburn would hear.

The woman must've been listening, for within seconds she magically appeared, still somewhat nervous at the teens' obvious displeasure. "Well folks," she said, "do you need anything copied? Can I be of any further service?"

"I think we're done here," answered T.J. diplomatically. Then he added, "At least for now."

They got up and left, and the door behind them had barely closed when Mrs. Rayburn picked up her desk phone and started dialing.

* * * *

"Well, it's only eleven, and we've got some time to kill before Chappy picks us up," said T.J. "How about an early lunch?"

"You know I'm up for that," said Bortnicker.

"Me, too," LouAnne chimed in. "Let's walk around and find someplace good."

They settled on Wahoo's Bistro on the waterfront, where LouAnne ordered the Bermuda fish chowder, while the boys shared orders of shark fritters and codfish cakes.

Chappy met them just as they emerged into the blinding sunshine. "A successful venture this morning?" he asked as they climbed in.

"Negative," said Bortnicker, rooting through Chappy's Beatle CD's. "It seems that some of the papers on Tarver had been removed, surprise, surprise."

"How unfortunate," the driver replied coolly.

"Chappy," said T.J., "I know this is your homeland, and that you're proud of it, just like everyone we've met, but I'm getting the impression that there's stuff we're just not supposed to know—"

"—Which makes us even more determined to know it," finished LouAnne.

"And don't take this the wrong way," continued Bortnicker, as he slid *Beatles for Sale* into the console, "but I get the feeling you're kinda holding back on us also." His words hung in the air as the distinctive opening to "No Reply" started up.

If Chappy was hurt or insulted, he didn't show it. "I'm sure I'm not the fountain of information you suppose me to be," he began.

"Remember, I'm a humble limousine driver, not an historian. But you have to understand the perception of people outside your country of the American media. The publicizing of lurid details and the sensationalism employed by your major media outlets can at times be off-putting and lead to caution, if not downright fear, when it comes to sharing the history of one's homeland.

"Bermuda is a country like any other. We've had our highs and lows, our heroes and scoundrels. We just downplay the scoundrels, whereas you Yanks seem to revel in them. For example, your gangsters of the 1920s and '30s — Al Capone, John Dillinger and the like. And I won't even touch upon the serial killers who have crossed the American landscape the past 25 or so years whose stories are chronicled on your various history channels. These people—these *concepts*—are disconcerting, if not frightening, to Bermudians. We are a peaceful, friendly people and would rather not speak of such things."

"I get all that," said T.J., as Paul McCartney warbled "I'll Follow the Sun", "but all we want to know is, where does Sir William Tarver fall? Was he a good guy or a bad guy?"

"My friends," said Chappy, "something tells me that you are going to find out, and more quickly than you think. But what you make of your finds, and how you plan to share them, should be a cause for great contemplation on your parts."

"Okay," said T.J., not wanting to offend their friend by pushing him too far. "Enough with this. Who feels like riding some waves down at Astwood Beach?"

"Cool!" said Bortnicker. "A little body surfing would be fun. How about you, LouAnne?"

"With that undertow? No way, José. But I will paddle around a little in Jobson's Cove and look at the tropical fish."

"Deal."

Chappy gave the teens a pickup time for that evening's trip to Hamilton and dropped them at the hotel. Within minutes they had changed into their beach attire and were on their way down to the breakers of Astwood Park.

LouAnne snapped pictures as the boys zoomed along atop the six foot swells, usually coming to a tumbling stop in the sea foam at the water's edge. There were others enjoying the sun, sand, and surf, but no one attacked the waves like T.J. and Bortnicker, trying to out-daredevil each other before their alluring female friend.

Finally, after forty minutes or so of crashing about in the ocean, the boys literally crawled to LouAnne's blanket where she sat placidly, reading a paperback.

"You guys done?" he said over her sunglasses.

"Stick a fork in us," moaned T.J., his hair dripping.

"I must have a pound of sand in my bathing suit," added Bortnicker.

"Too much info," said LouAnne, gathering her belongings. "Let's go over to Jobson's Cove so I can wade in the water. I even brought a mask and snorkel."

"LouAnne's going Jacques Cousteau on us!" cried Bortnicker. "She's even venturing into the murky depths by herself!"

"Ha-ha, Mr. *Deep Sea Detective*. Wrong on both counts. It's crystal clear and shallow. But even so, you guys keep an eye on me, okay?"

"Sure thing," said T.J., hoping Bortnicker wouldn't use that as an opening for a wise remark. They strolled up and around the rock formations that protected the small lagoon, and the boys spread out their blankets. Luckily, a Bermudian day camp group of kindergarten age kids was just leaving, their counselor picking up flip-flops and other belongings inadvertently left behind.

LouAnne cleaned her mask as T.J. had showed her, adjusted the snorkel, and pushed off into the shallow pool.

"This is nice," said Bortnicker, laying back with his hands behind his head. "But something's bothering me, Big Mon."

"What?" said T.J., his eyes locked on his cousin.

"I'm getting a strange vibe from Chappy. It's like he wants to tell us stuff, but something's holding him back."

"Yeah, I get that, too."

"I just don't wanna tick him off. He's such a good guy, not to mention a friend of John Lennon."

"Uh-huh."

"So, are you psyched for Harbour Night in Hamilton? Sounds like a cool time."

"No doubt. Are you inviting Ronnie to join us?"

"You think it's okay?"

"I'm sure Dad and Mike wouldn't mind—"

"I mean with your cousin."

"Nah. She's cool. Give Ronnie a call at the shop and tell her to meet us there around eight. We should be done with dinner by then. She could show us around Hamilton."

"Sounds like a plan." He took out his cell phone and started dialing the Blue Lagoon's number.

* * * *

Unfortunately, Ronnie Goodwin wasn't at the desk to take his call. She had been sent to Dora's Corners by her father to pick up a takeout lunch for him and Skeeter.

"Well, hello, Queen of the Deep!" sang out Dora as the girl breezed in. "What can I get for you this fine day?"

"Dad said to bring him whatever's fresh today, Miss Dora," answered Ronnie politely. "A double order for him and Skeeter."

"We've got a nice grouper, just come in. Give me a few minutes to fix it up."

"No rush, ma'am. I'll sit outside and wait there."

She had no sooner gotten comfortable when Willie B. and his sidekick Hogfish ambled across the crushed shell parking lot to her table. She tried to wish them away but had no such luck.

"Hello, Miss Ronnie," said Willie B., his forehead glistening in the noonday sun.

"Willie B., Hogfish," she answered, politely nodding.

"Hey, your daddy need any work done 'round the shop? I'm a little slow right now," Willie B. said, pulling up a chair.

"You know, he was talking the other day about the dock needing some repair. You might want to see him about that."

"That I will. Hey, Hogfish, fetch me a ginger beer, will you?" he said to his bulky companion, who sighed and waddled off to the restaurant entrance. Once he was out of earshot, Willie B. fixed his eyes on hers. "I see those American boys have hired out your daddy's boat. Was working on a neighboring dock and saw you all pull out of the lagoon the other day."

134

"Yes, that's right," she said guardedly.

"I had the pleasure of meeting them the other day, right here," he said genially. "Seem like good boys."

"They are."

"Told me they're here to do some ghost hunting. At least that's what the one with the glasses said."

"Oh."

"Well, he was right, wasn't he? No reason to tell me a tall tale."

"Yes, they've come to look into—"

"Hibiscus House. And all that nonsense about it being haunted."

"Who says it's nonsense?" the girl snapped, suddenly defensive.

"Ooh, sorry," he said soothingly, his teeth flashing. "Didn't know you saw it that way, Miss Ronnie. I'm sure they're very serious about it. So, when is the big investigation to take place?"

"Soon. They didn't say exactly," she lied.

"Well, we'll all be anxious to see what they found out on old Sir William," he said as Hogfish banged out of the shack's screen door with two frosty cans of Barritt's ginger beer. "You tell them I said good luck, okay?"

"Sure."

"Then good day, Miss Ronnie. I'll see your dad about that dock repair." The two started up the road, and Ronnie couldn't wait to get back inside and pick up her order.

"Just about to come get you," said Dora, handing over a brown paper bag bulging with Styrofoam containers of food. "That'll be £12." She read the look of consternation on Ronnie's face as the girl counted out her money. "What's wrong, girl?" she asked. "Willie B. bothering you?"

"He gives me the creeps," she replied, laying the money on the countertop.

"He's mostly harmless, and that Hogfish is just an imbecile. Pay them no mind." She scooped up the bills and coins and propped a meaty elbow onto the counter. "So, how is the investigation going?"

Ronnie rolled her eyes. Had the boys blabbed to *everyone*? "Okay, I guess," she managed. "Listen, Miss Dora, I've got to go. Daddy likes his food warm."

"Okay, dear. You just take care of yourself." As Ronnie snapped the screen door shut behind her Dora added, "And those cute boys, too!"

* * * *

Back at the Jobson's Cove Apartments, the teens parted to relax a bit, send emails home, and shower for the evening's festivities in Hamilton. Mike looked in on the boys to find how their morning research had gone and was annoyed to learn they'd come up empty. "So, you think some incriminating stuff on Tarver had been removed?" he said, rummaging through the teen's refrigerator.

"Definitely," said Bortnicker. "The archivist was really embarrassed."

"T.J.?"

"Bortnicker's right," he agreed, popping open a Coke. "And even if we go back, I don't know if we'll get any further."

Weinstein smiled. "Dudes, we're on to something. All this non-cooperation and secrecy have to mean something. But, see, they don't know we have secrets of our own. We found the bell. That's why tomorrow's dive and Friday night's investigation at the house could be enormous."

"Looks like it," said Bortnicker, flopping on the couch. "Hey, Big Mon," he said to T.J., "who's first in the shower, me or you?"

"You go first today," he answered. "I want to talk to Mike."

"Aww, and I was just getting comfortable.," he moaned, shuffling off to the bathroom.

"You joining us for dinner in Hamilton?" T.J. asked the senior *Ghost Chaser*.

"That I am," beamed Weinstein. "And the girl I met down here is meeting us at the restaurant your dad picked. Her name's Kim, Kim Whitestone, and her father's filthy rich. I've been hanging out on their yacht whenever I have some down time. But she's pretty down-to-earth, all things considered." He gave a sly smile. "And attractive, I might add."

"Way to go, Mike," chuckled T.J.

"And that's not all, dude," said Weinstein. "Word on the street is that your pop is bringing a date."

"Really?"

"Oh yeah. A lady he met at the golf club. We're going to end up with quite the entourage."

Outside, the engine of a moped could be heard in the car park. "That must be him now," said T.J., anxious to find out about Tom Sr.'s companion.

"Well, I gotta go shower," said Mike. "I'll tell your dad to drop in on you. Oh, by the way, he said collared shirts and slacks for tonight, gotta look presentable."

"So, no *Gonzo Ghost Chasers* attire?" joked T.J.

"Nah, we don't want to look *too* conspicuous," said Weinstein, who was probably only being half truthful. He exited, and seconds later T.J. was almost dozing, the steady hiss of Bortnicker's shower in the background, when his dad entered, energized and upbeat.

"Long day?" he asked, taking a seat next to his son.

"Well, the Heritage Trust was a dud, but we got some quality beach time. But, man, those waves knocked me out. So, Dad, Mike tells me you've got a date for tonight?"

The elder Jackson reddened a bit. "If you don't mind. She's a nice lady I met at the club. Handles their corporate bookings and such."

"And does this 'lady' have a name?"

"Oh, yeah. Lindsay Cosgrove. Grew up here outside of St. George's. She's been in on a lot of the meetings and we kinda hit it off."

"Is she pretty?"

"You could say that, yes," he smiled, which meant she was probably a knockout.

"Well, I'm glad to hear it, Dad," said T.J. "It's been kinda sparse since Wendy."

"Please don't mention that name," frowned Tom Sr. "And you'll be happy to know she's actually within a few years of my age."

"Who is?" said Bortnicker, emerging from the steamy bathroom.

"Dad's got a date for tonight," said T.J. proudly. "A Miss Cosgrove. It is 'Miss', correct?"

"Yes, it is," laughed Tom Sr., "and enough with the interrogation. Bortnicker, jeez, you're dripping all over the floor!"

"Oops, my bad," said the teen, holding a towel around his waist.

"T.J., your turn. But I was right. Wait'll you see all the sand that came out of me in the shower!" He padded off to the bedroom as both father and son shook their heads.

"Seriously, though, Dad, I'm happy you have a date tonight. Can't wait to meet her," T.J. said, heading for the bathroom. "Where are we eating, anyway?"

"I've decided on La Trattoria," said Tom Sr. "Pretty fair Italian food. You'll like it."

"Yeah, Chappy mentioned it, too." He closed the door and smiled broadly, happy to see the sparkle in his father's eye once again.

* * * *

"Skeeter, Dad, got your lunch!" Ronnie sang out as she elbowed open the front door to the dive shop.

"Your dad's out back, honey," Skeeter muttered while pouring over a scuba equipment catalog. "Meeting with that character Willie B. about some dock work."

Ronnie silently berated herself. "Me and my big mouth," she said under her breath. "He couldn't wait to get over here." She put the food down on a table and walked out back where Jasper was pointing to some rotted wood in one of the boat slips. Willie B. caught her eye and winked. She managed the barest of smiles.

"Are you back with lunch? I'm famished!" said the Divemaster, straightening up and wiping his hands on his cargo shorts.

"It's inside. You'd better get to it before Skeeter eats it all."

"Will do. And, oh, by the way, your friend Bortnicker called. He'd like you to meet him this evening at 8:00 in front of the cruise ship wharf in Hamilton. I told him I'd drop you there, but you might have to take the bus back."

"If it's okay with you," she said hopefully.

"Not a problem. But you can't stay out *too* late, and neither should those boys. We've got a big day tomorrow."

"Yes, sir," she answered, hating the fact that Willie B. had heard it all. "Well, it's kind of slow so I'll walk home and make myself presentable. Spend some time with Mum."

"You do that. See you later."

138

She bid good afternoon to Skeeter and hiked up the road to their cottage, all the while thinking of Willie B.'s knowing wink and hoping she wouldn't have to run into him again for a good long time. Of course, on an island as small as Bermuda that was pretty near impossible. But then she thought of her new friends, and the exciting possibilities of Harbour Night in Hamilton, and all was forgotten. By the time she walked in the front door, Ronnie Goodwin was singing.

* * * *

"You sure you want to do this, man?" asked a dubious Hogfish as Willie B. clicked off his cell phone.

Willie B. sighed and shook his head, adopting a tone one might take with a three-year-old. "Listen to me now. My cousin Dwight and his buddies hang out at Chumley's Pub on Court Street. All they're gonna do is keep an eye on those kids tonight. Dwight knows who Ronnie Goodwin is, so he'll have no problem finding them on Front Street."

"But what's in it for us, Willie B.?"

"Like I told you, man, they found *something* out on the water the other day. I'm sure of it. Maybe Dwight and his boys can get close enough to overhear something about it. Meanwhile, I think I just might take a ride over to Hibiscus House and set up a little surprise for their visit."

"Like what?"

"I'm still working on that. Time to bring those big-talking American ghost hunters down a peg."

Hogfish chuckled. "Willie B., you always up to some kind of mischief, you know that?"

"Yeah. And you know what else? I'm tired of doing the same old grunt work day in and day out, fixing docks and whatnot, so that rich Yanks can come over here and walk about like they own the place. And I'm disappointed Jasper Goodwin and his fine lookin' daughter are falling all over themselves catering to them, especially that goofy one. Lord, Lord if he doesn't deserve a righteous scarin'."

"But aren't you scared yourself of goin' in that house alone? Because you know I'll be havin' no part of that."

"Scared? Of what? Spooky stories about Black Bill Tarver's ghost walkin' the grounds? I'm surprised at you, Hogfish. Man your age believing in fairy tales. Everybody knows there ain't no such things as ghosts."

Chapter Eighteen

"A toast to our expedition, and to those who have joined us this fine evening!" said Mike Weinstein as he raised his wine glass.

"Hear, hear!" agreed Tom Sr., doing likewise as the others clinked glasses.

The evening had begun quite smoothly, with Chappy picking up the nattily attired Americans precisely at 6:00 p.m. for their night in Hamilton. The men were dressed in khakis, golf shirts, and sport jackets—though Weinstein's overly muscled torso threatened to split his navy blue blazer at any second—the boys in tropical shirts and slacks, and LouAnne in a peach-colored short sleeve pullover with white capris.

On the way to the city it was agreed upon that both Kim Whitestone and Lindsay Cosgrove were not to know of the discovery of the *Steadfast*'s bell, or anything beyond the basic information of the project. T.J. had his doubts, though; it only took a couple drinks to set Mike's tongue wagging.

La Trattoria, located in a walkway off Front Street, was quaint and not too pricey by Bermudian standards. The food was your basic Italian fare and quite tasty, though at one point Bortnicker leaned over and whispered, "I'll take Pizza Palace over this any day," to T.J.

From the conversation around the table T.J. could ascertain two things: that Kim Whitestone, though very attractive, didn't have too much going on upstairs and was star struck with Mike, who didn't mind at all playing the celebrity; and that Lindsay Cosgrove was quite taken with Tom Sr. Even LouAnne, who sat on his other side, nudged T.J. a couple times when the Bermudian woman complimented his father on his outstanding talent as an architect.

"So, T.J.," she said suddenly, fixing him with green eyes that accentuated her reddish-auburn hair, "tell us about this investigation of yours. It sounds quite the adventure."

The teen proceeded to give her a somewhat watered-down description of the events so far, leaving out all mention of the bell, of course. But then the inevitable happened, though it didn't come from Mike Weinstein, who was too busy making eyes at Kim Whitestone as they sipped their Chardonnay.

"We've been trying to do some research on the island, Ms. Cosgrove," complained Bortnicker, "but it's like nobody wants us to really get into the history of this Hibiscus House."

"How so?"

"Well, for example, we went all the way to St. George's the other day to meet this Mrs. Tilbury lady at the National Heritage Trust, and the old battle axe basically blew us off."

Lindsay's eyes widened. "Tilbury? Do you mean Constance Tilbury?"

"Yeah. You've heard of her?"

"Why, yes, actually," said Lindsay, regaining her composure. "She's my aunt, as a matter of fact."

At this Bortnicker went beet red, LouAnne shut her eyes and bit her lip, and T.J. wished he could slide under the table.

"Lindsay," offered Tom Sr., "I'm sure Bortnicker didn't mean to offend—"

But Lindsay merely waved him off. "No worries, Bortnicker," she assured. "Auntie can be a bit of a curmudgeon at times. She's just very protective of our island and its history, as you have obviously ascertained."

"Uh, yeah. But I'm sorry anyway," he said, flashing his crooked smile.

"You're very sweet," she answered, "as are you all. Let me have a word with Auntie. Perhaps I could sway her a bit to be a little more forthcoming."

"That would be great, Ms. Cosgrove," said T.J. with his winning smile.

"So, where to from here?" asked Tom Sr. as the waiter dropped off the bill.

"Well," said Mike, "if you don't mind, Kim and I are going to check out a couple of the clubs in town and I'll catch a cab back to the hotel, or I'll stay over on the yacht in Hamilton Harbor and get back early tomorrow."

"And I think, Mr. Jackson, that I should show you around our Harbour Night," said Lindsay, lightly placing her hand atop the architect's. "Maybe even partake in one of those touristy horse and buggy rides?"

"That would be great," he smiled.

"The three of us are meeting a friend down where the cruise ships are docked on Front Street," said T.J.

"Okay," said Tom Sr., checking his watch. "Why don't we meet back here at 10:30 and take a cab back to the hotel?"

"Oh, that won't be necessary," said Lindsay. "I have my Mercedes parked a block or so away. I'll give you all a lift home. It'll be a tight fit, but we'll make do."

"Sounds good. I'll call Chappy and tell him he's done for the night."

The group split up and the teens made their way down to Front Street, where Harbour Night was shifting into high gear. The waterfront, which was completely blocked off to motorized traffic, was awash in color and sound.

All of the upscale stores along the thoroughfare, such as Triminghams and Astwood Dickinson, were deluged with tourists, as were the smaller gift shops like Onion Jack's and Gosling's Liquors. Local vendors in gaily-colored outfits had set up stalls offering everything from homemade food to arts and crafts, clothing, and jewelry. There were jugglers, clowns and face painting for the children, and a reggae band was pounding out tunes from an elevated stage on the embankment near the motor scooter park. It was noisy, joyful, and alive.

"Too cool!" said Bortnicker above the surrounding din. "And there's Ronnie, near the band stage!" He waved madly and caught her eye, and she motioned them over. "Let's go!" he cried, and the three Americans took off at a jog to meet their Bermudian friend, who was looking good in a flowered top and short, white skirt that accentuated her finely-toned legs.

After hugs all around, Ronnie asked proudly, "So, what do you think? Can we Bermudians throw a party?"

"No question!" answered T.J., the band's reggae bass line throbbing through the nearby amplifiers.

"Can we hit some of the shops?" asked LouAnne hopefully.

"Why not?" said Ronnie. "Let's have a go!" She hooked her arm in Bortnicker's and pulled him across Front Street to the entrance to Trimingham's, one of the more traditionally British stores. They wandered around, rubbing elbows with hordes of Americans mostly, and some Canadians, before moving to the next shop down the street.

It was in Onion Jack's where LouAnne first noticed the thin black man with dreadlocks watching her from behind a display of Outerbridge's sherry pepper sauces, a Bermudian delicacy.

"T.J.," she whispered to her cousin, "don't look over, but there's a Rastafarian-looking guy on the other side of the shop who I could swear I saw in Trimingham's."

"And?"

"And I think he's following us."

"Really. Okay, let's go outside and get an ice cone and see if he follows. We're going outside!" he called to Bortnicker and Ronnie, who were looking for a Bermuda keychain to take home to Pippa.

"Give us a minute, we'll see you out there," replied Bortnicker.

T.J. and LouAnne ducked outside and made their way to the ice cone stand, where they both ordered the coconut. As they were paying, Bortnicker and Ronnie joined them. "Have you guys seen any police around?" asked T.J. casually.

"There were a couple way back on the other end of the block," said Bortnicker as he ordered a banana ice. "I love those British Bobby hats, but the navy Bermuda shorts gotta go. Why're you asking?"

"'Cause LouAnne thinks we're being followed."

"No way."

"I think she's right," said Ronnie quietly. "I've seen the same two or three men over and over since we started walking about."

"Including that guy coming out of Onion Jack's?" said LouAnne.

Ronnie nonchalantly glanced over her shoulder. "That would be one of them. Can't place him exactly, but he's a local."

"So, what do we do?" said Bortnicker. "Go after him?"

"Calm down, Rambo," said T.J., aware that his friend was out to impress his date. "Why don't we just work our way back up the street toward where we saw those Bobbies?"

"Sounds good, Cuz. Lead the way," said LouAnne.

They meandered up Front Street, pausing at the occasional vendor stall. T.J. kept taking furtive looks around, eventually picking out three faces that were keeping pace with the teens, trying to look casual as they clumsily shadowed them. All were dark-skinned men, though only the man in Onion Jack's sported the Rasta hairstyle.

They were nearly to the "Bird Cage" at the intersection of Front and Queen Streets from which a solitary Bobby conducted traffic during the daytime when T.J. realized the officers were nowhere to be found. "Any ideas?" he asked Ronnie. "You're the local expert."

"Hmm," she mused. "Ready for a bit of sport?"

"We were born ready," answered Bortnicker as LouAnne rolled her eyes.

"Then follow me." She strode briskly to an arcade off Front Street and darted inside, the Americans following close behind. "Now RUN!"

They took off at a sprint through the tunnel of small shops and came out on Reid Street, where Ronnie hung a right. Bortnicker was already panting as they crossed Burnaby Street and continued on Reid, glancing back over their shoulders every few yards.

"There they are!" cried LouAnne, easing into her cross country pace. "About a block back."

"Keep going!" said Ronnie, who had quite an athlete's stride herself. They passed the Cabinet Building and Sessions House of the Supreme Court.

"What now?" said T.J. as they neared another intersection.

"We don't want to go inland anymore, especially on Court Street," said Ronnie as they pounded along. "Lots of shady characters there, the type you never see in the travel adverts. I know an alleyway between here and King Street. Can you all hold up for another block?"

"We're okay, but Bortnicker's fading!" said LouAnne. "Those guys are closing on us!"

They kept running. Suddenly, Fagan's Alley appeared on their right. Ronnie took a sharp turn, and they followed in her wake, snaking through the passage. No sooner had they emerged on the far end of Front Street than T.J. spied a familiar face. "Hey, there's Dad and Lindsay on their carriage ride. Come on!"

The teens, now winded, waved and called to Tom Sr., who motioned to the driver to stop the carriage. With the last of their strength, the exhausted kids piled into the vacant rear seat of the buggy.

"So much for the romantic ride," said Tom Sr. "What's gotten into you kids?"

"We're being followed, Dad," wheezed T.J., wiping sweat from his brow.

"Oh my," said Lindsay. "By whom?"

"Don't know. Ronnie thinks they're locals."

Lindsay turned to face the brown-skinned girl, whose face was glistening with perspiration.

"Ronnie Goodwin," she said in introduction. "My dad owns Blue Lagoon Dive Shop."

"Oh yes, I've heard of it. Lindsay Cosgrove. Pleased to meet you, Ronnie. So, you recognize these men? Why on earth would they be following you?"

"Can't figure it, ma'am. We were just trying to enjoy Harbour Night and—"

Suddenly, a pounding, whooping sound came from way up Front Street in the area from which their flight had begun. Heavy drumbeats and shrieking whistles mixed with the roar of the crowd.

"It's the Gombay Dancers!" called out Lindsay. "Quite a show. Why don't we go have a look? The carriage ride's almost over, anyway."

"I guess so," said T.J., whose breathing had returned to normal. "Bortnicker?"

"Yeah, why not," said the other boy, clearing the moisture off his glasses. "Those guys won't dare bother us now, what with your dad here."

The carriage driver pulled up at the police barricade and Tom Sr. paid, with apologies for the extra last-minute passengers. They climbed off, still a little sore and winded from the merry chase of minutes before.

146

"Think I need another ice cone," said Bortnicker.

"We could all use one," agreed LouAnne.

They made it to the Front Street flagpole as the Gombay dancers paraded past, many of the somewhat inebriated tourists in tow. The Americans marveled at the wild feathered costumes of the Gombays as they dipped and swirled to the beat.

"It's a mix of Caribbean and African traditions," offered Ronnie. "Gets the heart pounding, doesn't it?"

"Like we really needed it," joked Bortnicker.

"I thought you did quite well, actually," said Ronnie, and she leaned over to give him a quick peck on the cheek. LouAnne and T.J. exchanged amused glances.

"Well, guys," said Tom Sr., checking his watch, "I'd say it's time to head back. I think we've had enough action for one night, and you all have a 10:00 a.m. appointment at the dive shop. Lindsay, are you sure that giving us a lift back is no problem?"

"Not at all," she said reassuringly. "I'll even run Miss Ronnie home. It's the least I can do after such a wonderful evening of food and friends—and a little intrigue!"

* * * *

As Lindsay and Ronnie turned out of the Jobson's Cove Apartments lot onto South Road, Tom Sr. huddled with the teens. "I'm worried, guys," he said somberly. "Why would anyone be following you kids? Do you think they found out about the bell? Maybe this whole investigation thing is getting out of hand."

"Dad, we can't stop now," said T.J. "We've put too much into it so far. And besides, if we quit on this it would reflect badly on Mike. This project is his baby."

"I agree, Uncle Tom," said LouAnne, her hair a bit askew from their earlier run through the streets of Hamilton. "I think we have to let this thing play out."

"We all think we're onto something," said Bortnicker. "Tonight just made me more determined to see it through."

"Okay, okay," said Tom Sr., surrendering in the face of overwhelming odds. "But do me this favor. First thing tomorrow, explain what happened to Mike and Chappy. I'm sure Ronnie is going to tell her dad. No matter where you go from here on in, keep your eyes peeled. Any trouble, you call me on my cell at the golf club."

"You got it," said T.J.

"So you all better get some sleep. Jeez, it's eleven already." He turned to LouAnne and said, "Please tell me you two aren't thinking of working out tomorrow morning."

"Sorry, Uncle Tom. Tomorrow's our last workout before Saturday's race. Tell you what, though. Since we did some running tonight, we'll cut down tomorrow's distance by half. Okay, Cuz?"

"Sounds great," said T.J.

"And then we go find Tarver's treasure!" sang Bortnicker.

Chapter Nineteen

"Followed, you say?" said Chappy as he helped the *Gonzo Ghost Chasers* stow their diving gear in the minivan.

"Dudes, I feel bad I wasn't there for you," lamented Mike, who looked a little worse for wear from his night of club-hopping with Kim.

"Not your fault, Mike," said T.J. "We handled ourselves pretty well. Even Bortnicker was zooming along like a track star. He actually wanted to go after those guys!"

"No way."

"Yes way," frowned LouAnne. "Sometimes he just flips into attack mode."

"Yeah, like when he chased you out onto the battlefield last year and almost got run over by Hilliard's horse!"

"Don't remind me," moaned Bortnicker.

"Shush. It was very heroic," said LouAnne primly. "Besides, my dad said you executed a perfect form tackle on me, and he should know." Indeed, Bortnicker had brought the girl down at the last second before LouAnne's father—a former Big Ten linebacker—had blown the horseman back into the past with his Sharps rifle.

"Well, I don't like the thought of people bothering you," said Chappy as they pulled out onto South Road. "Not a great show of hospitality, to say the least. If you don't mind, I'm going to ask around if anyone knows about this nonsense."

"You don't have to, but thanks," said T.J.

The ride to Blue Lagoon Dive Shop seemed to take forever;

everyone in the car was lost in thought and filled with anticipation. The sun beamed brilliantly overhead, and the views over the cliffs to the ocean below were something out of a Beach Boys oldie. The promise, however remote, of pirate treasure was palpable, and the boys had to fight their excitement to maintain a calm appearance.

Finally, Chappy pulled into the lot where the group was met by a beaming Ronnie and her father, who helped lug their gear to the *Reef Seeker I*. High spirits shone throughout, and when Jasper quoted famed treasure hunter Mel Fisher's immortal saying, "Today's the day!" it set off a chain reaction of fist bumps and high fives. Goodwin and Skeeter quickly stowed the dive gear and soon they were slipping out of the cove and headed for open water.

"Nervous?" said Ronnie, easing into a seat near Bortnicker, who was checking the band on his dive mask.

"Yeah, and really psyched, too," he said with his crooked smile. "What would you like me to find for you?"

"Hmm. How about one of those ornate golden crosses inlaid with emeralds on a thick chain? I'd fancy wearing that to the posh receptions you all would be invited to."

"Consider it done."

On the other side of the deck, T.J. was a little more reserved with his cousin. "Something is down there, Cuz, can't you feel it?" he said as she applied sunscreen to the back of his neck.

"Yup, though it's just hard for me to believe this wreck went untouched for centuries."

"Well, it just takes one powerful hurricane to stir up the bottom. I still can't believe we found the ship's bell."

"You think Mr. Goodwin's exaggerating what'll happen when this all goes public?"

"Hard to tell. He knows this island better than us, that's for sure. Tell you what, though, if we discover real treasure, it'll be incredible. When I think of the stuff Capt. Kenny found on the *Andrea Doria* and other wrecks, and how hard he had to work for it, the years he put into it … and then Bortnicker and I jump into the water on our first real dive and boom! I mean, what are the odds?"

"Well, there is something known as beginners luck," she smiled, spreading the cream around the tops of his shoulders.

"I guess. But if we come up with gold or silver it's a whole new ballgame."

"Well, whatever, it'll make good TV."

"You got that right. Even if the haunted house turns out to be a dud, the first ten minutes of the show might be enough to make The Adventure Channel buy the series!"

"And will fame and fortune change T.J. Jackson?" she chided in a dramatic voice.

"Nah ... well, maybe a little bit," he responded, allowing the faintest of smiles.

* * * *

"Dora, I have to speak with you," said Nigel Chapford, settling onto a stool at the counter.

The portly proprietor raised an eyebrow as she leaned on the chipped Formica, nearly nose to nose with the chauffer. "You look so serious, Dearie. Are you here to propose? And if so, what would the missus say?"

The sternness never left Chappy's face, despite her best efforts. "This is no laughing matter, Dora, not to me anyway. I have to ask you an important question: Do you have any knowledge of anyone bothering those American boys or Miss Ronnie?"

"And why are you asking me this, might I inquire?"

"Because last night in Hamilton, the kids were harassed—followed, actually—by three rather unfriendly looking men. They haven't been too many places in this area, so I'm asking you seriously, again: Do you know of anyone who'd wish them ill?"

Dora mopped her brow with a dishrag, then started polishing the countertop, breaking eye contact with Chapford.

"Well, to be honest, they might be bringing this all on themselves. Don't get me wrong—the boys are polite, though the one with the glasses tends to run his mouth a bit."

"To whom, may I ask?"

"Well, ah, that first day they did have a bit of an encounter with Willie B.—"

"I should have known!" cried an exasperated Chapford, throwing up his hands. "Probably the poorest example of all things Bermudian, though he fancies himself the champion of our island. Did he threaten those boys in some way?"

"Not exactly," she said cautiously, trying to avoid Chappy's ire. "Let's say he was just trying to discourage them from digging too deeply into some dark spaces."

"That's all?"

"And, uh, oh yes, I did notice him having speaks with Miss Ronnie yesterday afternoon outside the restaurant. What they discussed, I wasn't privy to."

Chappy puffed up his cheeks and slowly blew out. "And where might I be able to find our friend Willie B. this time of day?"

"How should I know? You give me too much credit, Nigel Chapford. I'm just trying to make a living here. Willie B. comes and goes. Where he lives, or stays, or whatever, is nobody's business but his own."

"Alright then, Dora, but let me tell you this. If he should happen by, please relay the message that I want to speak with him." He took out a business card and placed it on the counter. "And if anything comes up you think I should know about, call me on my cell. And I mean that seriously."

"Dear, dear," said Dora trying to lighten the moment, "what will Mrs. Chapford say if she learns a foxy lady like myself is making calls to you at all hours?"

"You'll notice I'm not laughing, Dora. I'm quite concerned, actually, that something regrettable is about to happen to these youngsters, and they deserve better. I hope to hear from you." With that he rose and walked out, the screen door smacking shut behind him.

Dora watched him all the way to his car and stood there many minutes after he'd left. Where *was* Willie B. anyway? He hadn't come by for lunch or a beer with his crony, that disgusting Hogfish, as was his routine. She sighed, shook her head, and went back to her stove, but not before she'd tacked Chappy's business card to the kitchen corkboard.

* * * *

"Okay, we're right over it!" sang out Jasper Goodwin. "Drop anchor, Skeeter."

"Aye, aye," came the response, as the first mate pressed the release button that lowered the anchor to the seabed.

The *Reef Seeker I* became a beehive of activity. Jasper and Ronnie helped the boys suit up and went through an equipment check as Mike and LouAnne prepared the underwater camera and dingy. Skeeter kept scanning the horizon for any intruders whose prying eyes might give their secret expedition away.

"I suppose you boys will want the metal detectors straight away?" said Jasper, adjusting a strap on T.J.'s oxygen tank.

"Might as well," said Bortnicker. "Why waste time just swimming around?"

"All right. I'll just have a look around the area surrounding the main wreck site, see if any debris was scattered about as the ship broke apart. You know, sometimes these wrecks were dragged around before finally coming to rest, though in water this shallow I rather doubt it. Just signal me if you find anything significant, like last time."

"No problem," said Bortnicker, his confidence growing by the minute. He turned to his friend. "You ready, Big Mon?"

"Let's do it."

They exchanged fist bumps with Ronnie and LouAnne and stepped off into the turquoise ocean.

It didn't take T.J. long to reacquaint himself with the wreck site. The piles of ballast and timbers that remained served as landmarks, as did the now partially-filled hole where the ship's bell had been buried. As Bortnicker glided toward the bow, T.J. concentrated on the stern, slowly waving the wand, trying not to be distracted by the rainbow of tropical fish that swirled around him. He would thoroughly cover a small area maybe four feet square, then move on. Precious minutes passed, with nary a blip. He was about to leave his third square when he got a hit. A loud one. He stood on the sandy bottom, located Bortnicker, and waved him over. His friend, kicking hard, was there in an instant. After pointing to a spot at his feet, the boys dropped to their knees and started digging, their excitement causing them to burn oxygen at an incredible rate.

Finally, T.J.'s hand found something hard and metal. Was it the handle to a box? Or the hand guard to a pirate cutlass? The two carefully excavated around the object, pushing the dug sand behind them. When T.J. pried it from the seabed and held it between them, LouAnne, who was intently following the whole procedure, muttered, "Oh my God. No way."

Lying between the kneeling divers was a finely preserved pair of wrist shackles. The two looked at each other. *Maybe this doesn't mean anything* reasoned T.J. Pirates were always taking prisoners from captured ships, sometimes offering them a chance to join their conquerors in a life of crime. He wanded the spot again, then widened his arc.

Hit. Hit. Hit.

Bortnicker was getting similar results. They began the task of clearing away the sand, only to find more of the same. Wrist and ankle shackles were everywhere. They'd found their treasure, but a cruel joke had been played on them.

The *Steadfast* was a slave ship.

Chapter Twenty

"Why are you coming back before the guys?" asked Ronnie as she and Mike helped LouAnne back onto the *Reef Seeker I*.

"Ran out of film," she lied, knowing the boys had called Jasper over and were uncovering even more slave artifacts as they spoke. "Mike, could I speak to you below deck?"

"Sure, LouAnne," he answered somewhat warily. "Is there a problem with the equipment?"

"I'm not sure," she said cryptically. "I'll tell you in a minute."

"Lead the way."

As they left a puzzled Ronnie behind, the boys, whose bottom time was nearly up, surveyed the excavation site with a clearly deflated Jasper Goodwin. Iron restraints of all types littered the area; T.J., doing some quick math, estimated that the *Steadfast* could hold anywhere from 50 to 100 slaves, depending on how tightly they'd been packed into the hold. And he also now had little doubt as to how William Tarver had managed to maintain one of the largest plantations on the island of Bermuda.

But as disappointed as T.J. and Jasper looked, they had nothing on Bortnicker, who appeared on the verge of tears. He had promised Ronnie gold and emeralds. How would she react to this stark reality? Jasper Goodwin shook his head sadly, checked his dive watch, and gave the boys the signal to surface. They kicked toward the sunlight, T.J. gripping an object whose last occupant had been torn from his or her homeland and forcibly transported to the island paradise called Bermuda.

As they broke the surface they were greeted by Ronnie, leaning over the gunwale, clapping with anticipation. "So, what fine baubles have you uncovered for me, Bort—"

T.J. issued their blunt reply, gently hoisting over his net bag containing the wristlets, which clanked on the deck at her feet. Ronnie, whose milk chocolate skin seemed to shimmer most days, went a kind of gray as she brought her hands to her mouth in recognition. Before Jasper could even get "I'm sorry, honey" out she was running below decks, sobbing as she shouldered past the emerging Mike Weinstein and LouAnne, whose own faces seemed set in stone.

Skeeter pulled the divers aboard and helped remove their gear. Minutes later they were seated around the small deck table, sipping bottled water and staring at the artifact before them.

"Bummer, dudes," said Mike, breaking the silence.

"Maybe we should've quit after the bell," muttered T.J., his shoulders sagging.

"Nonsense," offered Jasper, keeping the famous British "stiff upper lip". "I think you'll all agree that had we not gone back, we'd have all wondered as to what was really down there. I'm just sorry that our findings were so disturbing."

"So I guess he was a slave owner, then," said Bortnicker. "The famous pirate patriot of Bermuda. Yeah, right."

"Which might explain why there wasn't much in the archives," furthered LouAnne. "Tilbury or whoever removed any evidence that incriminated Tarver so his image as the romantic swashbuckler wouldn't be tarnished."

"Was slavery big here, Mr. Goodwin?" asked T.J. "I mean, if you don't want to talk about it—"

"No, no, T.J., it's quite all right. The slavery period is somewhat downplayed in our nation's history. In fact, upon your visit to the Maritime Museum a few days ago you'd have had to look hard to find it.

"The first slaves were brought to Bermuda in the 1600s, and this practice was accepted until slavery was outlawed in the early 1800s. Slaves initially worked under seven years of bond, to 'repay' the administrators for the cost of their transport. But as the size of the black population increased, those in power actually attempted to reduce its number by changing the term of indenture to 99 years. So, by Tarver's time his slaves were his property for life."

"Did any try to escape?" said Bortnicker, running his finger along the bumpy black iron.

"Oh yes, quite a few ran off and tried to hide in the caves along the coast. There were even some plots to overthrow the white masters, most of which failed, or so we are told, because of conspirators who lost their nerve tipping off the authorities.

"Today about 60% of Bermudians are described as being of African descent, though many have European blood mixed in."

"The question is," said T.J., "where does William Tarver fit in the big picture?"

"I guess the only way to find out is to ask him," said Weinstein matter of factly. "Which is why our investigation tomorrow night just took on a whole new meaning."

"I suppose," said Bortnicker. "Mr. Goodwin, I feel so bad for Ronnie. This really affected her. How come?"

"Well," said Goodwin gently, "Veronique is a very proud girl, both of her African heritage and of her country. However, she's always had a hard time coming to grips with the dark side, so to speak, of our island's history. She wanted so to believe in the romantic image of William Tarver, the adventurous buccaneer turned gentleman planter. What we've uncovered would indicate quite the opposite. I'd suppose she's disillusioned, and if you'll excuse me, I'm hoping that by this time she's cried herself out and that I'll be able to soothe her somewhat." He slowly rose from his deck chair. "Skeeter, there's no need for a second dive today," he said tiredly. "Raise the anchor and let's head for home."

As the engines started, Bortnicker went forward and laid out on some towels, trying to relax and wondering if his grand adventure with Ronnie Goodwin had been dashed upon the reefs of Bermuda. LouAnne, remaining at the table with her cousin, put a reassuring hand on his.

"It's gonna be all right, Cuz," she said evenly.

"Tell that to Ronnie. Or Bortnicker, for that matter."

"Listen, T.J.," said Mike earnestly. "We came here to conduct an investigation. Well, sometimes when you investigate stuff you find out things are not so pretty. Last year in Gettysburg you guys were willing to go all in to get to the bottom of Hilliard's story. And you did, which is why I had the confidence to get you on this case. Can I still count on you, or do you want to call it a day and fly home?"

T.J. looked him straight in the eye. "I'm not going anywhere, Mike. Not now. In fact, I really want to meet this guy Tarver."

"Me, too," said LouAnne.

"How about Bortnicker?" asked Mike, gesturing to the reclining teen up front who stared at the sky.

"He'll be okay. We can't do this without him, and he knows it."

"Okay, then," said Weinstein, clapping T.J. mildly on the shoulder. "I'm gonna help Skeeter steer the boat. Hope Jasper's getting somewhere with his daughter." He left them at the table, LouAnne never removing her hand from atop her cousin's, the both of them contemplating what lay ahead.

* * * *

"Good God," said Chappy as the minivan traversed South Road. "Sir William Tarver, a slaver. I'm disappointed, but not stunned. One always wondered how he maintained the workforce needed to keep such an estate in operation."

"Well, to say the least, it was a letdown for everybody," offered LouAnne.

"Especially Ronnie Goodwin," added T.J.

"The poor girl," said the driver, slowly shaking his head. "Ah well. I would assume, then, that this new information, like the bell, is also classified?"

"For now, yes," said Mike, relaying the expedition group's decision that had been reached upon their return to Blue Lagoon. (Ronnie had failed to emerge, however, preferring to wait until her guests had all left. Her father, though embarrassed, opted not to press the issue in light of her fragile state).

"My lips are sealed," promised Chappy. "But listen, I might have just the pick-me-up you all need. Why don't you come to the seafood buffet at the Elbow Beach Resort tonight as my personal guests? My band is performing, and I would be pleased if you could attend."

"That sounds great," said Mike. "I'll call Kim and tell Tom as well. Maybe that nice Ms. Cosgrove will feel a second date's in order. What do you think, T.J.?"

"Sounds good to me. How about you, Bortnicker?"

"I dunno," he mumbled.

"Oh, Bortnicker," admonished LouAnne, "don't be a stick in the mud. When we get back to the hotel, get your courage up and invite Ronnie to join us. I betcha she comes around and says yes."

"Really? After all that stuff today?"

"Women's intuition. I'll wager a lobster dinner on it."

The boy, who'd been in a funk since their dive, suddenly brightened. "Yeah," he said with renewed optimism. "Let's go out and have a good time. Chappy's rockin' out tonight!"

* * * *

"Wow," remarked Tom Sr., his forehead creased with concern. "Pretty heavy stuff, guys. The guy was a slave master. Does that change your investigation at all?"

"Not in the least," assured T.J. as he buttoned up his Hawaiian shirt. "In fact, it just gets me more psyched to try to make contact with the ghost, if there is one. How's the golf club deal going?"

"Fine. We're almost to the point where I can hand it off to the contractors and take off. Too bad, because by playing every day I've actually taken a couple strokes off my game!"

"Uh-huh. And what about Lindsay?"

Tom Sr. reddened a bit. "Well, we're certainly becoming more comfortable around each other. We might even keep this going after I leave. By the way, she'll be joining us tonight."

"Great." At that moment Bortnicker emerged frowning from the bedroom. "And speaking of dates, are you set for tonight or what?"

The teen adjusted his own tropical shirt in the hallway mirror. "I wouldn't count on it," he sighed. "She wasn't able to come to the phone, but her mom took the message and will tell her about tonight. Maybe she'll show."

"My cousin guaranteed it, so you never know."

"Either way, I'm pigging out. I haven't really eaten all day."

"Lindsay will be driving me, Mike, and Kim to Elbow Beach in her car. You mind if the three of you call a cab?" asked Tom Sr.

"Nah," said T.J. "I'm actually kinda anxious to see Chappy's band. I bet they're pretty good."

"To get booked at a place like Elbow Beach you'd have to be," agreed Tom Sr. "It's one of the swankiest resorts on the Island."

There was a knock on the door, and LouAnne made her entrance in the brilliant sundress she'd worn on her flight over. As always, T.J.'s breath caught in his throat as she glided into the room.

"Have you noticed all the cute green lizards around this place?" she said, flicking her blonde tresses over her shoulder. "I absolutely love them. They remind me of that gecko on those commercials back in the States."

"But do they have a British accent?" inquired Bortnicker in his Beatle voice.

"Well, *you* seem to be in a better mood," she observed wryly. "Does this mean Ronnie is coming?"

"Maybe, maybe not."

"She'll be there, you watch."

Chapter Twenty-One

As the Jackson entourage gathered at the front entrance of the sumptuous Elbow Beach Resort, strains of the steel drum music could be detected wafting from the beachfront patio beyond. It was a brilliant moonlit evening, with a soft breeze coming off the breakers down on the beach.

"Dudes, I'm starving," said Mike, who fell in with the others as Lindsay Cosgrove, attired in a chic sundress of her own, led them through the lobby to the spacious patio where the weekly seafood buffet was held.

"Ah, the Jackson party," acknowledged the white-jacketed maitre'd. "Please follow me, Mr. Chapford has reserved a table for you."

"Splendid," said Lindsay, and the group was escorted to a round table with a crisp white covering not twenty feet from where The Beachcombers, Chappy's six piece band, was working their way through "Yellowbird". Immediately they caught his eye, and he nodded happily as he gently tapped out a soothing Caribbean backbeat behind the lead vocalist, a younger, dark-skinned man with a goatee who sported the same blue tropical shirt with white slacks as his band mates.

"This is so cool," said LouAnne, who was turning more than a few heads in the 300 or so people attending the event. "Chappy's as smooth as I thought he would be!"

"And just look at that spread!" cried Bortnicker, eyeing the numerous tables laden with every variety of seafood, salads, and side dishes. "I can't wait to dig in!"

"Easy there, Hoss," said Tom Sr., a cautionary hand on the teen's shoulder. "Let's take our time and enjoy it. Why don't the ladies go up first, and we'll take our turn when they're done."

"Great idea, Uncle Tom!" said LouAnne, popping out of her seat while casting a sly wink back at Bortnicker.

"While they're up there," said Mike, sipping his table water, "let's discuss the plan for tomorrow. I'm going to be at Hibiscus House by 3:00 p.m. to start setting up the command post equipment. I've done it so many times on the show that it won't take me more than an hour to get the main console running and place DVR cameras in all the key rooms and hallways. Then, if you guys could show up between four and five, we could do a final check that everything's working, including your handhelds and walkie-talkies, and have a preliminary walk through."

"Will there be anyone there to show us around?" asked T.J.

"Not you guys. Our friend Mrs. Tilbury is meeting me at the house. Hopefully she'll be gone by the time you show up."

"Hallelujah," said Bortnicker. "Though I'd really like to grill her on those missing documents."

"We have to play this cool, dudes," advised Mike. "Remember, we might need a second night at the house. I don't want anybody to tick her off and make her throw us out."

"He means you, Bortnicker," chided T.J.

"Very funny. So this means we're kinda free until late afternoon?" inquired Bortnicker while eying the buffet tables longingly.

"Seems like it," said Mike.

"Would you guys like to play a little golf with me at the club?" asked Tom Sr.

"Nah, Dad, I think we'll pass," answered T.J. "Not our type of crowd. Besides, Bortnicker gets all bent out of shape when we play miniature golf at home. One bad putt and he loses it. I don't want him pulling a *Caddyshack* and flinging his club into the dining area. I think I'll just do an easy jog with LouAnne for the road race Saturday, and then we'll laze around the pool."

"Someone mention my name?" said his cousin, returning to their table with her plate heaped with crab legs and shrimp.

"Yeah, I was saying that tomorrow you and I will just loosen up with a jog for the race Saturday. Jeez Louise, Cuz, think you've got enough food there?"

"Girl's gotta keep up her strength," she retorted, placing a napkin on her lap as the other women returned with more moderately portioned plates.

"Can we *finally* hit the buffet?" pleaded Bortnicker. "This is torture!"

* * * *

As the men were attacking the seafood buffet at Elbow Beach, Willie B. was on a mission of his own at Hibiscus House. Annoyed that his knuckleheaded cousin and his cronies had bungled their surveillance of the teens, he'd decided to take matters into his own hands by trying to sabotage what was sure to be the impending ghost team investigation of the plantation house. What exactly that entailed, he wasn't quite sure. However, scaring the bejesus out of them seemed like a feasible idea. But to do that he'd have to scope out the mansion, and that was why he'd easily disabled the alarm system so similar to those he'd dealt with in his general handyman work around the island and was now prying open one of the numerous rear windows of the first floor gallery. With the implementation of no more than a simple putty knife he was quickly inside, hardly disturbing the white window frame paint.

"Let's see, now," he muttered to himself, "on that *Gonzo Ghost Chasers* show they usually stick to the biggest rooms and places where the owner hung about. Let's check out Black Bill's library, shall we?" He crept around, guiding his flashlight over the walls of books, Tarver's formidable desk, and the fireplace, above which a portrait of the captain himself glowered menacingly. However, there were no closets or secret compartments that would afford him a hiding place from where he might manufacture bogus sounds or taps that would drive the group's EVP recorders crazy and ultimately make fools of the entire bunch.

After a cursory search of the ornate dining room and a couple side rooms, he decided to venture up the winding mahogany staircase to the second floor, confident that the master bedroom would contain a concealed hidey-hole or two from which to conduct his mischief. But alas, even as Willie B. ascended the stairs, mentally patting himself on the back for his brilliance, his flashlight, whose batteries he'd not thought to change anytime recently, suddenly winked out. This threw the house into inky darkness, save for some moonlit beams emanating from random windows.

He held tightly onto the polished bannister with one hand while whacking the flashlight on his thigh to get it to work, but had no luck. Cursing his misfortune, he waited for his eyes to adjust to the gloom and made the decision to continue up the stairs, hoping there would be enough natural light in the bedrooms to help him see.

Willie B. reached the top step and peered into the darkness. Before him lay a long hallway with at least four rooms on each side. At the end was a small window from which a shaft of moonlight shone. As he set foot on the landing, though, something strange happened. A figure, really a black silhouette, seemed to step from one of the farthest rooms into the murky hallway.

They hired a security person? For a deserted house? he thought, panic starting a knot in his stomach. Willie B. grabbed a soiled handkerchief from his pocket and mopped his suddenly sweaty face. The figure had stopped moving. He had no choice but to try to brazen it out.

"What you doin' here, man?" he attempted in his harshest voice. "You a security guard or police or what?"

No answer.

"I ain't scared o'you, whoever you are. Show yourself!"

The answer, delivered in a Scotch-Irish accent, made his blood run cold.

"This is *my* house."

"*Your* house?"

"Quite right, *Boy*."

"*Boy*? Who you callin' *Boy*, man? You want me to kick your sorry butt right here and now?" he barked, his courage fueled by the racial epithet. Again he slammed the flashlight on his thigh, planning to use it as a weapon if necessary.

This time it blinked on.

He pointed it at the shadow figure.

It was the man's eyes that hit him first. Cold and hard and ice blue, like twin lasers. Longish hair pulled back into a ponytail capped a ruddy, bearded face accentuated by a strong nose and high cheekbones. The man's outfit was almost foppish, his blue velour waistcoat unbuttoned over a lacy white undershirt and tan breeches. Black knee-high boots of an expensive make gave him a height advantage over the stocky waterfront workman. The other thing that gave him an advantage was the flintlock pistol leveled at Willie B.'s chest.

"What is this, some kind of joke?" he managed. "You supposed to be a pirate or something?"

"I think you know who I am, *Boy*. And, as such, you also understand the consequence of being where you're not supposed to be, and giving your master backtalk besides."

"My *master*? You're-you're Black Bill Tarver? No way, man! You're long dead!"

The captain shook his head. "Dear me, aren't you the cheeky one. I can see you're one of the incorrigible. Too bad, as you're obviously capable of heavy work in the fields. I simply cannot deal with your insolence, so you will have to be made an example of."

Willie B. heard the flintlock's hammer clicked back and decided he'd had enough. Leave this maniac ghost to those snotty kids and let *them* deal with it!

He took a reflexive step backward but forgot he was barely onto the staircase landing. All Willie B.'s workboot found behind him was air and he pinwheeled down and down, coming to a smashing halt on the foyer floor, his neck broken, the flashlight still clutched in his hand. The last thing he saw before departing this world was the figure at the top of the stairs, hands on hips, and feet planted wide.

And he was grinning.

* * * *

"Jeez, Bortnicker," hissed T.J., "they let you go up for seconds here. Don't overload your plate so much. It's embarrassing!"

"Good point," acknowledged the famished teen, flipping a solitary Alaskan King Crab leg back onto a chafing dish.

They returned to the table where Mike and Tom Sr. had taken the liberty of ordering bottles of white wine for the adults and a pitcher of iced tea for the teens.

Everyone was digging into the expertly prepared seafood when the

Beachcombers went on break and Chappy strolled over to their table. "Everything okay, folks?" he inquired pleasantly, full well knowing the answer.

"This is fantastic, Chappy," wuffed Bortnicker through a mouthful of boiled shrimp. "My compliments to the chef."

"Yeah," agreed T.J., "I could easily get used to this."

"Thanks so much for your hospitality," offered Lindsay. "It seems I'm dining with some real celebrities!"

"That they are," grinned Chapford. "And how are you enjoying the music? We play most Caribbean standards, but there are a few original compositions we'll be working in, along with our take on some popular tunes."

"Any Beatles?" asked LouAnne eagerly.

"I think we can arrange that," he chuckled. "Well, I don't want your food to get cold. Just let Peter, the maitre'd, know if you need anything else. See you in a bit."

Bortnicker was just polishing off his third plate to the tune of "Bermuda is Another World" when T.J. nudged him in the ribs. "Wipe your mouth, man," he whispered, "somebody's here to see you." He looked up through his unruly bangs to find Ronnie, standing at the patio entrance with the maitre'd, offering a tentative wave. Even from a distance he could identify her red-rimmed eyes that a brave half-smile could not mask. His heart broke for her, and he navigated through some dancing couples to where she stood.

"I'm glad you made it," he said, awkwardly hugging her.

"I almost didn't, but my mum talked me into it. Said it would cheer me up."

"She's right. Come sit with us, okay?" He led her to their table where T.J. quickly pulled up another chair and introductions were conducted.

"So, how are you doing?" LouAnne discreetly inquired.

"Better now. Thanks," she managed.

"Well, I don't know about you dudes, but I feel like dancing," said Weinstein. He pulled Kim out of her seat and they were soon swaying together on the flagstone floor.

Tom Sr. looked at Lindsay. "May I have this dance, Ms. Cosgrove?"

he offered gallantly.

"I was thinking you'd never ask!" she chirped. They, too, joined the mostly adult crowd, leaving the four teens to share an awkward moment.

It was LouAnne, predictably, who broke the ice. "Well, I don't know about you all, but I want to move around a little bit. You gonna dance with me, Cuz, or do I have to ask one of the busboys?"

"I'm not much of a dancer," mumbled T.J.

"Doesn't matter. It's just Caribbean and reggae stuff. Just hold onto me and we'll shuffle around. C'mon!" With that she grabbed his hand and yanked him out of his chair. "Help me!" he mouthed over his shoulder as Bortnicker and Ronnie waved him goodbye.

"Uh, that leaves just us," said Bortnicker hesitantly. "So, would you, uh, want to go up there?"

"After today," she said, her lip trembling slightly, "I just want someone to hold me."

Her words hung in the air.

"I can do that," he said finally, offering his hand. "Let's go."

"Oh, good," said LouAnne, acknowledging their entrance to the dance floor.

"Jeez, first time I've ever seen Bortnicker try to dance with a girl," observed T.J. wryly.

"You're one to talk. Do you always stand two feet away during a slow dance?"

T.J. reddened and pulled her closer, finally experiencing the firm curves of her body he'd been admiring for the past year. Those around them could hardly ignore their nearly perfect complimentary appearances—T.J. with his doe eyes that gave him the appearance of a young Paul McCartney, LouAnne the blonde, all-American girl next door.

"That's better," she whispered softly, resting her head on his shoulder as the Beachcombers finished up "Everything's Gonna Be All Right".

After a round of applause Chappy stepped to the mic and announced, "We have a special number I've arranged for some good friends of mine who are here tonight, which was first done by another friend you might have heard of in your travels … Mr. John Lennon. It's called 'Imagine'." He shot Bortnicker a wink, and The Beachcombers drifted into the opening riff.

Ronnie eased her body into Bortnicker's, murmuring into his ear, "I'm so sorry about my behavior today. I overreacted, I guess."

He could feel a tear bleeding through the shoulder of his Hawaiian shirt and struggled for a response. "I don't blame you," he managed. "I mean, hey, I can't pretend to know what it's like to be bl- er, a person of color, but I know you thought a lot of this guy as, you know, a historical figure—"

"He was a low-rent piece of scum, Bortnicker," she said quietly. "I've come to terms with that."

"The thing is, Ronnie, with this Tarver situation, I feel like I can't make it better for you ... kind of helpless."

"Just holding me is good right now." She sniffled, then managed a smile. "Am I making you uncomfortable?" she said, as John Lennon's words described a brotherhood of man.

"No, no," he said shakily. "I'm just not ... used to dancing and stuff like that."

"You're doing fine."

"Thanks." He couldn't believe a girl so athletic looking could be so soft.

"I never asked, but do you have a girlfriend back in the States?"

His answer was, "Ah, that would be a no," but his eyes said *Are you kidding me?*

"Well, you should," she murmured, burying her face in his shoulder. "I think you're the kind of person who looks inside someone and appreciates who they really are, not just what they look like."

"Yeah, Ronnie, thanks for that, though if you don't mind me saying, you *are* kind of beautiful. You know that, don't you?"

"Listen," she said, "when you're in the tourist business you hear all kinds of things. You don't know how many jerks I have to deal with, and some of them are *a lot* older than you. But you're honest. And I think you have a good heart, Bortnicker."

He felt tears welling in his eyes and tried hard to blink them away. "That might be the nicest thing anyone's ever said to me," he managed.

"Good. Now stop stepping on my feet." They danced for a few

moments, Bortnicker conscious of not treading on Ronnie's toes. She looked up at him. "There's something you need to do for me—"

"Anything. Just name it."

"You're sweet," she breathed, kissing him lightly on the cheek, which nearly buckled his knees, "but don't say yes unless you can deliver on it."

"What is it?"

She pushed herself away to arm's length and looked hard into his Coke-bottle glasses. "I need to be there when you do the Hibiscus House investigation."

"Why?"

"*Why?* Because if that ghost shows up, I want to spit in his face, that's why." Ronnie's jaw was set, her blue eyes icy. "Can you do that for me?"

"Hey," he stammered, "I've got no problem with it but, you know, we're filming the TV show and all—"

She glared at him harder.

"B-but I'll talk to Mike. I think I can convince him. I don't think you'll be on the TV show, though—"

"Who cares about that? All I want to do is come face to face with that piece of garbage!"

"Okay, okay," he soothed, pulling her to him, "I'll take care of it. Please don't get upset again. It's too beautiful an evening to be sad."

As the Beachcombers deftly transitioned into "Bermuda is Another World", she locked on his eyes again, and Bortnicker's world stopped. Ronnie reached up and moved an unruly lock of hair from his glasses. "Thank you," she whispered, and kissed him, full on the lips.

"Holy cow, did you see *that*?" marveled T.J. across the dance floor. "Ronnie and Bortnicker are kissing, right in the middle of the party!"

LouAnne peered over her cousin's shoulder. "Wow," she giggled, "and me without my cell phone. This moment should be captured forever."

"No doubt." A few long seconds passed.

"T.J.?"

"Hmm?"

"Do you ever wonder about, uh—"

169

"About us?"

"Yeah."

"All the time, since Gettysburg. Do you think that's dumb?"

"I don't know," she said warily. "There's a lot of stuff at work here."

"I know what you mean. It's not your common situation."

"To say the least. But I want you to know something." She held him so tightly he could feel her heart beating through her sundress. "There's no one I'd rather be dancing here with under the stars than you."

He smiled. "Remember the first time we danced together?"

"Of course. The Civil War campfire last year. We were kinda waltzing around with my skirt swishing all over the place. It's amazing we didn't fall on our butts."

"It's amazing we're here right now, if you think about it."

"Yeah," she said, snuggling closer.

"Think we're gonna actually meet another ghost?"

"We seem to have a knack for it."

"And how about Saturday's race?"

"Don't be silly," she said sweetly. "You know I'm going to destroy you."

* * * *

That night before turning in T.J. finally lost his battle to avoid grilling his best buddy. "You were pretty quiet on the ride home," he began nonchalantly. "Anything up with you and Ronnie?"

Bortnicker gave him a *You've got to be kidding* look. "Was it that obvious?"

"Well, since you picked the middle of the dance floor to start making out with her—"

"Oh, you saw that," he acknowledged airily.

"A tremendous performance. LouAnne and I nearly applauded."

"Well, it was the least I could do to comfort her," he tried, suppressing a smile.

"The least."

"But listen, Big Mon, I wasn't the only one getting up close and personal on the floor. You and your cousin were so tight she was almost behind you!"

"Yeah," remembered T.J. fondly. "It was pretty sweet."

"The official beginning of something?"

T.J. smiled coyly. "Stay tuned. But don't change the subject. Did Ronnie say anything about Tarver?"

Bortnicker's face darkened. "Oh, about that. Do you think Mike will let her come with us on the investigation tomorrow night?"

"Don't know," said T.J., unbuttoning his Hawaiian shirt and placing it on a hanger. "Mike's pretty serious when it comes to anything connected to the show. I could be bribed to put in a word for her, however."

"It would mean a lot to her."

"All right. I'll grab him tomorrow morning. Seriously, yesterday must've crushed her."

"Yeah. She's still a little messed up over it. But I think I helped out a little."

T.J. chuckled. "I think you *helped* beyond your wildest dreams, buddy."

"Are you done yet?" Bortnicker cried with exasperation.

"I'm just playing with you. But next time could you go somewhere a little more private?"

"I'll try. Just remember, I'm new at this."

Recalling his own encounter earlier that evening, T.J. said wistfully, "All things considered, I'd say you did just fine. I'm actually kinda jealous."

Bortnicker removed his glasses and reached for the light, grinning from ear to ear.

Chapter Twenty-Two

"Let's get a good stretch this morning," cautioned LouAnne. "We don't want to be pulling a muscle the day before the race."

"Yeah," said T.J., looking toward the heavens, where dark clouds were scudding along. "Our first crappy day, though it's still pretty warm."

"That'll probably change," she said, bending forward in her hurdler's stretch. "Chappy said it could be raining on one end of the island and sunny on the other."

Once their jog began LouAnne was all business. No mention was made of yesterday's dive, the upcoming house investigation, or, sadly, the previous evening's romantic drama. With all that had been going on during their hectic few days in Bermuda he'd been able to avoid worrying about the road race. But now that it was 24 hours away, the usual trepidation that overtook him before any kind of athletic competition was beginning to creep in. He struggled to push it away, but the look of focus and determination on his cousin's face as they jogged along the Railway Trail this morning made it impossible. Did she really mean what she said last night about destroying him, or was she just trying to be funny?

Back at the apartments, he joined Bortnicker, Tom Sr., and Mike for a breakfast of cornflakes and sliced bananas.

"I'm still full from last night," groaned Tom Sr. as he sipped his coffee. "That was a royal feast!"

"At least the youngsters here got to burn off some of it on the dance floor," joked Mike.

"Are you kidding?" countered T.J. "I don't think Bortnicker left the two-foot square patch he started in."

Bortnicker, slurping up some soggy flakes, came right back at him. "Well excuse me, Mr. *America's Got Talent*. When did you become such a dance expert?"

"Enough, you two," chuckled Tom Sr. "I think you both did well enough. Neither of the girls ended up with broken toes." He checked his watch. "All right, I'll take the scooter over to the club. We're almost done hiring the contractors. The good news is I'll finally be able to join you guys tonight for the house investigation. I'll keep Mike company when he's at the command post. Another set of eyes on all those DVR screens couldn't hurt." He put his dirty cereal bowl in the sink and slung his briefcase over his shoulder. "Oh, and by the way, I'll be there tomorrow morning for the race. Figured I'd trail behind on my scooter. Bortnicker, you want to ride along?"

"Cool! You coming too, Mike?"

"Wouldn't miss it, dude. How many entrants did the say there are?"

"I think around a hundred overall," said T.J. "I just don't want to embarrass myself."

"That means get beat by LouAnne," cracked Bortnicker.

"You'll do fine," assured Tom Sr. as he opened the door to a still-threatening morning.

"I've got stuff to do, too," said Mike. "Kim is gonna help me buy some gifts in Hamilton for my friends back at home. It'll be good to see my *Gonzo* crew again. We start filming for next season in another week. The first case is a haunted saloon in Tombstone, Arizona." He rinsed his bowl in the sink. "So I'll see you dudes at around 6:00 p.m.?"

"Ah, about that," said T.J. cautiously. "Do you have any problem with Ronnie Goodwin being there with us?"

Mike sat back down. "I'm not sure. Why do you want her there?"

"Well," said Bortnicker, "she's been on both the dives, and you saw the effect this whole Tarver thing's had on her. I think it would mean a lot."

"Well, we'd have to get her dad's permission, but you've gotta understand the show's really built around the three of you guys. She could help out by filming, I guess, or holding one of the EVP recorders, but she can't really be on camera."

"That shouldn't be a problem," said T.J. confidently. "Besides, I think it'd be better that Bortnicker and I both buddy-up during the investigation rather than wander off alone in that big house."

Weinstein's brow furrowed as he thought hard for a few seconds. "Ah, what can it hurt," he said with a shrug. "Tell her if it's okay with Jasper she can meet us there at six."

After he left, the boys exchanged fist bumps as LouAnne entered, shuffling right to the refrigerator. "You guys got any OJ? I finished mine," she stated, her hair still damp from the shower.

"Don't know if we should," joked Bortnicker. "That would be like helping out T.J.'s opponent."

"A glass of juice isn't going to determine the race tomorrow, wiseguy," she said, pouring some out. "It's still yucky out there. Want to hang out by the pool until it clears up?"

"Why not?" said T.J. "Hey, I'll bet that nice Mrs. Maltby has some board games stored somewhere for days like this. I'll go ask her."

"See if she's got *Monopoly*," said Bortnicker. "It's my favorite."

* * * *

It was 11:00 a.m. and Nigel Chapford was washing his black minivan when his cell phone vibrated in his pants pocket. He checked the caller ID and saw "Dora's Corners".

"Good morning, dear," he said smoothly. "How are you this fine day?"

The tone of her voice told him immediately that the day was most certainly not fine. "You'd better get over here, Nigel," she said abruptly. "There's something happened at Hibiscus House you should know about, and I have someone who needs to speak with you. Now."

Chappy tossed the cleaning rag into his soap bucket. "Give me twenty minutes, Dora. I'm on my way."

He entered to find the proprietor commiserating with a younger woman who sat slumped in one of the chipped bistro chairs of the restaurant. Chappy pulled up a seat as Dora gave him a cautionary look that said Go easy.

"Good morning, Miss Dora," he began politely, then turned to the obviously distressed woman. "I'm Nigel Chapford," he said, extending his hand. "You look somewhat familiar. Have we met?"

She took his hand tentatively. "I'm Winnie Pemburton, Mr. Chapford," she said quietly. "You know my mother, Allison."

"Of course," he smiled warmly. "Your mum is one of the finest teachers on the island. Is there something I can do for you, Ms. Pemburton?"

She hesitated, then looked at Dora.

"Tell him, girl," said the proprietor.

"Mr. Chapford, word's gotten around that you are the driver for those teen ghost hunters from America and that they are going to be conducting an investigation on the island."

"That is so," he said evenly. "They're fine young people. But how does this concern you?"

"It's Hibiscus House they're going to visit, isn't it?"

"That's quite true, though I was trying to avoid broadcasting it."

"I understand. But I thought that before those kids go in there you could tell them what they're dealing with."

"Please explain, Ms. Pemburton," he said with his most reassuring smile.

She looked to Dora, who nodded. Winnie Pemburton then proceeded to tell Chapford the story of her encounter with Tarver's ghost at Hibiscus House that had left her running for her life. "I haven't told a soul what happened that night, Mr. Chapford," she whispered, again beginning to weep. "It's too embarrassing. You know how people on the island talk. But I'd heard rumors about those who'd worked there before me. I never paid them any mind until it happened to me."

"And you're sure of what you saw?"

"He was as real as you are sitting here with me."

"I'm so sorry you had to experience this," said Chappy, placing a comforting hand on hers.

"Well, it could have been much worse, apparently," she said, wiping her eyes with a table napkin.

"How so?"

Again she hesitated.

"Tell him the rest, dearie," said Dora.

"All right. My older brother is an orderly at King Edward Memorial. Early this morning the police were called by the cleaning crew who were sent to the house by the Bermuda Heritage Trust to straighten up for an impending visit. They found a dead man sprawled at the foot of the main staircase with a broken neck, like he'd fallen."

"Good Lord. And who was this?"

"The very man you've been looking for, Nigel," said Dora. "Willie B."

Chappy's eyes widened. "What could he have been doing there?" he wondered aloud.

"From what I've heard," said Winnie, "the police consider it a simple case of breaking and entering. They found no evidence of any others being there, so they removed the body and locked up. But I know better. This was no accidental fall during a botched burglary. I'd bet my life that Tarver's ghost got him."

"Why would Tarver have an axe to grind with a nobody like Willie B.?" asked Chapford.

"Because he was a *black* nobody," she said coldly.

Chapford tapped his fingertips on the chipped table a couple times. "Who knows about this? Are there next of kin on the island?"

"There's a man, Dwight Stanley, who Willie B. has referred to as his cousin, but they're not actually related," said Dora. "However, there is one other acquaintance." She turned to the back room of the restaurant and yelled, "Get your sorry butt out here, you."

The man known as Hogfish shuffled in from the shadows, his head bowed in fear. "Tell Mr. Chapford what you know about all this," Dora warned, "or you're going to have to deal with me."

Hogfish stood before them, his shoulders slumped, wringing his hands. "Willie B. felt those kids were up to no good from the jump," he said. "Ever since they mouthed off about their TV show thing right here at Miss Dora's lunch counter. Then he got it in his head that they'd found something valuable out on the reefs with Jasper Goodwin, so he started bird-doggin' Jasper's daughter, too."

"Was he following them a couple nights ago in Hamilton?"

"No, no, that wasn't him. He asked his cousin Dwight to do that, but he said Dwight's crew mucked it up. So he, uh, he decided to scare 'em

176

good at Hibiscus House. I told him I didn't want no part of that nonsense, so he just told me I was a chicken and went by himself."

"And what do *you* think happened to Willie B., Hogfish?"

The man lifted his head, tears spilling down his chubby cheeks. "Black Bill Tarver's ghost got him, Mr. Chapford, no doubt. I tried to talk him out of going, but he just wouldn't listen."

Nigel Chapford rubbed his eyes, processing all he'd been told. "Right," he said finally. "What I need from everyone here is to keep this quiet for the time being, though from everything I've seen the past few weeks it doesn't look like *anyone* on this island is capable of that." He looked around at the others' expectant faces. "In the end, Willie B. placed himself in a bad situation and paid the price for his foolishness. I've got to see how the authorities will play this, but my first responsibility is toward those young people who have put their trust in me and in the good intentions of the inhabitants of our happy little island. Miss Pemburton, you just go about your business and forget this meeting ever happened. Hogfish, let this be a lesson to you to choose your friends more wisely. I expect a low profile from you at least until the Americans leave." He turned to Dora, took her hand gently, and kissed it softly. "And to you, my sweet, many thanks for trusting me with this information. Let me see what I can do to help bring this affair to an acceptable resolution."

* * * *

"Aha!" crowed Bortnicker, slapping his hand on the poolside picnic table. "You have landed on my property once again, T.J. Let's see now…Park Place with a hotel, that'll be $1500, if you please."

"You're brutal," huffed the other boy. "Did we have to play *Monopoly*?"

"It's all Mrs. Maltby had around," apologized LouAnne. "Unless you wanted *Chutes and Ladders*, which I haven't played since like third grade."

"Well, that finishes me," declared T.J., counting out the last of his play money and handing it over to Bortnicker, who was rubbing his hands eagerly. "It's just you and LouAnne now."

"Nah, I'm done too," said his cousin. "This isn't fun anymore."

"Aw, c'mon, don't quit now," pleaded Bortnicker. "You could still win … with a little luck."

"Yeah, right," she snapped, looking at the sky. "Think it's gonna clear?"

"I don't know, man," said T.J. "A couple times the sun's almost broken through, but I still think we're gonna get a good storm sooner or later."

"I wouldn't mind this overcast tomorrow for the race," said his cousin, packing the *Monopoly* pieces back in the battered box. "With a cooling offshore breeze to boot."

"No doubt," agreed T.J. He looked at his waterproof dive watch. "Two hours till Chappy picks us up. Think I'll go upstairs and catch a quick nap, maybe have a snack."

"What, the grilled cheese sandwiches and chips I fixed you guys wasn't enough?" complained Bortnicker. "I made them extra thick! It was a lunch fit for a king!"

"They were great, Bortnicker," said LouAnne sarcastically, "the most wonderful grilled cheeses in the history of modern man. But T.J.'s right. We're not gonna eat again till maybe late, and I don't want a load of food sitting on my stomach during the race tomorrow morning. I'm going up to my room. Ta-ta." With a flip of her hair she was on her way, leaving the boys to finish boxing the game.

"To tell you the truth," said Bortnicker, dividing his stack of money into separate piles, "I don't know if I could eat much right now anyway. I'm really nervous about tonight, aren't you?"

"Yeah," said T.J., looking out over the cliffs of Astwood Park to the ocean and horizon beyond. "Tell you what, I've got the same feeling like the first time the three of us went on the battlefield last year to find Hilliard. It's as if he was drawn to us like a magnet."

"I remember. And, big as that house is, it's a lot smaller than the Battlefield Park. If Tarver's there, he'll come calling."

"I guess Mike'll let you and Ronnie buddy up," said T.J. "I'm sure she'll be able to work the handheld movie cam while you explore."

"Yeah, just me 'n her, and a lot of dark spaces," Bortnicker said, trying to be funny.

"Stop clowning around," shot back T.J. "We've got a job to do, and besides, she's so mad at this guy she's gonna be all business."

"You're right," relented Bortnicker. "This should be really interesting." He paused and crinkled his eyes. "Maybe I do have room for a snack after all. Let's go."

* * * *

Constance Tilbury watched Nigel Chapford's black minivan with the *Gonzo Ghost Chasers* vinyl decal turn into the driveway of Hibiscus House from the front entrance doorway, her lips pressed together so tightly they were bloodless. Her day so far had been disastrous, to say the least. First, she had been roused from her sleep by an inspector of the Bermuda Police to inform her of the discovery of Willie B.'s body. Then had come a terrible row with the members of the Bermuda Heritage Trust over whether to let the TV people go through with their scheduled investigation that evening. Of course, she had been outvoted again, the rationale of her colleagues being that the *Junior Gonzo Ghost Chasers* had only a few days left on the island and had been promised a couple visits by the authorities. Why should the accidental death of a thief dash their plans to jumpstart island tourism with worldwide exposure of Hibiscus House that a prime time show on The Adventure Channel would provide? When one of the younger upstarts on the committee had volunteered to take up the reins for her as the "go to" person for the remainder of the project, she had firmly declined, assuring them that she could handle it despite her misgivings. To acquiesce to their suggestions that she step aside would be an admission of her ineffectiveness as chairperson. And so she waited, standing proud and tall, as Nigel Chapford and Mike Weinstein began unloading the various black trunks and suitcases with *Gonzo Ghost Chasers* stenciled on the sides.

"Welcome, gentlemen," she managed. "Do you need any help with those?"

"Afternoon, Mrs. Tilbury," replied Chappy affably. "No worries ... we can bring these in easily enough."

Weinstein, sporting one of those ghastly *GGC* tee shirts, shook her hand gently. "If you don't mind, ma'am," he said politely, "we'll set them down in the foyer for a bit, along with a couple card tables and folding chairs we've brought along. If you could just show me where the closest outlets are, I can start hooking up the computer screens and such."

Tilbury suppressed a grimace as Chapford lugged a wind-up reel of extension cord into the house, then turned back to Weinstein. "Would you like a quick tour?"

"That would be much appreciated."

"All right then," she said primly, "come along."

He followed her around, taking notes in a small loose-leaf pad, as she went through the house's history, from its construction in the early 1700s to the dates of its various renovations and additions. Of course, he was given the sanitized version; no mention was made of slave ships or plantation cruelty.

When they entered Tarver's library, Weinstein was immediately struck by the size of the Captain's portrait, which hung above the fireplace. "He cut quite a dashing figure," said Mike tactfully, probing for information.

"That he did," was her clipped response.

"Uh, where is he buried?" inquired Weinstein, casting about for any nuggets. "Is there a family burial plot on the property?"

"No. Both the Captain and Mrs. Tarver are interred in the family crypt in the cemetery of St. Anne's Church in Southampton Parish, which dates back to the early 1700s."

"Really," said Mike, making a notation in his writing pad. "Is the crypt above ground, like a walk- in? Maybe we could—"

"Mr. Weinstein," she scolded irritably, "you apparently have neglected to research Bermudian burial customs. Here is the way it works: each family has a plot. A trench is dug for the first of the deceased, and the casket is lowered to the bottom. Then, a layer of palm fronds is put over the casket. This is done with each succeeding casket, until they reach the top of the crypt, which is covered with a slab of stone and perhaps a monument.

"When the hole is filled, it's everybody out. The coffins, or what's left of them, are discarded, as are the rotting clothes or whatever else is in there. The skeletons are removed and placed at the bottom of the hole, again covered with palm leaves, and the process begins again.

"Upon completion of the second 'stack', if you will, the original first layer of skeletons is pulverized and covered with the second layer. And then we repeat the alternating of coffins and palm leaves. Thus, you can have multiple generations piled upon each other." She gave a self-satisfied half smile as Weinstein wrote furiously.

"But ... I thought the Tarver's were childless."

"They were, unfortunately. Since there were no offspring, the only people in the Tarver crypt are the captain and the missus, who survived him by a good many years, at which time the estate was abandoned and then fell into a state of disrepair until it was rescued by the Bermuda Heritage Trust, restored, and established as a museum."

"You've been very helpful, Mrs. Tilbury," said Mike, closing the writing pad. "One last question. If you had to describe William Tarver in one sentence, what would it be?"

She gave him an icy look. "*Sir* William Tarver was a patriot and a cornerstone of our island's history. This house is a testament to his legacy. Now if you'll excuse me, I have to be off. What time do you estimate as the conclusion of your activities tonight?"

Mike blew out his cheeks and looked around. "Well," he said, "we have a lot of rooms to cover, but I can't see it going past 2:00 a.m."

"That late?"

"Believe me, Mrs. Tilbury, we've had sessions that have gone longer, sometimes till sunrise. But I'm factoring in the possibility of a second investigation, as per our original agreement."

"Oh, that," she sniffed. "Well, I don't have to tell you that I think you're on a fool's errand. My prediction is that you'll find absolutely nothing tonight that would warrant further activities. All this is, is a beautiful house."

"That may be, ma'am," he said as politely as possible, "but remember, you called *us*."

She breathed out slowly, holding her anger in check. "That we did. I'd only ask that you try to leave everything exactly as you found it, and tell your team that you will be held accountable for any broken or damaged furnishings. And please don't leave any windows or doorways open. We're expecting some rain tonight. Good day."

With that, Constance Tilbury marched out of Hibiscus House with a quick nod to Chappy, who offered a brief bow of respect as she blew by him.

"Wow," said Mike as Tilbury gunned her Mini and took off down the long drive. "She's not a happy camper. Any reason for her to be so defensive?"

"Mrs. Tilbury's set in her ways, Mr. Weinstein," said Chappy coolly, unfolding a card table. "She just wants this to be over, I'm afraid." He felt badly about not leveling with Mike at this point, but figured it was for the best.

"Well, whatever. Just help me get the tables set up here and you can take off. Bring the kids back around six and we'll get the show on the road."

"Will do."

Weinstein shot the driver a sideways look. "Can I ask you a question?"

"Sure."

"The thing is, I'm confused here. When our producers get contacted by the places who want us to investigate them, they're thrilled to be selected for the show. Then, when our team shows up on site they practically fall all over themselves making us feel comfortable, showing us around, and putting us in touch with people who have supposedly had experiences at the site so we can interview them."

"That's understandable," said Chappy.

"Of course it is, because once the show airs, whether the place is a fort or a prison or a hotel, the visitor rate increases by like 75 percent.

"Which is why, on an island that seems to pride itself on hospitality, this has to be the least amount of cooperation we've ever gotten. It's like they want us gone, and in a hurry."

Chappy snapped open a folding chair, searching for the right words. "I think you're doing a bit of generalizing," he said calmly. "Even on her best day, Constance Tilbury can be maddeningly disagreeable. Unfortunately, she's the point person for the Bermuda Heritage Trust when it comes to the various buildings. I apologize for her brusqueness."

Mike waved him off. "It's not your fault, Chappy," he said, uncoiling an extension cable. "I just get the feeling there's stuff going on we don't know about but should."

"In all fairness," countered Chappy, "your group, of which I am a part by association, is withholding information itself, or have you forgotten about the discovery of the *Steadfast* and its cargo?"

"You got me there," admitted Mike. "Oh well, we'll just make the best of it. I think the kids are gonna do a great job."

"I would agree," said Chappy. "I'll have them back here by six, as promised."

"Thanks, Chappy," said Mike, extending his hand. "I can't tell you how much of a help you've been, man."

"No worries," he said reassuringly, hoping the nervous sweat that was now running down his back wouldn't be visible on the way out of Hibiscus House.

Chapter Twenty-Three

The teens, attired in their black *Gonzo Ghost Chasers* tee shirts and shorts, were waiting when Chappy pulled into the Jobson's Cove Apartments lot. "T.J., your father phoned to say he'll be meeting us at Hibiscus House," said the driver as they piled in. "He was having a late lunch with Ms. Cosgrove."

"Uh-huh," said Bortnicker devilishly as he popped *Yellow Submarine* into the console. "Hey, Chappy, your band was amazing last night. Thanks for inviting us."

"Yeah," agreed T.J., "it was a great time."

"You *know* it had to be great if these two would actually get on the dance floor," joked LouAnne.

"Oh, I don't know, Miss LouAnne," said Chappy wryly, "I believe the young gentlemen comported themselves quite admirably. There was a sense of romance in the air, I think." He gave Bortnicker, who turned beet red, a conspiratorial wink.

"Do you think it's gonna rain, Chappy?" said T.J., tactfully changing the subject.

"I think you can count on it before the night's out," said the driver. "Hopefully it will blow through quickly."

"Think Sir William's going to show up?" asked LouAnne as she watched the swishing palm trees fly by.

"I couldn't say. I'm just sitting here watching the wheels go round and round."

"Hey, that's from a John Lennon song!" remarked Bortnicker proudly.

184

"And where do you think *he* got the phrase?" smiled Chapford.

* * * *

"Wow," said Bortnicker as the minivan began its climb up the driveway. "Looks like the captain was living large."

"It's the most beautiful house I've ever seen," marveled LouAnne. "Like a fairy tale."

"Yeah," cautioned T.J., "but remember, we're looking for what's inside, and it might not be too pleasant."

As they pulled up to the ornate, hand-carved teak door, Mike came outside, his body exuding nervousness and excitement. "Welcome to Hibiscus House," he said with a grand sweep of his arm, "home to Bermuda's very own slave-driving pirate, William Tarver."

As the kids got out, Weinstein jogged around the car to the driver's side window. "What's your plan, Chappy?" he said.

"I think I'll just park off to the side and wait it out," he said calmly. "No sense in going all the way back home. I brought a book, and I might just take a nap as well." What he didn't say was that he wanted to be right there if someone was injured or the police had to be summoned quickly.

"Fine with me," answered Weinstein.

As if on cue, Tom Sr. cruised into the estate entrance, followed by Jasper Goodwin's vintage Toyota, from which Ronnie alighted. Jasper parked near Chappy and approached Tom Sr., who was removing his helmet. "So good to see you again, Tom," he said. "Seems like a lot has changed since our merry feast a few nights ago after we found the bell."

"Yes," said Tom Sr., shaking his hand in greeting. "The kids told me all about the slave find. Sorry it came out that way."

"What's done is done. I'm just concerned about my daughter's well-being now. Will you be sure to keep an eye on her tonight? She's been rather agitated since that last dive."

"We'll all keep our eyes open tonight, don't you worry. And I'll make sure she gets home safely."

"Thank you." The Divemaster looked skyward at the gathering storm clouds. "Even so, Veronique has my cell number, if I can be of any assistance."

"I'm sure it'll go just fine," Tom Sr. said. "Mike's an old pro at conducting these investigations."

"You're probably right," sighed Goodwin. "It's just that ... there's something *wrong* with this house. I just can't say quite what." With that he returned to the car and eased off down the driveway.

"Glad you made it," said Bortnicker to Ronnie, who was dressed in a black tee shirt and shorts.

She gave him a quick hug. "Wouldn't miss it for the world."

"Okay, dudes," said Mike, calling the teens together on the front entrance landing. "Time for us to film our intros. I'm going to do the greeting, which will play before the dive sequences when we put the show together. Then, each of you give a good sound bite of what you'll be looking for tonight in our first investigation. Got it?"

"Got it," they said in unison.

"Okay, then," he said, handing LouAnne the camcorder. "If you'll do the honors, I'll get things started."

She took the camera and counted in from three, then gave a quick thumbs-up.

"Behind me is Hibiscus House, the palatial mansion built by Sir William Tarver on the idyllic island of Bermuda in the 1700s. For many years it has been one of the most visited spots on the island, but it has been vacant for the past six months.

"Hibiscus House has always been active in the paranormal sense, but apparently things have ratcheted up to the point where nobody wants to work here.

"Is Hibiscus House cursed? Is the ghost of William Tarver haunting these grounds, and what secrets are there to discover about Bermuda's most famous pirate?

"We're here to find out. I have assembled a team of talented teenaged ghost chasers who will try to get to the bottom of this mystery—"

A rumble of thunder briefly interrupted Weinstein, who then added, "A perfect evening for a haunting, wouldn't you agree? Welcome to *Junior Gonzo Ghost Chasers*, Bermuda."

"Great job, Mike," said LouAnne, clicking off.

"Yeah," agreed Bortnicker, "and the background thunder was cool!"

Weinstein took the camcorder from LouAnne. "Okay," he said, "you're up first, babe. Smile big and tell us what you're looking for tonight."

"During tonight's investigation I want to contribute a little more than I have been," she said confidently. "Since I wasn't a participant on our two dives, I hope to find out more about Sir William by actually recording him."

Bortnicker shot a wink to Ronnie, who stood behind Mike, and said, "We've found out some pretty nasty stuff about William Tarver on our dives, like the fact that he owned slaves. I want him to show up so I can confront him on this and find out how he felt living like a king while others suffered."

T.J. offered, "William Tarver seems to be a man of contradictions who's always been looked at as a Bermudian hero. I want to find out his true colors and set history straight."

"Outstanding, dudes!" cried Mike. "If this is any indication, tonight's gonna be awesome. Let's go inside and I'll show you the layout."

The entourage, save for Chappy, who lowered the seatback of the minivan for a snooze, ventured inside as the first soft rain of the storm proceeded to fall. They began on the second floor and toured the various bedrooms and suites, gradually making their way back down the grand staircase where, unbeknownst to them, Willie B. had met his demise the previous night. Then it was on to the sumptuous bedroom of William Tarver, which looked out on the rear gallery and provided sweeping views of the fields where his slaves toiled in the Bermuda sun. They finished in the library under the glowering eyes of Tarver's portrait.

The house itself was immaculate; not one piece of furniture or the Irish lace doilies that protected them was out of place. The entire mansion smelled of old wood and polish.

"Get your bearings now," reminded Mike, "and try to remember where everything is, because when we go 'lights out' for the investigation it's going to be pretty weird, at least at first." He led them back down the long ground floor hallway to the entrance foyer, where he'd set up a bank of computer terminals that would monitor virtually every passageway and room in the house. With Tom Sr. looking on he pointed out the locations of static night vision cameras he'd set up that afternoon. "They'll constantly be recording, so we'll pick up any anomalies that surface. If Tom or I see something on the DVR's, say, in one of the upstairs rooms, we'll direct one of you teams to get right on it."

"What about handhelds?" asked T.J.

"Each team will have one infrared camcorder and an EVP recorder."

"Could you explain that to me?" asked Ronnie. "I don't watch too many ghost shows over here."

"No problem," smiled Mike. "EVP stands for electronic voice phenomena. It's been found that spirits can manifest themselves through sound waves that are not readily picked up by the human ear. These recorders are tuned at a much higher frequency so that if you ask a question, and there's a spirit present, you might just hear a response when you play back the tape."

"For real?" asked Ronnie skeptically.

"Oh yeah," said Mike assuredly. "We get some feedback almost every investigation. Now, in some cases the words or sounds might be garbled or very faint, but with computer enhancement, we've actually captured intelligent responses."

"And have you actually had a ghost, you know, show up?" she questioned, her eyebrow arched.

"Over the first few seasons of the show we've had shadow figures, knocking, and stuff falling or even being thrown around in the dark, but we have yet to experience a full manifestation. But your three buddies here are living proof that ghosts exist. Right, dudes?"

"I know it sounds crazy, Ronnie," said T.J., "but believe me, last year we were talking to a ghost who seemed as real as you or me."

"I know," she said. "Bortnicker kind of filled me in on your adventures from Gettysburg, although I'd still have to see it for myself to become a believer."

"Well, that's why you're here, isn't it?" said Bortnicker.

"That's why we're *all* here," said Mike. "That's why millions of people tune into *Gonzo Ghost Chasers* every week, and other paranormal shows. We all want to be the first to capture a full body apparition on video. It's the holy grail of paranormal investigating. And you guys, based on what's happened to you already, have as good a shot as any to be the first." His passionate words hung in the air.

"But no pressure, right?" joked Bortnicker, breaking the tension.

Another rumble of thunder rolled across the island, causing vibrations throughout the house. "This could be problematic," grumbled Mike. "Lots of extraneous noise outside can wreak havoc on the audio, and if we get a lot of lightning there will be shadows flying all over the place."

"What if we lose power?" asked Ronnie. "That happens a lot here with tropical storms."

"Well," sighed Mike, "the one thing we weren't able to lug over here was a generator, and I couldn't find one on the island that would suit our needs. My bad."

"Aw, c'mon, Mike," said Bortnicker. "You couldn't think of *everything*."

"I agree," said Tom Sr. "The command post you've established here is pretty impressive."

"Yeah," said T.J., "and it's not like the famous Bermuda National Heritage Trust was killing themselves to help you out."

Mike held out a hand to stop them. "Listen, dudes," he said, "it's as simple as this. If we lose power, you'll still have the small light on your camcorder, and I'm going to give LouAnne and Ronnie a flashlight to stick in their pocket. T.J. and Bortnicker will also have a walkie-talkie clipped on their belts, so we'll always be in communication." He looked at his watch. "With the stormy conditions outside, I estimate that we'll lose most of our sunlight within the hour. Then we'll go lights out. Until then, I want both teams to take all their equipment and become comfortable with it. We'll also do a walkie-talkie check. Okay?"

"Got it," said T.J., offering Bortnicker a high five.

As the two teams separated, Ronnie latched on to Bortnicker's arm with a force that made him flinch. "Oww!" he cried. "I didn't know you were so strong."

"It's all those years of lugging diving tanks, I guess," she said apologetically. "And maybe because I'm, ah, a bit afraid of the dark."

He turned to her, his eyes widening behind his Coke-bottle glasses. "You wait until *now* to tell me? Are you sure you're up for this, Ronnie?

You can still back out—"

"Just stay close to me," she whispered, and brushed his cheek with her lips.

"No problem there," he smirked.

* * * *

It was just before 8:00 p.m. when the team gathered around the command post. All the equipment had been checked and re-checked; it was time to get underway.

"Okay, dudes," said Mike, as rain drummed on the windows, "we've got ten rooms upstairs: five on each side of the hallway, and eight down here, five and three. Bortnicker and Ronnie, you start up top. T.J. and LouAnne, cover the first floor. Then you'll switch." He paused, as if searching for the appropriate words.

"Now remember," he began, "that this is a serious investigation. We've done a lot of amazing groundwork already, with our two dives. But don't forget that the thing that makes *Gonzo Ghost Chasers* different than the other paranormal shows out there is our style. We like to be provocational and confrontational. When you're asking questions on the EVP recorders, don't be afraid you'll hurt the feelings of William Tarver or anyone else. Make sure your questions are stated in a way that can be answered with simple responses. Also be sure to allow long pauses after questions so the spirit can respond clearly. You want to be a little on the dramatic side? Hey, go for it. This is Hollywood, after all."

The last comment drew nervous chuckles from the teens, except for Ronnie, who remained stone-faced.

"If there's an emergency, both of you boys have the walkie-talkies. Tom and I aren't going to move from this post unless you need us. Comprendo?"

They all nodded.

"Okay then, at the beginning of each investigation we have a custom with our team. Everybody huddle up and put your hands in."

This they did, their bodies trembling with excitement.

"Gonzos rule, on three. One, two, three."

"Gonzos rule!" they cried aloud, and the sound of their cheer echoed throughout the halls as the first crack of lightning cast an eerie flash of light on Hibiscus House.

* * * *

As they made their way slowly among the downstairs rooms, the cousins couldn't help jumping each time thunder boomed. "Sure is different now that we've gone lights out," said T.J. "Mike wasn't kidding."

"We'll get used to it, Cuz," said LouAnne bravely. "Those lightning flashes are freaking me out, though."

They found themselves in the bedroom of Lillith Tarver, which was only slightly less grand than that of her husband. "You think it's strange she had her own room?" mused T.J.

"I don't know," she replied, panning the infrared camcorder around. "Seems that back in the day if you were very wealthy you got your own bedroom, married or not. Want to ask Lillith some questions?"

"Let's do it."

They settled gently on the somewhat lumpy mattress of the elaborately carved mahogany four poster bed. T.J. clicked on RECORD and spoke into the EVP unit. "We're trying to contact Lillith Tarver. My name is T.J. and this is my cousin LouAnne, and we're visiting your island from America. Are you here, Mrs. Tarver?" He paused for a response, then continued, "Is your husband here with you? Are you aware that we have found him to be a slave master? ... Do you have any regrets about your lives in this house?"

T.J. rewound the tape and hit PLAY. But there was only dead air in the response spaces. "Oh well," he said, "let's keep going. Remember, when the TV show airs, people only see a few highlights out of hours of footage."

"You're so encouraging, Cuz," she replied sarcastically.

* * * *

Upstairs, Bortnicker and Ronnie weren't faring any better. "I can't get over all the woodwork in these rooms," marveled the boy. "It must take hours to polish it."

"Not if you've got slaves," Ronnie bitterly retorted.

"Good point. Let's try to bring him out. Sir William," he announced, raising his voice, "we've come a long way to meet you and hope not to

191

be disappointed. Are you annoyed that we are in your home? … Are you trapped here, or is it just that you don't want to leave? … Are you ashamed that you subjugated others to live so well?" He rewound the tape and they both put their ear to the miniature speaker. Nothing.

"Oh well, on to the next room," he sighed.

At 11:00 p.m. Mike radioed the teams to meet back at the command post for a break. "So you thought ghost chasing was easy?" he said, noting their sense of frustration.

"There's nothing, Mike," complained T.J. "Not a peep on the EVPs, or a knock, or anything. Once I thought I heard a rap on the window, but it was only a palm frond blowing in the storm breeze."

"Which by the way keeps picking up," added LouAnne.

"You dudes don't want to quit, do you?" Mike challenged.

"No way," said Bortnicker doggedly. "Let's just switch floors and see if our luck changes." He turned to Tom Sr. "Mr. J, have you seen anything at all on the monitors?"

"Sorry, Bortnicker," said Tom Sr., "Mike and I are practically going cross-eyed looking at these screens. We've seen a few dust motes and stuff, but outside of the occasional lightning through the windows, it's been dead. No pun intended."

"I've been listening to your questions," said Weinstein, "and you're doing good. But maybe it's time to get a little nastier."

"Not a problem," said T.J. "Let's get after it."

* * * *

Outside in the car, Chappy was getting a little edgy. Not only had the storm intensified to the point where wind damage was probable, every minute more that those kids spent in the house was pushing their luck. After hearing Winnie Pemburton's story and the news of Willie B.'s demise, he was convinced that something was certainly wrong in that house. However, being a rational man, he was reluctant to give in to his gut impression. He checked his watch. "Just a couple more hours," he said to himself, "and it will all be over."

Then the lights went out.

* * * *

"Uh oh," said LouAnne, suddenly clutching her cousin after a particularly nasty crack of lightning. "That sounded way too close."

Almost immediately T.J.'s walkie-talkie crackled, making him almost jump out of his shoes.

"Come in, T.J. and LouAnne," said Weinstein. "Can you hear me? Over."

"We-we're here," answered T.J. "Jeez, Mike, you scared the crap out of me. What's up?"

"We've lost power, dudes. The computers are all down. You want to call it a night?"

T.J. looked at LouAnne, who shrugged with an *It's up to you* look. "Nah, our handhelds are still working. I'll just flip on my flashlight. Over."

Bortnicker gave Mike pretty much the same response. "Okay, then," said Weinstein, "Tom and I will be here if you need us."

"Hey," said Ronnie. "Why don't you give me a try? Maybe it will change our luck."

"Well," reasoned Bortnicker, "it's not in the script, but I don't see why not." He handed her the EVP recorder in exchange for the video cam. Suddenly he froze. "Do you smell tobacco, like a pipe?" he said.

"Now that you mention it, I do catch a whiff."

"Maybe it's him. Let 'er rip."

"William Tarver!" she called. "I will not refer to you as 'Sir' because you don't deserve my respect, or anyone else's for that matter. Are you here? Come forward, you coward. Are you in our presence?"

She paused and then proceeded with her line of questioning: "Did you die in this house? ... Are you aware of the despicable nature of your deeds?"

"Play it back," said Bortnicker.

"Okay, here goes," she said after rewinding.

"William Tarver! I will not refer to you as 'Sir', because you don't deserve my respect, or anyone else's for that matter. Are you here? Come forward, you coward. Are you in our presence?"

"Yes." The voice was somewhat faint, but clear. The teens' eyes widened in horror.

"Did you die in this house?"

"No."

193

"Are you aware of the despicable nature of your deeds?"
A chilling laugh was the only reply.

"Wow!" cried Bortnicker, hugging Ronnie excitedly. "We've broken through! He's really here! Keep going!"

"Okay," she answered, then shivered. "Bortnicker, are you cold?"

"Now that you mention it, yeah," he replied. "It's like the temperature's dropping by the second. I've seen this all the time on ghost shows. When a spirit is trying to manifest itself it could lead to an extreme temperature drop where it is. Let me check the thermal imaging camera," he said, pulling the device from his pocket. "Holy Toledo! The temperature's at 70...65...50...45..."

"Get T.J. and LouAnne up here," she said hurriedly. "I think something's about to happen!"

"I'm on it!" He fumbled with the walkie-talkie, then clicked on. "T.J., come in."

"What's up?"

"You got anything going downstairs?"

"Not really, and this lightning outside isn't helping any."

"Well then, you'd better get up here, 'cause things are getting weird."

"Really? How?"

"We got a response on the EVP recorder, it's getting colder in here, and—"

"Bortnicker? Bortnicker!" T.J. turned to LouAnne, who looked on pie-eyed. "His walkie just cut out. Remember last year in Gettysburg how Hilliard drained the batteries in the tape recorder when he manifested? It could be happening upstairs, right now!"

"Come on!" she cried, grabbing her cousin's hand. "Let's get up there now!" They took off running through the darkened hallway toward the grand staircase.

* * * *

"T.J.? Bortnicker? Can you guys hear me?" Mike shook his walkie-talkie, listened, then gave it a whack. Nothing. "We're out, Tom," he said with concern. "The storm shouldn't affect them, since they run on batteries. Something tells me Tarver is trying to manifest himself...but to drain all our radios is pretty extraordinary. Takes a lot of energy for

194

something that dramatic."

"Think we should go find them?"

Mike thought a second. "Nah, let's sit tight. These kids can handle themselves."

* * * *

T.J. and LouAnne burst through the doorway to find Bortnicker and Ronnie literally shaking in their sneakers. No sooner had T.J. uttered the words "Jeez, it's freezing in here!" than the door behind them slammed shut, prompting them all to jump.

"Think the wind caused that?" said Bortnicker shakily.

"Are you serious?" answered LouAnne. "Have you checked out how heavy the doors in this place are?"

"Okay, okay, everyone calm down," said T.J., bringing his voice down a few octaves. "Ronnie, tell me what's happened."

"W-well, we've been trying to make contact all night," she said, holding herself against the chill, "but it wasn't till I started asking the questions that we got a hit on the EVP."

"Could you play it back for me?'

"Sorry, Big Mon, the batteries went dead," said Bortnicker. "But believe me, he responded."

"Okay, then. Ronnie, he seems to be reacting to you. Why don't you try again."

"If you want." She cleared her throat. "William Tarver! We've all assembled here to meet you. The least you could do is show yourself. Or are you—"

"No need to scream, lass," came a burly voice from another part of the room. "I can hear you just fine."

The teens froze, then slowly turned to see a figure silhouetted against the huge balcony window, sheets of rains sliding down the outside glass. He was large, over six feet, boots planted wide, shoulders thrown back and balled fists on hips. His long hair, tied back, nearly reached his shoulders. Flashes of lightning revealed a weathered, somewhat handsome face framed by a prodigious dark beard. A cutlass hung from his wide belt, and the butt of a flintlock pistol protruded from his brass buttoned waistcoat.

"C-Captain Tarver?" said Ronnie, her voice quivering. "Captain William Tarver?"

"In the flesh," he replied, chuckling at his own joke. "And what brings this group to my humble home?"

T.J. stepped forward. "Captain, we've come here from America to speak to you—"

"All that way across the ocean. My, my. What is it you seek?"

"Some information," said Bortnicker. "Specifically, about your life and death."

"Really, now." He looked directly at Ronnie, who was doing her best to appear unruffled. "And you, young miss? Are you the personal attendant to this other lass? You seem rather mouthy for a slave. A more respectful tone is in order here, I think. But I must say, I love the color of your eyes. A wonderful shade, that. Too pretty to be a field slave."

"Why, you—" She stepped forward, but LouAnne put herself between the black girl and the ghost.

"Ronnie is most certainly *not* our slave," she said firmly. "What's more, she is a full member of our team, and we don't appreciate the tone you're taking with her."

"Is that a fact?" said Tarver with mild amusement. "Let me remind *you*, lass, that you're in my home, and you'll watch your tongue when addressing me." His voice turned harsh. "Now, state your business plainly before I lose patience."

Sensing that the situation was escalating, T.J. again took the lead. "Sir William," he said calmly, "your house is regarded as a historic landmark, a national treasure of the Bermudian people—"

"As well it should be," he growled.

"Then why are you chasing away those who visit this place?"

The pirate glowered. "There are those who belong here and those who do not," he replied.

"Like me?" asked Ronnie indignantly. "And to think, I considered you a hero. I remember being so sad when I visited your tomb years ago, and proud at the same time when my teacher told our class about your brave exploits. She never mentioned how you worked people like me to death, all for your own benefit!" Bortnicker tried to rest a calming hand on her shoulder, but she shook it off.

196

"You know," he said with a hint of admiration, "I like you. Cheeky one, you are. And I must say, I'm somewhat honored that you took the time to visit my grave. But there's a problem with that, I'm afraid."

"Which is?" asked Bortnicker.

"Well, I'm not actually buried there."

"Wait a minute," said LouAnne. "According to the official records, or what's left of them, you died of natural causes and were buried in the St. Anne's Church cemetery. Your wife was later buried with you."

He sighed. "Sorry to disappoint you, but while she is indeed there, I am not."

"Did you go down with the *Steadfast*?" asked T.J.

"How do you know about my ship?"

"We found it, Captain Tarver, off the South Shore."

"Indeed? And how long ago was this?"

"My father discovered it, actually," said Ronnie proudly. "About seven months ago."

"Well, that would explain it then," he replied.

"Explain what?" asked Bortnicker.

"Why I've been…returned."

T.J., remembering back to the previous year when Major Crosby Hilliard had come back to the Gettysburg Battlefield as a result of his remains being accidentally dug up, figured Jasper Goodwin's fateful dive in November had similarly awakened the pirate's spirit in some way. "Captain Tarver," he said, "if you're not buried in the St. Anne's Cemetery, then where are your remains?"

Suddenly there was a hammering on the door of the room. "Dudes! Are you in there?" yelled Weinstein. "Hey! Are you guys all right? Let me in! This door's locked or something!"

The teens looked to the ghost, whose density seemed to be thinning. "It appears I must be going," said Tarver. "But since you seem so interested in my whereabouts, I'll make you a proposition. Return to this place tomorrow night and all will be made clear."

Bortnicker had barely managed a "But—" when Mike blasted his way into the room and went sprawling as the pirate vanished.

Picking himself up, the Senior *Gonzo Ghost Chaser* eyed his young protégées. "Dudes, what was going on in here?" he said agitatedly. "And why did you lock me out?"

"He showed up," said T.J. excitedly. "We were actually speaking with Tarver's ghost!"

"And we didn't lock you out," added Bortnicker, "he locked us in!"

"So I missed him? I can't believe it!" moaned Weinstein.

"It's not your fault, Mike," said LouAnne. "I mean, the electricity's out and it looks like Tarver drained every battery in the house."

"But we got his voice on the EVP recorder," said Bortnicker. "A couple responses to Ronnie's questions before the battery went dead. We can pop in some new ones at the hotel and play it back for you. Betcha we can use it on the show because it came through pretty well."

Just then there was a buzz from downstairs. "We've got power!" called Tom Sr. from the command post.

"Let's go down and debrief there," said Mike. "Looks like the show's over for tonight."

By the time they'd made it downstairs, Chappy was sitting with Tom Sr., marveling at the bank of computer terminals and other equipment that Mike had set up.

"Quite a lot of kit you have here," he said as the group gathered around. "Did you catch anything?"

"Not on the video," said Tom Sr., "but—"

"We made contact!" blurted Bortnicker, who was met with admonishing glares from Mike and his teammates.

"Is that so?" said Chappy coolly. "With the Captain himself?"

"Yeah, Chappy," said T.J. "He showed up. It's funny, though…we didn't get any hits until Ronnie tried to bring him out."

"Hmm, interesting," he replied, the realization becoming clear that this ghost only reacted to those of African descent. "And what did he tell you?"

"Basically, that he isn't buried in the Tarver crypt at St. Anne's Cemetery," said Bortnicker, handing over the video recorder to Mike.

"Well then, where is he, Mr. B?"

"He wants us to come back for another visit," said LouAnne. "Maybe he'll tell us then."

"And you actually…saw him?" asked Chappy, an eyebrow raised.

"Most definitely, Mr. Chapford," said Ronnie. "He was somewhat transparent, but we could make out his features, which were dead on to the portrait in the study."

"Quite remarkable. And did you actually document this conversation?"

"I'm afraid the only thing we might have are his original responses to Ronnie's inquiries," said Bortnicker. "Then the power in the house went down, and he drained the batteries in our flipcam and EVP recorder to boot."

"We'll give a listen back at the hotel," said Mike. "I have a stash of extra batteries there. One thing's for certain, though. We've gotta come back for a second visit. While you guys are doing the road race tomorrow morning I'll drop by Mrs. Tilbury's office and tell her we need another night. Think you'll be okay for tomorrow night? Not too tired from the running?"

"Nope," said LouAnne confidently. "We'll be back at the hotel by noon, and we can chill out at the pool or the beach all afternoon."

"Sounds like a plan," said Mike. "Now, let's all pitch in and break this stuff down so we can get back to the hotel at a reasonable hour. Our marathoners need some sleep!"

"I'll run Ronnie home on my scooter," offered Tom Sr. "See you all tomorrow morning bright and early for the race."

It was a happy crew that loaded the equipment into Chappy's minivan that night. Having an actual exchange with a ghost was Mike Weinstein's holy grail, and the possibility that their next encounter could be documented on film would be a groundbreaking event in the paranormal community, not to mention a smashing pilot episode for the new TV series.

* * * *

T.J. and Bortnicker were just about to turn in when Mike knocked on their door, excited. "We've got the audio, dudes!" he piped. "Sir William Tarver, clearly responding to Ronnie's questions. And after we clean up the tape a little, it'll be perfect for the show. So I'll go see Mrs. Tilbury while T.J.'s doing his running thing and catch up with you guys tomorrow around noon." He high-fived the boys and strode out, obviously fired up.

"How are you gonna be able to sleep after all this, Big Mon?" asked Bortnicker. "Between the investigation tonight and the race tomorrow, my mind would be spinning!"

"Just watch me," said T.J. "I'm really exhausted. And I'll bet my cousin next door is sleeping like a baby already."

"'Cause she thinks she'll kick your butt?"

"Exactly. But she just might be surprised come race time."

"You psyched to talk with Tarver again?"

"Oh yeah. And I have a feeling this whole deal still has a ways to go. We're gonna break this case wide open!"

Chapter Twenty-Four

Saturday dawned sunny and breezy, ideal running conditions. The previous night's storm had blown out to sea, and all that remained were a few downed trees and palm fronds everywhere. After a light breakfast Mike was on his way to St. George's for his rendezvous with Constance Tilbury. Bortnicker rode the scooter toward the Royal Naval Dockyard, the race's starting site, with Tom Sr. while T.J. and LouAnne stretched out in Chappy's minivan for the twenty minute ride.

"Splendid day for a road race, folks," said the driver. "I'm assuming you're both in peak running trim?"

"You know it," said LouAnne, adjusting the laces on her Nikes.

"Didja sleep okay, Cuz?" asked T.J., adjusting his seatback into a semi-reclining position.

"No reason not to," chirped his cousin confidently, which is what he figured.

The starting area was awash with volunteers manning registration tables and handing out water bottles. T.J. and LouAnne picked up their paper number tags emblazoned with an American flag, which a worker promptly pinned to the back of their tee shirts. They had both decided to wear their *Junior Gonzo Ghost Chasers* shirts in honor of the team. The cousins found a quiet area to do some last minute stretching while eyeing the crowd.

"Looks like we have quite a few countries represented," said LouAnne, as she settled into a hurdler's stretch.

"Yeah," said T.J., leaning forward into a standing calf stretch. "I'd say overall we've got over a hundred runners."

A portable PA system crackled to life. "Would all runners please assemble at the starting line for a playing of 'God Save the Queen'?"

"Here we go," said LouAnne, rising. "See you at the finish line?"

"Yeah," joked T.J., "I'll be there waiting for you."

"You wish." She gave him a quick peck on the cheek. "Good luck, Cuz."

"You too."

"Go get 'em, you guys!" screamed Bortnicker from the side of the road, where he and Tom Sr. were waving madly. "We'll be right behind you on the scooter!"

T.J. waved back in acknowledgement. "Too bad Ronnie couldn't make it. She had to work at the dive shop this morning—"

At that second the crowd of runners hushed as the Bermuda Regiment, resplendent in their red tunics, black pants and white pith helmets, began a stately rendition of the anthem. Famous the world over, their performance was both dignified and inspiring. At its conclusion, a cheer rang out from the runners and hundreds more tourists and residents who'd turned out for the event and would be lining South Road all the way from Dockyard to Hamilton, where the race would conclude on Front Street.

"Runners to the mark…" intoned the starter.

The cousins bumped fists.

"Ready…steady…"

"Luv ya, Cuz," said LouAnne.

"Back atcha."

"Go!"

And they were off.

The first mile or so, as the road wound its way through Sandys Parish toward Somerset Village, was glorious. Puffy white clouds dotted the sky, and the flowers had opened up after the rain. Gradually, the bunched-up runners of all sizes and colors began to thin out, and T.J. found himself alongside his cousin, their smooth gait no different than on the Railway Trail or the Gettysburg Battlefield the year before. However, T.J. noticed a difference in his cousin on this run. Her jaw was set, her entire being focused on running the perfect race. *That's where she's got me*, he thought. *She goes to a place I've never been, a higher level of consciousness*. He envied her.

Almost as if reading his mind, LouAnne sang out, "Okay Cuz, gotta jet. See ya!" and took off in another gear. Determined not to fall into the trap of trying to match her unquestionable superiority, he kept his normal pace, which wasn't all that bad, either.

T.J. crossed over into Southampton Parish, now following the curve of South Road that overlooked the cliffs and afforded purely majestic views that distracted him from any fatigue he was feeling. He had left the Gibbs Hill Lighthouse behind and was on the way toward Astwood Park when he first caught sight of his cousin sprawled on a grassy shoulder of the road. As he sprinted toward her, heart racing, he noticed she was clutching her lower leg and writhing in agony. She saw him approaching and cried out, "Charley horse in my calf! Omigod it hurts."

He fell to his knees in the grass before her. "What can I do—"

"Nothing!" she hissed between clenched teeth. "There's nothing you can do, and it'll just have to work its way out. Get going!" She pounded the grass in anger.

"But I can't—"

"Listen, T.J.," she rasped, "Your dad will be along and see me. I'll be fine. Now get your butt back into gear and finish the race! You're losing time!"

"But—"

"You're seriously ticking me off here. I'll see you in Hamilton. Now go!"

"Okay," he said, affecting a retreating jog toward the road. "See ya later." He got back into the race, looking over his shoulder intermittently until he rounded a bend and lost sight of her completely.

The rest of the course was run in a fog, with T.J. wondering numerous times if he should give it up. But he was actually more afraid of incurring his cousin's wrath for quitting than of getting embarrassed by the other runners, who at first were blowing by him at an alarming rate. Gradually, though, he regained his composure and equilibrium and started making up some ground. By the time he began his descent toward the city, whose shops on Front Street twinkled in the morning sun, he'd found his second wind and overtaken a bunch of contestants. Stronger by the second, T.J. went into his kick and sprinted the length of Front Street, whooshing by docked cruise ships and cheering crowds, and crossed the finish line just behind the first clutch of racers. Accepting a bottled water from a backslapping tourist screaming "USA! USA!" he deliberately walked past the horse and buggy stand and found a small palm tree to lean against while his breathing equalized. The sun shone off the water of the harbor, and the salty air revived him. He was extremely proud of himself for sucking it up and finishing, but he worried about his cousin. It was at this moment, as he looked out over the Harbor where sleek sailboats cut the waves under an azure sky, that he realized just how hopelessly in love with LouAnne he was. Which was not altogether a bad thing.

"Big Mon! You did it!" cried Bortnicker, who embraced him after a sprint across still-congested Front Street.

"Thanks, man," he said. "I'm pretty whipped. Where are Dad and LouAnne?"

"We got to her first on South Road; then Chappy came along and we put her into the minivan. Everyone's parked on a side street because Front Street's blocked off."

"How is she doing?"

"Physically, not bad. Just a bad cramp we slapped some ice on. But *mentally*? Boy, is she cheesed off."

"Because of me?"

"No, no, nothing like that. She's just mad at herself because—"

"Because that's never happened to me before," said LouAnne, suddenly materializing behind his friend. "I'm really proud of you, Cuz," she added before giving him a heartfelt hug.

"Watch it, I'm kinda yucky," managed T.J., looking over her shoulder to where Bortnicker was grinning and flashing a double thumbs-up of approval.

"And I'm not?"

They parted, and T.J. asked about her leg. "It's no big deal. I've already kinda walked it out."

"Yeah, but I didn't win anything."

"Oh, yes you did," she said with a wink. "Now, let's get some lunch with your dad and Chappy."

"A capital idea!" said Bortnicker in his best John Lennon voice, and the trio made their way back across Front Street.

* * * *

"You most certainly may *not* conduct another investigation at Hibiscus House," snapped Constance Tilbury from behind her desk, the color rising in her powdered cheeks.

"But we were promised—" spluttered Mike, who was having a hard time keeping from vaulting over the desk to choke her.

"You were *offered* two investigations. From what you've described, your first investigation was a smashing success, affording you ample material on which to base an episode of your ridiculous show."

"But this isn't fair!" he cried.

"Fair? It's more than fair, when you understand that there were certain circumstances unbeknownst to you that should have precluded any visits whatsoever!"

"Like what?"

She rose, leaned across the table until practically nose to nose with the muscled ghost hunter, and hissed, "Like the man who was found dead in the house the morning of the same day you conducted your search. You're lucky we let you in at all!"

He sat back with a thud into the leather chair. "Someone was murdered in Hibiscus House?" he asked incredulously.

"The cause of death is deemed accidental at this time," she sniffed. "You should be thanking me."

Mike pondered for a moment. "May I ask a question about the man?"

"You can try, but I'm sure I cannot divulge what you want."

"White or black?"

"Pardon?"

"I'm asking if he was Caucasian or African."

"He was a black man, and that's all I can say. In fact, it's too much. As far as I am concerned, your business is done here, especially your dealings with the National Trust. Any further attempts to enter the grounds of Hibiscus House will be considered trespassing and open you and your group for prosecution to the fullest extent of Bermudian law. Good day, Mr. Weinstein. Please close the door behind you on the way

205

out."

T.J.'s group was just finishing a light lunch at the Hog Penny Pub in Hamilton when a thoroughly demoralized Mike Weinstein shuffled in. After finding Tom Sr. via cell phone, he'd made the scooter trip from St. George's to the capital in record time, his knuckles white on the handle grips from anger.

"Mike, what's the matter?" asked LouAnne with concern. "You look like your dog just died."

"Well," he said, pulling up a chair, "my dog didn't die, but the second investigation did. Mrs. Tilbury just pulled the plug on us."

"What! This is an outrage!" cried Bortnicker, springing to his feet.

T.J., who was sitting next to him, reached up, grabbed the back of his tee shirt, and yanked him down onto his seat while the Hog Penny's patrons gawked. "Tell us what happened, Mike," he said quietly.

After Weinstein's recap, Tom Sr. let out a low whistle. "Wow, a guy found dead the same day you investigated. We're lucky they permitted the first investigation."

"That was her opinion as well," said Mike forlornly.

"So that's it?" said Bortnicker, somewhat more composed. "We're outta here?"

Mike let out a heavy sigh. "The Adventure Channel made it clear that we're to fly out the day after our investigation is concluded. So, I'm gonna try to book us a flight for late tomorrow afternoon."

"Can you produce the show based on just what we've done so far?" asked LouAnne.

"Oh yeah. Between the dive stuff and the EVP's you guys picked up last night, which came out pretty clear by the way, we have enough to make a show. But it could have been so much better. We were so close!"

"Oh well," said T.J. "Them's the breaks. So, we still have this afternoon and tonight, right?"

"No question. I'm gonna motor over to the marina and say my goodbyes to Kim. Her family is sailing out on their yacht for Charleston later this afternoon. Hey, let's make the best of tonight. Tom, what do you say I pick up some steaks and we have a farewell feast by the pool with the kids? You can invite over Ms. Cosgrove to join us. And Bortnicker, why don't you give Ronnie a buzz and invite her family as

206

well? We've got to discuss how Jasper's going to announce the *Steadfast* find anyway."

"Okay," the boy said glumly, realizing that his time with Ronnie was about to be cut short.

They left the Hog Penny and split up, Mike heading toward the marina and Tom Sr. taking the scooter back to the Jobson's Cove Apartments. Rather than bother Chappy, whom they'd see on their upcoming ride to the airport, the teens volunteered to ride the pink bus back from Hamilton. As they headed up the hill from Front Street toward the terminal, Bortnicker suddenly wheeled on his friend. "Well, *you* certainly took that well, if you don't mind me saying."

"Yeah, Cuz," chimed in LouAnne, "aren't you ticked off over this?"

"Yup," he answered.

"So why are you smiling?" asked Bortnicker.

"'Cause we're going back to that house tonight, that's why."

* * * *

If Mike and the kids thought they were having a bad morning, they weren't alone. Breakfast at the Goodwin residence had reached epic proportions of *bad*.

It all started innocently enough; Claudette had prepared a breakfast of sweet buns and tea before father and daughter were to take a dive group out on the *Reef Seeker II* for some "fish peeping", as Ronnie called it. As the girl described the previous night's exploits, including the encounter with Tarver that her prompting had induced, her mother grew distant and looked away, seeming to wish the conversation over. "But he said some things that were strange, Mum," Ronnie remarked as Jasper sipped his tea and looked on. "He commented on my eyes and said I looked familiar. How could that be if he's never met me? It was creepy, like he was looking right into my soul. Does that make sense? Mum? What's the matter?"

"Oh child, child," she whispered, tears welling in her eyes. "There's so much you don't know, so much I've tried to shield you from. Your father's always thought I was too protective but—"

"Daddy, what's this about?" Ronnie said with alarm.

Jasper Goodwin sighed, then picked up his tea cup and saucer to bring them to the sink. "Tell her, Claudette," he said calmly. "It's time."

Mrs. Goodwin reached across the weathered wooden table and took her daughter's hand. "Veronique," she said calmly, "we live a good life that we've worked hard for, in a wonderful place that many consider a paradise. But there was much sadness here, years ago. Horrible things happened that we, as a black Bermudian people, have managed to recover from, most of the way, anyway.

"You are a beautiful girl, a mixture of myself and your father's people, and I wouldn't trade or want to change anything about you. Your eyes, as mine, are the brightest blue. But there is a reason for everything, as they say, so let me explain.

"When your father and I were courting, he told me about his family's background, which made me uneasy because my own parents, who sadly died when I was barely out of grade school, were always vague or evasive when I brought up the subject. So, I decided to start digging through my ancestry on my own.

"To make a long story short, the ancestors on my mother's side were among the first slaves brought, against their will, to the island to work on the plantations of the time."

By this point Jasper had sat down again and handed his wife a napkin, with which she dabbed at her eyes. Ronnie sat entranced, her eyes locked on her mother's, as Claudette resumed her story.

"Among that first wave of slaves brought in was a woman named Maruba, whose name was later Anglicized to Maria by her master…William Tarver."

"My God," whispered Ronnie, fearing what would come next.

"In those days, child, it was not uncommon for the masters to take a shine to a pretty face in their crowd of workers. These women were sometimes shifted to easier jobs rather than toiling from dawn to dusk in the fields. A position as cook, nanny, or personal attendee to the mistress of the house was coveted by all, but at times it came at a price.

"As the story goes, Captain Tarver, who remember was a pirate to begin with, saw just such an opportunity and elevated Maria to the kitchen. Well, one thing led to another, and Maria made the decision to accept his advances despite the very presence of Mrs. Tarver—who by all accounts was a decent woman—in the house.

"Unfortunately, Maria became pregnant, and gave birth to a boy with the mocha-colored skin of my side of the family, and—"

"Blue eyes."

"Yes."

Ronnie took a deep breath, her anger barely in check. "What happened then?"

"From then on, things get hazy. Of course, slavery was eventually abolished on the island, and my family, whom I traced all the way back to Maruba, was assimilated into the island's population. I guess if you'd really want to know the details, you'd have to ask *him*."

"Maybe someday I will," she snarled.

"But what I *do not* want, Veronique Goodwin, is for you to hold hatred in your heart going forward. What's done is done, and you can't change it. Your father and I have made a good life for you, and we must always look forward to a better day."

"Which is why I've got to be going, my sweet," said Jasper, tapping his watch.

"Okay," said Ronnie. She walked around to her mother's side of the table and kissed her lightly on the forehead. "Thank you for telling me, Mum," she whispered. "I'll try to take your advice." With that she walked outside to the car park.

"It had to be done," said Jasper Goodwin to his wife. "She'll get over it."

"I don't know," said Claudette. "Please keep an eye on her today."

"As always," he said, scooping up his car keys.

* * * *

Nigel Chapford frowned as he hung up his cell phone after Mike's disappointing news. Begging off from Weinstein's invitation to join the group for a farewell dinner, he agreed to be on call for an afternoon drive to the airport the following day. The phone immediately rang again and Chappy clicked on, thinking Mike had perhaps missed something. But it wasn't the ghost chaser on the other end.

As early as was politely possible that morning Chappy'd rung up his friend Ian Burton, the caretaker at St. Anne's, to ask for a favor, and was surprised to receive a call back this early afternoon. "You were right,

Nigel," he said. "Me and the boys had a burial this morning and waited until the mourners had left. We had a backhoe handy with which to lift the slab off Sir William's crypt. I told the boys I wanted to check for water damage inside, or some such nonsense, and told them to go grab a cup of tea while I did the inspection.

"Anyway, it appears that although Mrs. Tarver's safely tucked away, the good Captain, as they say about Elvis, has left the building."

"The coffin's empty?"

"What's left of it, yes. Funny thing, though. It would appear he was never there in the first place."

"So you'd say there was no evidence of body snatching or something of that sort?"

"None whatsoever. Now, the boys came back from their tea break none the wiser, and we replaced the slab, so no one knows about this but you and I."

"And the Captain," said Chappy pointedly.

"Aren't you the card," said Burton. "Just keep it between us, all right? I rather like my job here."

"Consider it done, Ian. I owe you one."

"That you do, Nigel. Have a nice day."

* * * *

The three *Junior Gonzo Ghost Chasers* had barely settled into the back seat of the pink bus when T.J., in hushed tones, began to explain his plan.

"Okay, here's how I see it," he said. "We've got 24 hours, give or take, to solve this mystery. Tarver told us last night that if we returned he'd tell us the true story. I say we have our grand farewell dinner tonight and then sneak out to visit the Captain."

"You mean like we did the first time in Gettysburg last year?" said LouAnne excitedly.

"Exactly," smiled T.J., remembering how the teens had climbed down from their second-story bedrooms at LouAnne's house to meet up with Major Hilliard in a wooded area of the battlefield.

"Sneaking out's the easy part, Cuz," said LouAnne. "Everyone's going to be tired, and I'm sure Mike and your dad will have had a couple of glasses of wine on top of that. But how do we get to Hibiscus House? It's a few miles away."

T.J. nodded knowingly. "That's why we're taking the motor scooters. Bortnicker, I'm sure I'm not the only one who's observed how to start and drive them. You were just on one with my dad this morning. Think you can use a bike and not kill yourself?"

"No problemo, Big Mon. And if I'm correct, your dad and Mike leave the keys with their helmets in the car park storage box, which is unlocked."

"Bingo."

"I don't know," said LouAnne. "I get a queasy feeling about this. First, despite what you two think about your driving skills, all you've ever done is sit on the back. *And* it's gonna be dark. *And* you're both underage. *And* it could be me who gets thrown to my death from the bike if you wipe out going around one of those hairpin curves on South Road."

"Does that mean you're out?" said T.J. with a lifted eyebrow.

"Not a chance."

"We'll have to roll the bikes up the road a ways before we start them up so we don't wake your dad or Mike," said Bortnicker.

"No doubt," answered T.J, "but if we're really serious about seeing Tarver, we've got to be willing to take risks. Do you want to call Ronnie and ask her if she's in? She can't breathe a word of this to her father or anyone else."

"I'll give her a buzz right now. Who even knows if he'd talk to us without her there? It's like he was attracted to her last night."

"Yeah," said LouAnne, "like he's still caught up in the whole slavery deal. Yuck."

"So we're set," said T.J. as the bus chugged along. "I propose that we spend one last glorious afternoon lounging on the beach so LouAnne and I can rest our aching muscles, enjoy a tasty steak dinner by the pool, and then have a little talk with our pirate friend."

* * * *

"I'm gonna miss this," said Bortnicker as he lay back on the beach blanket, his battered Red Sox ball cap tilted down over his glasses.

211

"We do have beaches in Fairfield, you know," yawned T.J., stretched out alongside his friend and LouAnne.

"Not the same. Where else are we gonna see pink sand?"

"Guess you're right. And speaking of pink, you've got a pre-lobster tint going on there. Didn't you put on sunscreen?"

"Oops. Only one thing to do." He removed his hat, tossed his glasses in, and took off at breakneck speed for the surf, diving headfirst into a pale green wave before disappearing.

"Your leg still sore from the race this morning?" T.J. asked LouAnne, who had begun kneading her injured calf.

"Nah, it's pretty much worked out, more like a cramp. Maybe I wasn't properly hydrated."

"Yeah. You would've rocked it otherwise."

"You're sweet, Cuz, but I'm still gonna be mad at myself for what happened. That's just the way I am."

"I've noticed."

"Are you saying it's a bad thing?"

"Not at all. I admire how you hate to lose. Wish I was more like that."

"Don't sell yourself short. When the chips are on the table you always seem to come through. I just can't believe that within 48 hours I'm gonna be back in Gettysburg in my Civil War getup, entertaining the touristas at the Charney Inn."

"That's why we've gotta make tonight count," her cousin said earnestly.

Bortnicker had by this time dragged himself from the ocean's undertow and staggered back up the beach, where he collapsed in a sodden heap on their blanket. "Let me call Ronnie again," he said between rasping breaths. "She must've been out on the boat before and couldn't take my call." He punched in her number, put one finger in his ear to drown out the sound of the pounding surf, and shuffled out of earshot of the other teens.

He returned a few minutes later after what appeared to be a fairly intense exchange, his face ashen despite the sunburn.

"Bortnicker, what's the matter?" said LouAnne concernedly. "Is Ronnie alright?"

"Well, depends on what you consider 'alright'. Listen to *this*." He related the revelations of the Goodwin family tree as his friends listened with a mixture of sadness and horror.

"So, does that mean she'll be joining us tonight?"

"What do you think, Big Mon? This isn't just a ghost hunting expedition to her anymore. This is *personal*."

* * * *

Despite noticeable overtones of disappointment, the gathering at the poolside barbeque of Jobson's Cove Apartments was a success. After Bortnicker explained that the Goodwins had a prior commitment and would see them off the following day at the airport, the jovial Mrs. Maltby kicked off the event with a large bottle of non-alcoholic champagne to commemorate the visit of the *Junior Gonzo Ghost Chasers*. The steaks were sizzling and the breeze was mild as the sun started to set on the island of Bermuda.

T.J. observed with interest the interaction between his dad and Lindsay, who seemed to be sharing many quiet asides. This trip had been good for him. Not only had he swung a huge deal for a golf resort that would probably make him an honorary lifetime member; he'd met an attractive woman close to his age with whom he might be able to cultivate a relationship beyond this trip. T.J. had a feeling that the poolside dinner might not be the end of their evening, as Ms. Cosgrove had driven over in her Mercedes.

As for Mike, who quickly switched over to a more potent beverage to drown his sorrows over the cancellation of the second investigation, it seemed as though he had enough to cobble together a workable pilot episode for the series based solely upon the diving footage and last night's EVPs. He had already begun packing the equipment for shipment home and would probably finish tonight. This, of course, presented a problem for the teens, who would need camcorders or EVP recorders for their meeting with Tarver. However, they still had their flashlights.

They were sitting around a large poolside table, making small talk and eating like there was no tomorrow, when Bortnicker suddenly excused himself. "Probably calling Ronnie," said LouAnne. But Bortnicker had other ideas. Making sure nobody was looking to the upper level, he quietly slipped into Mike's room, gently lifted the lid to one of the two equipment trunks, and removed one of the pocket-sized EVP recorders from its box, along with a couple batteries. "Tarver might drain these tonight, but it's worth a shot," Bortnicker whispered to himself as he pocketed the device. He then crept back to the apartment door, checked to see the coast was clear, and slipped outside, returning to T.J.'s side at the dinner table within minutes of his departure.

"Got an EVP handheld for tonight," he whispered in his friend's ear.

"Way to go."

At around ten o'clock, as T.J. had expected, his dad and Ms. Cosgrove went for a last night drive into Hamilton. "Get a good night's sleep, kids," Tom Sr. cautioned. "Tomorrow you can get some pool time in before we head to the airport. Mike, what time's the flight?"

"We're booked for a 6:00 p.m. flight to JFK. I told Chappy to be here around two. LouAnne, I have you booked on a connecting flight out of Kennedy to Philadelphia, arriving at 10:30 p.m."

"I'll call your dad with all the particulars," added Tom Sr.

"Thanks, Uncle Tom," she said. "I think I'll turn in."

"Us, too," said the boys in unison. They helped Mike and Tom Sr. clean up and then said their goodnights. As they shuffled up the stairs, Mike couldn't help but apologize again for the aborted second investigation. "Dudes," he said, his speech a little slurred, "it's still gonna be a good show, but we were really onto something there. Maybe when Tilbury retires they'll let us come back to finish the job."

"I wouldn't bet on it," said Bortnicker. "Don't blame yourself."

"Yeah," said T.J. "There's no guarantee Tarver would've shown up again, anyway."

"Well, whatever," said Mike with a dismissive wave. "I just want you to know you guys went beyond my expectations. If The Adventure Channel picks up the series, I wish you could be the permanent team."

"We could never do that, Mike," said LouAnne seriously. "Not with school and sports and whatever."

"But that doesn't mean an occasional guest spot isn't possible," said T.J.

"You're on," the host smiled for the first time all evening. "Well, I've gotta finish packing the equipment. I'll probably be sleeping a little late tomorrow morning, so I'll see you at the pool around noon...maybe." He went inside his apartment, leaving the teens alone.

"Okay, it's 10:30," whispered T.J. "We'll meet back here at midnight. Whatever you do, keep it quiet!"

"I'll call Ronnie and tell her to meet us at Hibiscus House a little after midnight," said Bortnicker furtively.

"And how is she supposed to get there?" said LouAnne.

"Let's put it this way," said Bortnicker. "We won't be the only ones stealing a motorbike tonight."

Chapter Twenty-Five

"Did you hear that?" said T.J. to Bortnicker as they lay on their beds resting. "Dad just got in." He looked at his dive watch, purchased from Capt. Kenny's. "A quarter to twelve on the button. Let's give him about twenty minutes and take off."

"Good thing Mike scheduled the rental bike pickup for tomorrow," said Bortnicker, pulling on his beat-up Reeboks, "or we'd be up the proverbial creek."

Minutes later there was a quiet tapping on their door. "It's my cousin," said T.J. "Let's get after it."

They crept down the stairs to the first floor and followed the poolside terrace to the steps leading to the car park. The full moon shone brightly, a complete opposite to the stormy night of 24 hours ago. T.J. and Bortnicker gently lifted the kickstands to the hefty scooters as LouAnne rummaged in the storage box for the keys and three helmets. The teens then walked the bikes down to South Road and started pushing along the shoulder of the gently sloping macadam.

"How far we going before we rev them up?" asked Bortnicker, who was already panting.

"Let's at least get around this next bend in the road and we'll be okay," answered T.J. "Cuz, you want to help Mr. Muscles with his bike?"

"No problem," she said, grabbing one side of Bortnicker's handlebars.

They cleared the bend; thankfully, no other cars had come by. The last thing they needed now was some friendly Bermudian to offer assistance—or worse—radio the police of a breakdown.

"Okay," said T.J. finally. "Let's do it."

"Gentlemen, start your engines!" cracked Bortnicker, hopping on his bike and turning the key.

"I think I'll ride with you, Cuz," said LouAnne, climbing onto the back of T.J.'s scooter and wrapping her arms around his waist. "I don't trust Bortnicker one bit."

Feeling her warmth behind him, T.J. was never going to disagree. He turned the ignition key, and the throaty engine roared to life. After revving the motor a couple times he tentatively eased onto the road, Bortnicker following at a safe speed and distance behind him. "And away we go," he said with a conviction that belied his terror over the thoughts of accidents or arrests. In fact, at this point, the prospect of being alone with a ghost gave him the least amount of fear. Maybe he was just becoming good at the whole paranormal thing.

The two bikes glided along South Road in the moonlight, the ocean clearly discernible past the cliffs below. As they passed the Gibbs Hill Lighthouse, which cast its powerful beam in sweeping arcs that could be seen for miles, T.J. was sure he could pinpoint the area where the *Steadfast* lay amid the reefs. Some fifteen minutes later, they turned up a tribal road and began their ascent to Hibiscus House.

Upon entering the winding approach road, the teens were struck with the massive size of the structure silhouetted against the moon. They felt small and insignificant, perhaps like the slaves who had suffered here centuries before. T.J. steered his bike around the house toward the service shed in the back, and Bortnicker followed suit. No sense in leaving them out front where a police car might happen by.

Ronnie Goodwin must have had the same idea, because she was parked near the shed removing her helmet, her corkscrew curls exploding forth, as they pulled up.

The boys switched off their bikes and dismounted, as did LouAnne. "Smooth ride," she said with admiration. "You're a natural."

"I was shaking the whole time," T.J. confessed sheepishly.

"Well, *I* wasn't scared," boasted Bortnicker. "In fact, I could see myself on a big old chopper someday."

All the kids chuckled at the image. "Hey, those are smashing bikes," complimented Ronnie. "My dad's here is just a little putt-putt."

"Mike and my dad went for the top-of-the-line," said T.J. "They're as big as a lot of motorcycles I've seen. I'll be happy when they're back all safe and—"

The kids froze as the headlights of a large, dark automobile came around the back corner of the mansion, blinding them.

"Busted," was all LouAnne could say.

Then the lights switched off, and the driver's side door opened. Figuring he'd brazen it out, T.J. said, "I don't know who you are, but we have just as much right to be here as you-"

"Oh, I'm quite sure of that, Mr. J," said Nigel Chapford, smiling thinly.

"Chappy!" cried Bortnicker. "My man!"

"In the flesh, as it were," he chuckled.

"What are *you* doing here?" marveled LouAnne.

"Well, Mike called with the bad news at midday, and like you, I was disappointed. However, after getting to know you young people, I had a feeling you weren't going to take Mrs. Tilbury's 'no' for an answer, and I figured you might need some 'backup' as they say on those American police programs.

"But before we venture inside, I have some information I have to get off my chest, so bear with me.

"First, you boys and Miss Ronnie here have had the misfortune of meeting a man known on the island as Willie B. Well, he was found on the morning of your investigation at the foot of the grand staircase inside, quite dead."

"What!" gasped Ronnie.

"Was it an accident," said T.J. warily, "or was he pushed?"

"That has yet to be determined."

"Wow," said T.J. "And did Mrs. Tilbury know about this?"

"Oh yes," Chappy answered coolly, "so it's a wonder you even got inside that one time. But I'm afraid that's not all.

"I was recently put in touch with the latest of a succession of Hibiscus House tour guides who was forced to quit her job out of fear. Apparently, she was threatened by the good Captain—"

"Because she was black," said Bortnicker. "Er, African. Like Willie

B. and Ronnie, right?"

"I'm afraid so."

"But that's not the worst of it, Mr. Chapford," snarled Ronnie through clenched teeth. "I had the pleasure this morning of being told that I am actually one of his descendants!"

"My word."

"Well, Chappy," concluded T.J., "you're with us now. Care to do a little ghost hunting?"

"Not before I share this last tidbit. On a hunch based on your findings from last night, I discretely placed a call this morning to a friend who's the caretaker at St. Anne's Church Cemetery. He took a quick peek into Captain Tarver's crypt at my behest and found his coffin vacant."

"Wow, Chappy," said Bortnicker, "you're a pretty good ghost chaser yourself."

"Hardly. Just a curious old man. So lead on, Mr. J. Let's see what this is all about."

Chapter Twenty-Six

"How should we get in?" said T.J. "This place must be locked up tight. I hope we won't have to break a window."

"Mike said last night that the alarm had been disabled because of our investigation," said LouAnne. "Hopefully they haven't turned it back on yet."

"We'll know soon enough when we get inside," said T.J. "But the question remains: where?"

It was at this moment that something odd occurred. Bortnicker started snapping his head around, back and forth, like he was being bothered by a mosquito. He then looked at Chappy, who stonefacedly nodded. "Follow me," said the boy. He led them onto the rear gallery where a corner window was open a crack.

Ronnie managed a "How did you—" before Bortnicker shushed her.

T.J., who was equally perplexed, shrugged his shoulders, said, "Quietly now," and gently lifted the sash. One by one they climbed over the waist-high sill into the pantry. When no alarm sounded they breathed a sigh of relief.

"Okay," said T.J. "Bortnicker, you and I will carry the flashlights. LouAnne, why don't you man the EVP recorder. And Ronnie, you were the only one who managed to draw him out last time, so do your thing."

"From here? The pantry?"

"No," said Bortnicker with that odd tone in his voice again. "Follow me." He led them down the hallway to William Tarver's massive library. When they were all inside he said, "Chappy, please close the door." With an acknowledging nod, the driver complied.

Almost immediately, the temperature in the room began to drop, and the tobacco smell became apparent. The Americans turned to their friend. "William Tarver!" cried Ronnie. "Are you here? If so, show yourself and stop the drama!"

From a corner of the room a low, rumbling chuckle sounded. Bortnicker and T.J. swung their flashlights toward the sound, but there was nobody there. It got colder. LouAnne started to shiver involuntarily.

"We're waiting, Sir William!" called Ronnie, "and we'll wait all night if we have to, if you insist on playing games!"

The boys' flashlights winked out simultaneously.

"Uh-oh," said T.J.

"I do not appreciate being addressed this way in my house," came the voice from another corner. This time as they turned toward it the source was discernible. In the pale moonlight that streamed through a backing window, the figure of Sir William Tarver, sitting at his opulent desk, was eerily clear.

"Well, it's about time," said Ronnie, stepping forward bravely.

"My, my, aren't you the spirited one," said Tarver in a sarcastic tone. "And I see you've brought along another one. What's your name, *boy*?" he said to Chappy.

"I am not a *boy*, sir, I am a *man*," replied Chappy with only the slightest hint of fear. "Nigel Chapford, at your service."

"Indeed. Well, *Nigel*, so nice you could join us. Actually, I am pleased you all have returned. It appears we have some unfinished business to attend to."

"You bet we do, you monster!" screamed Ronnie. Before anyone could grab her she'd scooped up an inkwell from the front of Tarver's desk and hurled it at his face. Her aim was true, but the clay pot passed right through him and smashed against the teak straight-backed chair in which he sat.

"Oh dear," he said mockingly, "I rather liked that piece. The governor himself gave that to me as a gift."

Ronnie stood there, chest heaving, until T.J. put a comforting hand on her shoulder and eased her backward to where Bortnicker gently embraced her as she sobbed quietly.

"Sir William," said T.J. calmly, "we've returned as you requested, at

221

great danger to ourselves. We're anxious to hear your story because, as you suggested, we found your crypt empty. Would you like to tell us what happened?"

"Finally, a person with a civil tongue," snapped the Captain. "Very well, I'll tell you the tale." He shot a look at Ronnie. "And I'd appreciate not being interrupted." He stood and pushed his chair back, and it was plain that he was at least a bit transparent, as T.J. could make out the outline of a moonlit palm tree through the window behind him.

"I grew up in Bristol, England—no, let me amend that. I was born there and grew up at sea. My parents had abandoned me at a young age, and I survived on the streets much the same way a rat does, on guile and tenacity. Of course, I had no formal schooling—the back alleys and taverns of Bristol were my classroom. As soon as I was able, I lied about my age and signed on as a cabin boy on an East India Company trade ship bound for the West Indies.

"Having never been away from what I called home, the seafaring life was a dramatic, often brutal, change. I was given every disgusting menial task the crew could think of, but I did the work with great relish, for I saw myself, as ridiculous as it may have been at the time, as a commander of my own vessel one day.

"Gradually I adjusted to life at sea and was accepted as a trusted member of the crew, both by our captain—who ran a tight ship—and my shipmates. And, I was allowed to see parts of the world I never dreamed existed.

"Our merchant ship was grand, and we were able to cram the holds with spices, silks, and other treasures from the East that would bring untold wealth to the East India Company's coffers. Then one day we spied a sloop on the horizon, flying what we believed to be a British flag. We were relieved in that there were ongoing problems with other nations such as the Spanish, French, and Dutch. But when the sloop drew near, it took down the Union Jack and ran up the Jolly Roger—specifically, a black flag with a white skull and crossed swords underneath. It was a privateer, commanded by none other than Calico Jack Rackham, whom I consider the greatest of all captains.

"Calico Jack's ship, the *Treasure*, came alongside us smooth as you please and before you knew it, we were boarded and captured. Any of our crew who resisted was shot on the spot and fed to the sharks. Those who did not express a desire to join Calico Jack's crew were put in a longboat with some water and bread and sent on their way, probably never to be seen again, as we were in the middle of nowhere. I was one of the few who opted to join the *Treasure*'s crew. And what a fortuitous decision it was!"

Tarver was pacing now, punctuating his sentences with sharp hand gestures as he warmed to his story. His eyes seemed to glow like cobalt, and none of the ghost hunters dared move a muscle so as not to distract him.

"We sailed the Caribbean, taking whatever we pleased, from whomever we pleased. I was quickly accepted as a crew member and was instructed in the use of the flintlock and cutlass by my mates. In no time I was even participating in hand-to-hand battles as we captured ship after ship, and Calico Jack himself lauded me for my bravery under fire. And when we came to port in such places as Port Royal, I drank and caroused with all the gusto of a much older man. Ah, those were the great times!"

He paused, wistfully looked out the window, and continued: "Although our ship was entirely democratic, with every man receiving an equal share of the spoils, of which there were many, something came along to ruin it.

"Shortly after I came aboard, Calico Jack found a woman, Anne Bonny, who as it turned out was every bit the pirate he was. She became, more or less, his wife, and joined us in our exploits. Now, some of the men were uneasy with that; it is a well-known fact that a woman on board a ship is bad luck. But since she earned her keep, they looked the other way. And I surely didn't mind, because she always was kind to me, as well as being easy on the eyes." He chuckled then shook his head.

"But things became complicated when we captured a Dutch merchant bound for the West Indies. As was the custom, we invited, so to speak, those who did not want to be set adrift to cast their lot with us. Among them was one Mary Read, a woman with a buccaneer's heart as well; but she was in disguise at the time, affecting the dress and mannerisms of a man! She was able to keep this secret for a time, but she came to be close friends with Anne Bonny, which seemed to rankle

Calico Jack. This dissention filtered down through the ranks, and by the time we docked in Bermuda to repair a hole in the keel, there was a faction of us who felt disaster was just over the horizon.

"So, I made a bold decision. I gathered together a group of ten good men who pledged to follow me through the gates of hell, and deserted Calico Jack's ship at St. George's. We purchased our own sloop and began a new career, with me the elected captain, which had always been my dream.

"My crew, though small, became a scourge of the seas, venturing as far south as the coast of Africa and the Dry Tortugas, taking ships and raiding Spanish settlements. My ship, the *Steadfast*, was sleek and quick; the big, bulky merchant traders were clearly overmatched by our cunning and ruthlessness in battle. In the pursuit of riches my men and I took more lives than I'd care to count.

"But after a few years, I began to realize that an age was coming to an end. Even old Calico Jack, the greatest of them all, was captured and hanged for his deeds. I knew it was time to begin a new existence. So, on a trip to Bermuda I approached the governor and offered my assistance as a protector and defense advisor, to which he was all too happy to agree. In fact, he was so taken with the idea of a buccaneer defending his interests that he introduced me to his niece, who later became Mrs. Tarver, and whose father was a wealthy landowner in Southhampton Parish. As a dowry we were given this very house and the surrounding acres, which I determined would be the perfect size for a tobacco plantation. And this is how I became a gentleman farmer, while running the occasional privateering errand and designing fortifications for the island." He paused, then frowned.

"Alas, a plantation needs workers to make it profitable, and so I was forced to follow the custom of importing slaves from the West Coast of Africa to fill the need."

"Forced?" managed Bortnicker, his words creating vapor in the freezing room.

A steely look from Tarver silenced him. "If my business venture was to succeed, I needed manpower. Apparently you do not understand that there is a certain order in this world. But how could you? A callow youth who's probably never had a blister on his hands…" He sat back down. Clearly this effort was exhausting him, and T.J. wondered how much longer Tarver would be able to manifest himself.

"And so, the *Steadfast* made a few runs to the African coast, and we brought back as many workers as we could, who by the way were sold to us by other, conquering African tribes who desired our money.

"Things went well for a time; the plantation was successful, and Mrs. Tarver and I were relatively happy. The governor, in gratitude, bestowed my title, and all the trappings of nobility that came with it. Unfortunately, as was the case with old Calico Jack, a woman would prove to be my undoing."

At the mention of this, Ronnie stopped her sniffling and listened intently.

"We had a field worker named Maruba, a true beauty who was sturdy yet alluring. As Mrs. Tarver was, unfortunately, unable to bear a child, which strained our relationship, I turned to Maruba for comfort, and in the process she conceived my child. Of course, that ended it for me and my wife. We would continue to live in the same house as strangers, but even so, I was pressured to return Maruba to the fields.

"Upon hearing of the pregnancy, the workers, whom I had always treated fairly and to whom I had rarely raised my hand in anger, revolted. One stormy night they came for me, overpowering my overseer and house staff, and dragged me outside by torchlight. I doubt if my wife had the power, or the desire, to stop them. I was paraded to the back of the property to a secluded area and brought to a formidable cedar tree. Along the way, the rabble-rousers of the group spoke of commandeering the *Steadfast*, which lay at anchor off the beach close by, and making a run for it to Africa. Of course, there were no sailors among them. If they did take the ship, they probably dashed it on the reefs. The last thing I remember as I danced at the end of a rope was their angry faces, glowering at me with an unfathomable contempt."

"Oh my God," breathed LouAnne.

"They lynched you?" whispered Bortnicker. "On your own property?"

"Until I was good and dead. And then, after inflicting spiteful atrocities upon my corpse, they buried me at the foot of the tree from which I was hanged."

"And are you still there, sir?" said Chappy, who had regained his composure.

"That I am. And that is why we are all here. For some reason, there was an occurrence that had caused me to reappear in this place of both pride and sorrow. I feel that if I could only be properly interred with my wife, it just might put things to rest. Forever."

"You want us to do you a *favor*?" blurted Ronnie.

He smiled thinly. "Girl dear, it's the least you could do for an old ancestor, don't you think?"

"How…did you know?" she managed, her voice a child's whisper.

"Because, my love, you're the very image of her. A little lighter in tone, perhaps, though it's hard to tell in this infernal gloom. But you most definitely have her spirit, and thereby her allure."

"I'd never let you lay a finger on me," she spat at him.

"Don't be so quick to judge. Life's circumstances sometimes put us in … precarious situations." His words hung in the frosty air.

"But enough about me. This whole experience tonight has been exhausting, and I don't know how much time I have left. So I ask: Are you curious enough to find my grave?"

"That's why we're here, sir," said T.J. "If you'll lead the way."

"Good lad, but there could be a problem. I don't know how far beyond the walls of this house my … existence … reaches."

"It's worth a try."

"That it is. Follow me, then." He seemed to glide walk from behind his desk to the doorway, becoming more transparent by degrees as the seconds ticked. The group looked at each other for a moment; then T.J. took the lead and they followed, Chappy bringing up the rear.

Tarver made his way toward the back of the house and a rear servant's entrance that must have led to a long since destroyed cookhouse. Amazingly, he passed right through the wooded door, which T.J. quickly yanked open so as not to lose the pirate on the rear terrace. But by the time they had all exited, the apparition was barely visible.

"Bah, it's as I feared." He turned to T.J. "There's a rather large cedar tree five hundred paces or so straightaway from this door, in a fairly wooded area. You'll locate me somewhere near, I'm sure."

"And what if we find you?" asked LouAnne.

"Dear lass, I want nothing more than to be properly interred with my wife. It's my sense that if this occurs, you'll not see me again." He turned to Ronnie, who held Bortnicker's hand. "And as for you, girl dear, understand that I truly loved Maruba, and that I am sure she had the compassion to forgive me before she left this world. I hope to see her again, wherever I'm going—"

"But—" said Ronnie, as with a chilling breeze, the pirate vanished.

"He's outta here," said Bortnicker.

"Remarkable!" gasped Chappy.

T.J. took a long breath. "Okay, so what now?" he said, searching his teammates' eyes.

"I say we go find him," volunteered LouAnne.

"But how?" said Ronnie. "We don't have any equipment."

"There's a maintenance shed near the garden," said Chappy. "Come on."

Luckily for them, the shed was unlocked and contained shovels and even a large flashlight, which the boys quickly scooped up.

"We're good to go," said T.J. "But his directions were pretty vague. A big tree in a wooded area? Jeez Louise."

It was then that Bortnicker had another one of those head-jerking fits.

"What's *up* with you, man?" said T.J.

"Nothing," he replied after another unnerving exchange of nods with Chappy. "Just follow me."

They started walking across the large expanse of the back lawn, eventually reaching and passing the remains of foundations of the slave quarters, then entering an area which reminded T.J. of the Railway Trail he had run with LouAnne in the mornings. It was disorienting, but Bortnicker seemed sure of himself, picking his way over fallen branches and around bushes.

"What's the deal on Bortnicker, Cuz?" LouAnne whispered sideways as they walked along.

"Don't know. Just stay with him."

Finally they came to a small clearing which featured the truncated remains of what must have been an immense cedar. "This is it, Big Mon."

"How can you be sure?" asked Ronnie, swatting a mosquito on her neck.

"Trust me." Then he brightened a bit. "Hey, T.J., remember when we read *Treasure Island* in fourth grade? That scene when Long John Silver's men went to dig up the loot, shovels over their shoulders? This is just like it!"

"Except we're digging up a corpse."

"Well, yeah."

"What say we get started, gents?" suggested Chappy, who'd brought a pickaxe himself. "Miss LouAnne, if you'd be so kind as to shine the torch for us?"

And so the three males bent to their work, which at first was easy as they broke through the loamy surface, occasionally throwing a small rock to the side. But it became more difficult the deeper they went, and the width of the hole began to widen when they had no luck at the initial target. Time passed. The girls, sitting together on a rock, made small talk, and LouAnne tried to comfort the still-traumatized Ronnie, who had learned more about herself and her country in the last week than she ever probably wanted to know.

"Fifteen men on a dead man's chest," sang Bortnicker.

"Yo ho-ho and a bottle of rum!" countered T.J.

"Drink and the devil had done for the rest—"

Clink!

"Blast it," muttered Chappy, "we've hit a rather large rock."

"Wait a minute," said T.J. "Maybe they covered him with stones before they threw the dirt on top. Bortnicker, help me move this."

The two boys worked their fingers over the two-foot square slab and flipped it away. Something white lay beneath.

"I see bone!" cried Bortnicker.

Immediately the girls sprang to the edge of the hole and peered in.

"There's more rocks!" said T.J.

"Can we help?" asked Ronnie.

"Come join the party," replied Bortnicker.

The girls hopped in the hole and heaved aside more stones as Chappy and the boys uncovered the dirt topcoat. In a matter of minutes an entire skeleton, which appeared to be buried face down, was visible.

"Whoa, Nellie," was all Bortnicker could manage.

"But how do we know it's him?" asked LouAnne, her hands smeared with dirt.

"Give me the light right here, Cuz," he said, pointing to a spot. "I think I see something shiny."

She directed the beam to the area of one of the skeleton's hands. A gold ring encircled the bones of the middle finger. T.J. gently removed it. "Shine the light on it, Cuz," he whispered after brushing the ring off. A close examination of the inner band revealed the initials "WT".

"Bingo," said T.J.

"Incredible," said Chappy as they all knelt around the skeleton. "I would never in a million years have believed—"

"Freeze!" came a stern voice from behind them. "Hands on your heads, the lot of you!"

"Uh-oh," said Bortnicker.

Two men stood above them with large, blinding flashlights. "And who are you?" asked the smaller, older one, who had a neatly trimmed, grayish goatee and a blue uniform with a tie. His tone was firm, his elocution perfect.

"We're the *Junior Gonzo Ghost Chasers*," said LouAnne defiantly. "Who are *you*?"

"*I*, young lady, am Inspector Thomas Parry of the Bermuda Police, and this is PC Harold Crocker." Parry nodded to a husky Afro-Bermudian police bobby, complete with tall hat, light blue short-sleeved shirt, and navy Bermuda shorts. He leaned over the hole. "Dear Lord, who is *that*?"

"*That*, Inspector Parry," said Bortnicker in his best Beatle accent," is the earthly remains of the great Bermudian pirate Sir William Tarver!"

"Stop fooling around," said T.J. to his friend. He looked into Parry's flashlight beam. "Inspector," he said in his most even tone, "how did you know to find us here?"

"I received a call from Mrs. Tilbury at the National Heritage Trust that an inspection of the house might be in order given that an unfortunate occurrence took place here recently — that, and her suspicions trespassers might be about this evening. We saw the minivan and motorbikes and looked around. The house was empty, but then we

229

came out back and heard some ghastly singing—"

"Busted," whispered Bortnicker to T.J.

"And wait...Nigel Chapford, is that you in the hole with these intruders?"

"Afraid so, Inspector," said the popular Chappy, wiping his hands on his trousers. "If you don't mind me asking, could we move this conversation to a more appropriate place? We're all getting rather gritty in here."

"Yes, of course." Parry turned to Crocker, who awaited his orders. "Contact HQ and have them send some vehicles to cordon off this area. We'll also need a forensics team, an ambulance, and the coroner."

"Yes, sir!" said Crocker smartly and hurried off to radio in what would be the most interesting event to occur on the island in years.

* * * *

"So, wait a minute," said Tom Sr. as the dirty group sat around a large table at Police Headquarters in Hamilton. "You guys took it upon yourselves to steal the bikes and go up to that house alone? Are you crazy?"

"Dudes, that wasn't in the script," agreed Mike, whose hair looked even more disheveled than normal.

"It's lucky they allowed you one call," continued Tom Sr., "but after realizing what you did, I'm not sure I shouldn't have let you spend the night in the clink, which you still might."

T.J., who had never seen his father this angry, tried to smooth things over. "Dad," he said calmly, "we weren't going to leave this island without finding the truth. When Mrs. Tilbury cut us off so close to our goal, we had to give it a shot on our own. And it *worked*! We actually talked to the ghost of Sir William Tarver!"

"No way!" moaned Mike, slapping his forehead. "I blew *another* chance to see a ghost?"

"'Fraid so," said Bortnicker. "But Ronnie here brought him out all over again. Heck, she even found out she's related to him!"

"No way."

"Yes way! But, unfortunately, it'll never make the TV show."

"Don't be so sure," said LouAnne with a sly smile. "While Parry

230

was walking us back to the house I hung back a little and listened to the EVP recorder, which I'd switched on when we entered the house and just left running. And I gotta tell ya, even though it was in my pocket, *I've got the whole conversation on tape*."

"Tarver's whole story?"

"Every last word, Cuz," she smiled, holding up the player. "And you can bet—"

"I'll take that, young lady," said Parry, entering the questioning room. "Are there any other recording devices on your person? Any of you?" He plucked the recorder from LouAnne's hand.

The group shook their heads sullenly.

"Right. Well, I've spoken to Mrs. Tilbury. She is not pressing charges, though you're all underage anyway—except you, Nigel, who should have known better—but your presence is requested at a meeting in the Heritage Trust office at 9:00 a.m. sharp. Until then you are free to go on your own recognizance, but under no circumstances are you to divulge a word of this to anyone or attempt to leave the island. Do I have your word on this?"

"Yes, sir," said Tom Sr.

"May I drive them back to their hotel?" asked Chappy.

"Yes, you may, and you will drive them tomorrow morning as well, because I'm positive Mrs. Tilbury will have some choice words for *you*, Nigel Chapford."

"I'm sure she will," he replied with the faintest hint of a smile.

"Mike and I will take the bikes back," said Tom Sr. as they exited the building ahead of the breaking dawn. "Ronnie, Inspector Parry said he'd have an officer run you back home, but we'll need you tomorrow morning as well, I think."

"No problem, Mr. Jackson," she said. "I think my dad will want to come, too. That is, if he doesn't kill me when I get home."

The teens tiredly piled into Chappy's minivan, and he gunned the motor. "Quite an evening," he observed in his typical understated manner.

"Ya think?" said LouAnne with a yawn.

Chappy maneuvered the car down Front Street and left the downtown for South Road.

231

"There's just one thing I don't get," said T.J. "What was going on between you and Bortnicker at the house, Chappy?"

"What do you mean, Mr. J?"

"Aw, c'mon, Chappy, I saw you guys giving each other those looks." He turned to his friend. "Spill it, Bortnicker. How did you know where to go every time? What was up with *that*?"

"Well," said Bortnicker, removing his thick glasses to give them a polish with his tee shirt, "you might not believe this, but somebody was whispering in my ear the whole time. At first it was weird, but then it was kinda cool."

"Who was it?"

"To tell you the truth, Big Mon," he said with a crooked smile, "it sounded a lot like John Lennon."

"No way!" cried T.J. and LouAnne together.

"I'm afraid he's quite right, folks," said Chappy, his eyes on the road. "Old John loved it here. Maybe, like Captain Tarver, he's decided to pop in occasionally."

"Wait a minute. *He's talked to you before*?" said T.J. incredulously.

The driver turned and looked him dead in the eyes. "All the time."

"Now I've heard it all," said T.J., throwing his hands in the air.

"I think it's the perfect occasion for some tunes," said Bortnicker.

"Agreed, Mr. B," said Chappy. "Might I suggest *A Hard Day's Night*?"

Chapter Twenty-Seven

Taptaptaptaptaptaptaptaptap...

Constance Tilbury hated to be kept waiting. As she sat at her enormous desk, drumming away with a pencil on its polished top, she again checked her wristwatch. 9:06. Her anger rose with every second.

How *dare* these film people come to *her* island and take advantage of Bermudian hospitality? How *dare* they go back to that house, in the dead of night like common thieves, *against her orders*, and start trashing the grounds? How *dare*—

"Mrs. Tilbury?" The young man at the front desk, who looked terrified, had stuck his head in the door.

"Yes, what is it?" she snapped.

"Your, uh, guests are here to see you."

"Well, it's about time," she harrumphed. "Send them in."

"*All* of them?"

"Yes, of course, all of them. We have some serious business to conduct!"

"Yes, right, I'll fetch them," he said, regaining his Bermudian polish.

Seconds later the door flew open, and in stepped the obnoxious Weinstein fellow, who at least had the decency to leave that ghastly black tee shirt of his behind, followed by the American teens, led by the cute one with the good manners. But who were these other people? A fortyish white man with a stylish haircut, blue shirt and khakis; a black man she knew as a taxi driver on the island; a rather large black woman in tee shirt and jeans, accompanied by one of Tilbury's former employees—what was her name? Pemburton? There was also a roughhewn, bald black man who smelled like he'd washed up on the beach; a trim black man in boat captain whites accompanied by a striking mocha-colored girl with bushy corkscrewed hair; and—thankfully— Inspector Parry from the Bermudian Police. By the time he stepped inside her roomy office seemed to have shrunk.

"Oh, Charles!" she called to the front desk man. "We'll need some folding chairs, I believe."

"Good morning, Mrs. Tilbury," said Mike cautiously. "Before you say anything, I'd like to thank you on behalf of my team for allowing them to go home early this morning and not have to spend time in jail."

She waved him off as the chairs arrived, all of the visitors grabbing one and snapping it open. Within seconds, they were all seated before her.

"If everyone's comfortable, let us proceed—"

No sooner had the words left her lips then there was a knock on the door.

"What now?" she cried.

"Hello, Auntie," said Lindsay Cosgrove. "Sorry I'm late." She opened a folding chair she'd been handed in the lobby and set it down next to Tom Sr.

"You're *with* these people?"

"Oh, yes. Tom here, who is T.J.'s father, is overseeing a rather extensive renovation of the clubhouse over at the Coral Bay Golf Club. We've become good friends these past few days." She reached over and squeezed Tom Sr.'s hand, at which point Bortnicker nudged T.J. in the ribs.

For a few moments the elderly woman was speechless. Then she cleared her throat and plowed ahead. "We are here today to discuss the deplorable behavior of these young people—who were apparently aided and abetted by our own Mr. Chapford—as they not only trespassed on the grounds of Hibiscus House but proceeded to dig up the back lot! I'd like an explanation, and I'd like it *now*." She sat back in her seat, waiting for some brave soul to step forward.

As always, it was T.J. who led the way. Rising, he began, "Mrs. Tilbury, when Mike Weinstein contacted Bortnicker, LouAnne, and I last winter and told us we had an opportunity to go ghost hunting and be on TV in beautiful Bermuda, we jumped at the chance. Your island, and its people, have given us some of the greatest experiences of our lives." When he saw her blush slightly and almost smile, he went on:

"We had a lot of work to do to prepare for this project—tons of research on Bermuda and its history—we even took a six week SCUBA course to learn to dive, which we passed with flying colors.

"So we came here ready to investigate Hibiscus House and try to make contact with Sir William Tarver, its famous owner. The problem was, from the minute we got here we noticed that nobody really wanted to talk about the Captain except to say what a hero he was."

Suddenly, Bortnicker was at T.J.'s side. "But when we came to this very building to do research, it was clear some old records had been pulled. But this made us even more determined to find the truth."

When T.J. saw Tilbury's eyes open wide and her nostrils flare at the accusation, he gently placed his hand on Bortnicker's shoulder and eased him back down into his seat. "Mrs. Tilbury, what got this whole thing started was the fact that your staff refused to work at Hibiscus House anymore—"

"That Captain Tarver chased me out! Scared me half to death!" blurted Winnie Pemburton.

"You can't be sure—"

"Oh, yes she can!" said the woman next to her in a belligerent tone.

"And you are?"

"I'm Dora Pedro, owner of Dora's Corners, the best little restaurant on this island, as anybody'll tell you. Winnie's mom and I are friends, and she came to me with her story. I'm here to support her because you're obviously a non-believer!"

"That will be quite—"

"Mrs. Tilbury," said T.J. smoothly, "may I continue? Anyway, it seemed that what touched off the questionable paranormal activity of the house was the discovery of a shipwreck on the reefs off Gibbs Hill Lighthouse on the South Shore. We contracted with Mr. Goodwin, who owns the Blue Lagoon Dive Shop, to take us there because he's the one who'd found it. Well, we must've got lucky because we found the ship's bell on the first dive. The *Steadfast*'s bell."

Tilbury leaned forward, her mouth agape. "You found ... the *Steadfast*?"

"My father found the wreck," said Ronnie proudly, "but T.J. and Bortnicker found the bell."

"And you have it?"

"Yes," said Jasper Goodwin. "It's secure in a saltwater bath at my shop."

"Remarkable."

"But that's not all, Mrs. Tilbury," said T.J. "And you might not like what I've got to say next, but here goes. We did a second dive, hoping to find gold and silver and jewels—you know, pirate's booty—but instead we started bringing up slave shackles for wrists and ankles. The fact is, the *Steadfast* was a slave ship, and its owner, Sir William, was a big slave trader and owner on the island." He added gently, "But ... you knew that, didn't you?"

She nodded slightly and said, "Proceed."

"So we figured that the only way we were really going to get to the bottom of this was to see if we could draw Sir William out during our investigations—"

"Because we *thought* we were getting two!" blurted LouAnne.

T.J. gave her a quick look, then went on. "What happened was, Ronnie Goodwin came with us because finding the slavery stuff had a big impact on her, and—" he looked directly at her— "because she's a descendant of Tarver ... and she's our friend."

That annoying Dora woman then spoke up. "What they didn't know, ma'am, was that a man was murdered in that house the night before."

"And he was my friend!" added Hogfish.

"That unfortunate fatality is classified as accidental," said Inspector Parry from the back of the room in an awkward attempt of support for the beleaguered Mrs. Tilbury.

"Which is why we never should have allowed the first investigation!" Tilbury hissed. "But I was overruled on that one," she added bitterly. "Please continue, Mr. Jackson."

"So, anyway, the first night there was that storm, which made all the sound stuff difficult, especially EVPs—"

"EVPs?"

"Electronic voice phenomena, Mrs. Tilbury. We have devices which can pick up the sounds of spirits communicating with us."

"Nonsense."

T.J. let that one go and went on. "All of a sudden we lost power—whether it was from the storm we didn't know, because right after that all our battery operated devices went dead. Then it started getting really cold where Bortnicker and Ronnie were—which can be a sign that a ghost is about to manifest—er, show up. So they called us to help them and then, there he was."

"There *who* was?" said Tilbury with a raised eyebrow.

"Sir William! He wasn't exactly solid, kinda partway vapory. But he talked to us."

"Oh really? And what was his message?"

"That he couldn't rest until he was properly buried in his crypt at St. Anne's."

"But he is!"

At that point, Chappy spoke up. "I'd have to respectfully disagree, ma'am. I have it on good notice that the Captain's body is not interred with his wife's."

"Then where is he?"

"That's what he wanted to tell us on our second visit, which was why we just had to go. Don't you see?" T.J. was becoming exasperated with the stubborn woman.

"And when you went back—illegally—what happened?"

"With Ronnie's help, we brought him out again, and he told us his life's story."

"My, my. An entire narrative. And I'm supposed to just take your word for it?"

"We wouldn't expect that, ma'am," said LouAnne, "but I did get it down on the EVP recorder." She turned to the policeman. "Inspector Parry, did you bring it?"

"Yes, miss, I have it here," he said smartly, producing it from his pocket.

"If I may?" she asked hopefully.

After an affirming nod from Tilbury, Parry handed the recorder to LouAnne, who rewound it to the beginning, then set it on Mrs. Tilbury's desk.

"Shall I?" said LouAnne sweetly.

"Please do," replied Tilbury through clenched teeth.

LouAnne hit PLAY and took her seat. The tape began with Ronnie's insulting provocations but then, after a pause, came the words that sent chills up the spines of all who were present:

I do not appreciate being addressed this way in my house.

At that point T.J. sat back down and patted his cousin on the knee.

It was a strange scene; all the visitors sitting ramrod straight with a forward lean, Mrs. Tilbury looking as if the very life were draining from her. When the tape ended with *I hope to see her again, wherever I'm going*, the congregation let out a collective breath.

Then Bortnicker said, "Pretty cool, huh?"

Tilbury gave him a look that shot daggers. "So, I would assume, then, you went to dig him up, stealing equipment from the tool shed."

"We *had* to, Mrs. Tilbury. It's what he wanted," said T.J. sincerely.

"And this skeleton that the Inspector said you found. How do we know it's Sir William?"

"Because of *this*," said T.J. as he placed the initialed gold ring on her desk. "*WT*...William Tarver. It couldn't be anyone else."

She sat quietly for a few moments, her fingers tented in front of her face. An antique clock ticked on her wall. "We have a delicate situation here," she said at last. "Sir William Tarver is a central figure in Bermudian history, which, to be fair, has treated him in a manner far beyond what he actually deserves.

"This being said, I do not see how it could possibly be in the best interests of our nation to try to rewrite his legacy at this point. Whose interests would this serve? No one's."

"So you're not going to re-bury him?" said Bortnicker.

"Oh, we will. Quietly. With no fanfare."

"But what about the *Steadfast* discovery?" asked Jasper Goodwin. "It's the historical find of the century for Bermuda."

"I have no problem with you announcing the finding of the ship's bell," said Tilbury. "What I ask is that the exact site coordinates — which only you probably know — are kept a secret. Besides, the reefs around our island are littered with wrecks. Without the bell, what remains down there from the *Steadfast* could be attributed to any number of vessels."

"But what about the *show*?" complained Mike, who'd managed to restrain himself throughout the meeting. "Are you saying we can't reveal the true story of the greatest paranormal investigation ever conducted?"

"That's *precisely* what I'm saying," shot back Tilbury. "Remember that what you came back with that second night was illegally acquired. Or do we have to start arresting people?"

"Lady, you've gotta be kidding—"

"Stop it!" cried Ronnie, springing to her feet. She took a breath, then lowered her voice. "Just stop it. She's right.

"Listen, everybody. No one hurts over this more than me. Can you imagine how I felt yesterday when my mother had to tell me that I'm descended from a man like *that*? But she also told me that hating people serves no purpose. And so, let them take that pirate's bones and put them in the crypt and be done with it. Hopefully, that will be the end of him bothering people at Hibiscus House. Winnie here can go back to work; thousands of tourists will visit based on just the first part of the investigation, minus the slavery information, televised for all to see; and the rest of us—regular people like my dad and Dora and Mr. Chapford, can get back to living our lives."

"Hear, hear," agreed Chappy.

Tilbury took a few seconds to let Ronnie's impassioned words sink in, then nodded. "The girl makes sense. You have quite a daughter there, Mr. Goodwin.

"This, then, is our agreement. Mr. Weinstein, for your TV show you will use only footage from your diving expedition and the first visit to the house, with no mention of slavery. I'm sure you can fashion a slam-bang program from that. This EVP tape," she said, popping open the cassette player, "belongs to the Bermuda Heritage Trust, as does his signet ring. Sir William Tarver will be interred, quietly, with his wife. And no one—I mean, *no one*—will breathe a word of this for the rest of their natural lives."

"You've got *my* vote," said Dora.

"Mine too, Mrs. Tilbury," agreed Hogfish, wiping his sweaty pate with a handkerchief.

"Thanks for everything, Mrs. Tilbury," said T.J., extending a courtly hand across the desk. "Overall, we had a great time in Bermuda."

As she shook it, she said with a faint smile, "When are you supposed to be departing our island?"

"We have a flight booked for 6:00 p.m. today," said Mike.

Tilbury's smile vanished. "Make sure you're on it."

* * * *

Once outside, the group said their goodbyes and broke up. The meeting had taken over an hour, and it seemed even longer.

"It's still early, Cuz," said LouAnne. "Lots of time before we go. What do you say to a little snorkeling in Jobson's Cove?"

"*You* want to snorkel? I can't pass that up."

"Guys," said Ronnie, "would you mind if I bring Bortnicker home for a farewell lunch? Send him off with a proper Bermudian meal. We'll have him back in plenty of time. Right, Daddy?"

"Sure," said Jasper. "It will be fun."

"You youngsters go enjoy yourselves," said Tom Sr. "Lindsay and I will grab a bite in Hamilton and see you later."

"And I'm just gonna veg by the pool," said Mike. "It's been a long week, er, eight days."

Said Beatle Bortnicker, "I think there's a song in there somewhere."

Chapter Twenty-Eight

"This must be boring to you," said LouAnne as she and her cousin took a break from their shallow-pool snorkeling in Jobson's Cove to sit on a submerged rock.

"Why do you say that?" asked T.J., tipping back his mask so it rested atop his brown locks.

"Are you serious? After wreck diving on the reefs and making a historic discovery? All we're doing is paddling around in three feet of water and looking at pretty fish."

"It's still fun, Cuz. Maybe we'll come back someday."

If there was any acknowledgement of T.J.'s veiled insinuation, LouAnne didn't show it. "I'm going back in," she said, adjusting her mask. "You coming?"

"In a sec."

As she paddled away in her orange one-piece, blonde tresses trailing behind, he felt that same warmth for her as had occurred during the road race. It was so maddeningly wonderful.

* * * *

"Bortnicker, so nice to see you again," said Claudette Goodwin, clasping his hands in hers. "I'm so appreciative of the way your little band took Veronique in and made her feel welcome." Mrs. Goodwin and the teen were soon chopping peppers next to the kitchen sink while Jasper and Ronnie ran over to the dive shop to check on things.

"No problem, Mrs. G," he said, his curls partially obscuring his glasses. "We couldn't have done it without her. I mean, with her knowledge of the island and all the boat stuff. I just feel bad about everything she had to go through with her ancestry and Tarver."

"I wouldn't worry about that, Bortnicker," she said. "Veronique is a strong girl. She'll come through this just fine and be better for it. And I hope this isn't the last we'll see of you around here?"

"You mean it?" he said, brushing the curls from one eye.

"Without a doubt," she answered, and gave him a peck on the cheek. "You're the first boy she's really liked. Or hasn't she told you that?"

Lunch went by all too quickly, with Jasper and Ronnie recounting some hilarious tourist-related diving tales and Bortnicker sharing highlights of the previous summer's Gettysburg adventure that had brought the *Junior Gonzo Ghost Chasers* together.

When it was done, Jasper looked at his dive watch. "Two thirty. We should be getting Bortnicker on back soon."

"We've still got time, Daddy," assured Ronnie, taking Bortnicker's hand. "See you in a bit." She led the boy out of the kitchen toward another area of the cottage. "Come with me," she said coyly, "there's something we have to do."

* * * *

"Where *is* he? It's nearly four o'clock," moaned T.J. as the group of Americans stood around Chappy's minivan. "I had to pack his junk and everything."

As if on cue, Jasper Goodwin's battered Toyota turned into the Jobson's Cove Apartments driveway. Goodwin switched off the ignition and got out. "All I will say is that I had nothing to do with this."

Ronnie was the next to exit, a mischievous smile on her face. "Ladies and gentlemen, I give you the star of the new program, *Bermudian Makeover*!"

Bortnicker emerged from the backseat, and his friends' mouths fell open. In place of the scraggly, out-of-control curls that usually framed his face there were Rasta-style dreadlocks. Sunglasses and a multicolored knit cap completed the shocking tableau.

"Bortnicker," stuttered Tom Sr., "Is that really you?"

"Oh yeah," he said confidently. "What do you think, Big Mon?" he asked T.J., who was still in shock.

"I don't know exactly what I think," he replied, "but I have a feeling your mom's gonna *love* it."

* * * *

The scene at the airport was fairly hectic, with Mike overseeing the shipping of all the equipment and Tom Sr. double-checking the transfer flights for Mike and LouAnne. Weinstein would connect at JFK for a night flight to LA, where he and the honchos from The Adventure Channel would review the tapes and see if they had enough for a killer pilot episode of *Junior Gonzo Ghost Chasers*.

Jasper Goodwin had said his goodbyes at the hotel, with Chappy volunteering to drop Ronnie at home after seeing off her friends at the airport.

The ride to Bermuda International Airport had been surprisingly quiet, the usually talkative teens deep in their own thoughts, looking out the windows of the minivan at the wondrous landscape of Bermuda much the same way as they had upon their arrival, trying to seal it into their memories.

Only Mike and Tom Sr. had made small talk, and T.J. heard his father say that he and Ms. Cosgrove would probably be visiting each other in the near future. He was glad.

As they made ready to board the plane, T.J. and LouAnne tried to look away as their dreadlocked friend said his farewells to the island girl he'd obviously fallen head over heels for. But Bortnicker was full of surprises, and today was no different.

"Er, uh, Ronnie, I—we—want to thank you for being a member of the team, and ... I have something to give you." He pulled a wad of tissue from his pocket and unwrapped it. In the center was a thin, crudely fashioned golden ring.

"I found this on the very first dive, when I thought we were going to end up with tons of treasure. When we found the other stuff, the bad stuff, I figured I'd just keep it to myself, maybe give it to my mom. But, the way I figure it, this could've belonged to one of your ancestors. I'd like you to have it ... if that's okay with you. Because if you don't, you—"

He never got a chance to finish, because Ronnie Goodwin embraced

243

him and rendered a kiss that made the one at Elbow Beach look lame. Many tourists in the area applauded.

"Wow," said T.J. as LouAnne smiled broadly.

"You go, Bortnicker!" she cheered.

After they had parted, Bortnicker a beet red, Chappy spoke up. "Time to go, folks. Your plane's boarding."

"Chappy," said Mike, "we can't thank you enough." There were handshakes all around.

"I look forward to seeing you all again," said the amiable driver. "Bermuda is a magical place that calls you back. And, Mr. B, if and when you do return, I'll try to dial up old John for another visit." He put his arm around Ronnie, whose eyes were glistening, and led her out of the terminal.

* * * *

The flight itself was uneventful, with the teens, who sat together, dozing amid the stares from returning tourists that Bortnicker drew for his Rasta look. But, as is usually the case, there were delays coming in to JFK, and at customs, and at the luggage carousel, so that both Mike and LouAnne were going to have to hustle to make their connecting flights.

As they caught their breath, Mike bid them farewell, assuring them that the show, when given the Hollywood Treatment, would be a hit, and promising to let them know when something was decided. "Problem is, dudes," he said, high-fiving them, "how am I ever gonna find another team like yours?"

"We said we couldn't do a *series*," replied T.J. "An occasional special might be possible, though."

"Solid! I'm outta here," said the *Gonzo Ghost Chaser*, running to catch another plane.

Tom Sr. and Bortnicker went to hit the restroom, which left T.J. alone with LouAnne.

"Think they really had to go?" she said.

"Probably not." He searched for words. "Just think, tomorrow night you'll be back at the Charney Inn, dressed in your Civil War stuff, telling your tale of woe and making tips. And Reenactment Week is around the corner."

"Don't remind me," she smiled. "But I do miss Mom and Dad. I feel like I've been away for ages. So much happened in so short a time."

"Did you have fun, Cuz?" he said expectantly.

"No, T.J.," she replied. "I had an adventure. And life with you is *always* an adventure." With that she cupped his face in her hands and kissed him sweetly on the lips. "Until our next adventure," she whispered as her uncle and Bortnicker exited the restroom. She produced the small glass bottle he'd found for her on their first snorkeling dive at Treasure Beach. "I'll keep all my wishes in here until then."

The intercom blared for the departure of LouAnne's flight to Philadelphia. "All right, guys, they're calling me. Gotta jet." She hugged Tom Sr. and Bortnicker and shot her cousin a wink. In a second she'd slung her carryon over her shoulder and, with one last flourishing toss of her hair, was on her way down the ramp, wearing the gorgeous sundress she'd sported upon her breathtaking arrival in Bermuda.

"I love that dress," said Bortnicker.

Epilogue

A soft, steady rain shrouded the people who had gathered around the crypt of Captain William Tarver on the first of July. No brass bands played, and there was little in the way of pomp or circumstance.

The group itself was a rather odd representation of the social strata of Bermuda: the Governor was there with some aides, as were Constance Tilbury, accompanied by her niece, and the Police Commissioner; but the Goodwins were present as well, joined by their driver of the day, Nigel Chapford. They had been invited, somewhat surprisedly, by a rather contrite Constance Tilbury, who had orchestrated the announcement of Jasper Goodwin's incredible underwater find that had, as predicted, made front page news on the island and elevated both him and his business to celebrity status.

As the pastor of St. Anne's administered the rites of burial, Ronnie Goodwin, dressed all in black, involuntarily shivered, though her father's free arm was draped across her shoulders, the other holding a golf umbrella aloft that barely sheltered the family huddled tightly underneath. She stared down into the whitewashed crypt, whose cover had been slid aside for the internment of the simple coffin that would house the bones of the pirate. On her other side Claudette Goodwin emitted a lilting sigh every few seconds.

At the end of the ritual the Goodwins and Chapford turned toward the black minivan that would return them to their cottage in Somerset.

"Ah, Miss Goodwin?" a voice called from behind. Ronnie turned to face Mrs. Tilbury, whose niece dutifully held a stylish, ivory-handled, black umbrella above her perfectly coiffed head.

"Yes, ma'am?" she replied, an eyebrow raised in curiosity.

"I am glad you and your family could attend," she said primly. "I realize that your … connection to Sir William has been a source of consternation for you, but I thank you and your American friends for helping to return him to his rightful place here."

"Thank you, Mrs. Tilbury," she managed, her eyes filming. "The Captain was, I guess, a man of his times. But, like it or not, a part of him lives on in my mother and me. As for my friends, quite honestly, you might have been a bit more civil to them—"

"Veronique!" broke in her mother. "This is not the place—"

"No, no," said Tilbury quietly. "Let the child speak."

"My friends came to our island with only the best of intentions. They wanted to find the truth about a major figure from our history. We should have done more to help them."

"I agree, young lady, and I want you to tell them that they are always welcome to return for a more pleasant visit."

"Maybe you should tell them yourself," was her quiet but resolute reply. With that, she turned on her heel and marched toward the minivan, leaving her parents to sheepishly say their goodbyes and follow.

It was Chappy who reached her first, suppressing a chuckle as he closed his umbrella in deference to the sun, which had broken through, sending a cloud of steam skyward from the wet pavement of the church parking lot.

"Well done, Miss Ronnie," he quipped. "And do you think we will, indeed, see your comrades again?"

"Come on, Mr. Chapford," she replied, breaking out a smile. "Don't you know that Bermuda always calls you back?"

"It does have that reputation." He opened the door of the minivan as Ronnie's parents came up behind, then craned his neck to squint into the brilliant deep-blue sky. "Ah," he grinned, "another day in paradise."

Author's Note

Many of the historic sites, restaurants, beaches and resorts mentioned in this novel do exist, although Hibiscus House and Dora's Corners do not. I did play around a bit with the date of construction for Fort St. Catherine, which was initiated before William Tarver's supposed existence. However, he theoretically could have assisted in one of its renovations. Constance Tilbury is a figment of my imagination, and the National Heritage Trust does a wonderful job keeping their various museums and facilities in pristine condition for habitual tourists like myself. As far as the natural beauty of the flora and fauna, and especially the beaches, you'll just have to experience it for yourself. But most of all, be sure to enjoy the warmth and friendliness of the Bermudian people. It will, as Chappy says, keep calling you back.

About the Author

Paul Ferrante is originally from the Bronx and grew up in the town of Pelham, New York. He received his undergraduate and Masters degrees in English from Iona College, where he was also a halfback on the Gaels' undefeated 1977 football team. Paul has been an award-winning secondary school English teacher and coach for over 30 years, as well as a columnist for *Sports Collector's Digest* since 1993 on the subject of baseball ballpark history. Many of his works can be found in the archives of the National Baseball Hall of Fame in Cooperstown, New York. His writings have led to numerous radio and television appearances related to baseball history. Paul lives in Connecticut with his wife, Maria, and daughter, Caroline, a film screenwriter/director.

Visit him at www.paulferranteauthor.com.

Also by the author at Melange

Last Ghost at Gettysburg, A T. J. Jackson Mystery

Coming Soon!

Roberto's Return

Book Three of the T.J. Jackson Mystery Series

CPSIA information can be obtained at www.ICGtesting.com
Printed in the USA
LVOW08s0710071113

360211LV00003B/24/P

9 781612 357133